ONCE IN A BLUE MOON

a novel

Vicki Covington

Once in a Blue Moon

Vicki Covington

John F. Blair, Publisher
Winston-Salem, North Carolina

John F. Blair, Publisher
1406 Plaza Drive
Winston-Salem, NC 27103
(800) 222-9796 | blairpub.com

Library of Congress Cataloging-in-Publication Data

Names: Covington, Vicki, author.
Title: Once in a blue moon / Vicki Covington.
Description: Winston-Salem, North Carolina : John F. Blair, Publisher, [2017]
Identifiers: LCCN 2016047235 | ISBN 9780895876799 (hardcover : acid-free paper)
Subjects: LCSH: Interpersonal relations--Fiction. | Birmingham (Ala.)--Fiction.
Classification: LCC PS3553.O883 O53 2017 | DDC 813/.54--dc23 LC record available at https://lccn.loc.gov/2016047235

10 9 8 7 6 5 4 3 2 1

Cover design: Brooke Csuka
Book design: Anna Sutton

For Haden Marsh

ALSO BY VICKI COVINGTON:

Bird of Paradise
The Last Hotel for Women
Night Ride Home
Gathering Home
Cleaving: The Story of a Marriage (with Dennis Covington)
Women in a Man's World, Crying

MR. KASIR

Sometime during the late sixties, Abraham Kasir began buying up property on the south side of Birmingham. He collected turn-of-the-century homes that had fallen into disrepair, built when industrialists from the North realized that the three main ingredients for producing steel—iron ore, coal, and limestone—were nestled together in Jones Valley. An impressive railroad system was already in place, and the industry exploded. Rapid growth propelled the city into the national spotlight and attracted a bounty of new residents, construction, and development. Wealthy investors built their mansions in Southside. The skyline burned brightly with furnace towers. Birmingham acquired a nickname, "the Magic City." And yet as quickly as it had rocketed upward, the city began to decline. The industry changed. Factories closed. The once-splendid pieces of architecture that had been homes to the titans of industry were abandoned.

But while others were leaving the city behind, Mr. Kasir saw an opportunity to build something new. He gathered properties, dividing each home in half, generally a downstairs and upstairs with separate entrances, and began renting them out. By the 1990s, he owned more than twenty properties sprinkled along the hills and forests of Red Mountain; six of them were clustered along Cullom Street. Despite Southside's beginnings, its grandeur declined along with the city at the end of the twentieth century. And yet Mr. Kasir's community of renters thrived. Hippies, artists, and other free spirits found solace in his collection of duplexes.

During showings, when a potential renter met Mr. Kasir, the landlord often said, "I think you'll find everything you need here."

What he meant was that the back of the house was a junkyard of sorts—old tools, two-by-fours, bedframes, pieces of fencing. The renters had to be a particular kind of scavenger to appreciate his words, and his properties. Yet he taught them to appreciate what was at hand, like how to piece together a makeshift dog pen or cut their grass with the ancient manual lawn mower that the neighbors shared.

Mr. Kasir's tenants knew they'd pay way less than with other landlords. Perhaps they knew family or friends who had rented from Mr. Kasir. Or maybe, while attempting to navigate around rush-hour traffic, they'd driven past one of the generic red For Rent signs that Mr. Kasir fished out of the back of his truck on the rare occasions when someone moved out. Maybe they intended to cross the mountain to the suburbs on the other side, but life had made other plans.

Living over the mountain meant that you were guaranteed a good school system for your kids, that the neighborhoods were well kept, that doctors and attorneys lived alongside you, that you were safe in your home and didn't find it necessary to keep your doors locked all the time. Indeed, Mr. Kasir himself lived over the mountain. But he had noticed that his tenants saw the suburbs merely as a reminder of their place within the city, which bred in them a strange sense of pride.

Vulcan was a straight shot up the mountain from the cluster of Mr. Kasir's duplexes on Cullom Street. The towering statue—a burly, bearded, bare-assed man, the Roman god of fire—lorded over the city. Still the world's largest cast-iron statue, *Vulcan* was built by an Italian named Moretti for the 1904 World's Fair in St. Louis and found a permanent home on Red Mountain in 1938. Visitors could enter through the pedestal on which Vulcan stood and climb the steps to a landing that gave a view of the entire city stretching east to west, with Southside directly below.

LANDON

The story of how Landon Cooper's address came to be 1627 Cullom Street was a lament.

And this wasn't unusual. Many of Mr. Kasir's tenants landed in this part of Southside via trauma or loss. Landon, for example, had just signed divorce papers. After nearly three decades, she'd left her marriage, kicking and screaming. To make matters worse, she and her husband had lived beyond their means for years, and the recession had necessitated a quick sale of the home in which they had raised their daughters.

In her new life, she was going to be alone, without so much as a familiar hallway to comfort her. She had envisioned herself in one of the sleek new lofts downtown, but they were too expensive and too small to hold all that she was moving. She considered the faceless suburban apartment complexes, but their thin walls would do little to mask the sounds coming from the adjacent units. Finally, she decided to drive around Southside. When she got to Cullom Street, she spotted a For Rent sign in front of an aging Victorian with a front porch swing, two private entrances, and the remnants of a garden she knew she might salvage.

She called the phone number on the sign immediately.

"Kasir here."

They agreed to meet at the house the following day.

Landon woke the next morning feeling hopeful. Even if the house was in slight disrepair, it appeared to have a lot of space, and space was what she needed, since she was moving an entire family history. She arrived a few minutes early and sat on the porch swing.

Moments later, a red truck pulled up to the curb. She watched a man—Mr. Kasir, she assumed—open the door and pull his legs out to rest on the running board. Then he slowly put his feet on the asphalt, using a cane. He was a tiny man, clearly old.

"Abraham Kasir," he said, extending a gnarled, arthritic hand.

"I'm Landon," she replied, taking his hand gently.

She watched him fumble with a big set of keys. When her family lived in Homewood—over the mountain—they had felt so safe that they locked the door only if they were vacationing.

Mr. Kasir found the key he was looking for and unlocked the door. When Landon followed him into the foyer, she was taken aback. The home felt like a cathedral. The ceilings must have been fifteen feet high, and most doors had a transom. Sure, they were in dire need of dusting, but she'd take care of that. The floors were wood and recently waxed.

"It's beautiful," she said to Mr. Kasir.

Already, she was mentally placing her dining-room table, china cabinet, buffet, secretary, and, most importantly, her piano in the big parlor. These were all heirlooms from her grandmothers. Their history began to merge with what she imagined of the room she was staring at. Blinds were on every window. They were askew in a few places, but she figured she'd take them down anyway and hang some long ivory curtains or white eyelets.

"How old is this house?" she asked.

"More than a hundred years. Older even than me."

"Those pocket doors," she swooned.

"You like those?"

Mr. Kasir walked over to the heavy mahogany sliding doors, which could close off the parlor from the next room. He pulled one door out a few inches, then tucked it back into its pocket. The second room, a living room, had a fireplace that was boarded up. Yet it still held its charm, thanks to its black tiles and carved mantel. In this room, Landon would put her television, her sofa, bookshelves, and comfortable armchairs.

"I can't believe the space here."

"You have a family?" he asked.

"Yes," she replied, then corrected herself. "But my children are grown, and my husband and I are divorced." She hated saying those words, unnatural on her tongue. She felt it was a confession of failure, a dark place she now was sharing with this stranger.

Mr. Kasir nodded, allowing Landon to take the room in. She started walking forward and he followed, his gait compromised by whatever was ailing his legs.

Behind the big parlor and living room were three bedrooms, a kitchen, and a bath.

"Well, I can take this master bedroom. And fix up the other two with what the girls left behind—you know, beds, clothes, artwork. In case they ever come back home," she told him, her voice catching.

They stood in the hallway that connected the bedrooms.

"You have kids?" she asked him to steer the conversation away from herself.

"One son," he replied.

Mr. Kasir was waiting patiently.

"I have a dog," she told him.

"That so?"

"A small one. He's a wire-haired dachshund. His name is Alejandro."

Landon expected him to quote her a fee for having a pet, but he said nothing. He smiled, took a handkerchief from his pocket, and wiped his brow. It did feel a bit stuffy, but she had taken note of the many window air conditioners. Right now, the power was off.

Landon walked into the kitchen. It was spare, not big enough for a table. The one redeeming feature was a stained-glass window over the sink. It stood out, so bright and colorful next to the tiny white refrigerator and old gas stove.

"Here's your washer-dryer hookup," he noted.

She was relieved.

"The smaller units don't have them. Like the girl who lives upstairs. She and all the others," he said, making a small, sweeping gesture with his cane, "they all go to the Laundromat just around the corner, by the market."

Landon nodded, already sold.

When she and Mr. Kasir returned to the parlor, she turned to him. His eyes looked big behind his glasses, magnified by the Coke-bottle lenses.

"I want it," she said. "I want to live here."

"That's good news, Ms. Cooper. Let me get the lease from my truck."

They went back outside. Landon sat on the ledge of the porch and watched him limp toward his truck, open the door, and retrieve the papers from the passenger seat.

"Sorry. I have a hard time getting around. Old war wound," he said when he returned to the porch. "Shrapnel. Omaha Beach."

He reached into his pocket and retrieved a jagged piece of steel, dull gray, the size of a tiny pocketknife. "This is what they cut out of my leg. I carry it around with me for good luck."

Landon wanted to ask more, but he was handing her the lease. She skimmed it. Still no mention of a pet fee. *What luck*, she thought, feeling for the first time somewhat hopeful about the future. She signed her name, reached into her purse, and retrieved her checkbook for the deposit.

Afterward, she asked how soon she could move in.

"Tomorrow?" he asked, grinning.

She laughed. "Well, maybe not that soon."

A yellow maple leaf floated softly to the porch tiles. She let her eyes travel up the street, then down again. She liked the feeling of living in Southside, living in a house that was old, the feelings of change and of history.

Mr. Kasir took her check and handed her the key. "It's yours," he said.

·After he left, she went back inside and walked through the two smaller bedrooms. Maybe the girls would be pleased with her for saving their things. They'd move back in. They'd sit on the porch swing at night and listen for the trains in the distance as the crickets and cicadas sang a descant. The scent of fresh mint from her garden, the rustling leaves of the maple, the stars overhead—all those things would carry them back to how it was before they grew up.

. . . .

A week later, after an ill-fated attempt at packing up the Homewood house, Landon caved and hired movers.

She sat on the porch after the movers left, not knowing what to do with herself. She heard footsteps coming down from the upstairs unit. A girl appeared, locking her door behind her. She was wearing a T-shirt and workout pants. She jumped when she turned to see Landon sitting on the steps.

"I'm sorry. I'm Landon, your new neighbor."

"Oh, hi!" the girl said, and smiled at her. "I'm Abi."

She was tall, very tall. And slender. Her green eyes carried a look of wanting, but her smile was confident and unyielding. Landon saw that Abi was the kind of woman who could take a room, as her mother used to say.

Abi sat on the ledge, pulling her long legs up until her chin touched her knees. "What's your story?" she asked Landon.

"I'm not sure anymore."

"I know what you mean."

Landon tried to guess how old Abi was. She looked to be in her thirties but had a youthfulness about her. She wore no makeup, her curls were natural, and she carried a raw, sharp beauty that Landon associated with Appalachian girls—poor but proud.

"Do you have pets?" Landon asked, not sure where to go with the conversation as the two women took each other in.

"A cat. Her name is Cinderella," Abi replied.

"I have a dog," Landon told her. "You know, Mr. Kasir never said anything about a pet fee."

Abi pulled her curls up and secured them with a clasp that she'd been holding in her hand. "He doesn't charge for pets. He doesn't care if you're late with your rent payment or scratch up the floors moving furniture. The flip side is that you're kind of on your own. It takes him awhile to get here from over the mountain, and he's so old, you know. But he does love to teach you how to fix things. I've learned a lot from him," she said, and smiled her winning smile. "You will love the neighbors."

"Will I?"

"Really, we're like a family. I didn't mean to pry when I asked what your story was. It's just that most of Mr. Kasir's tenants have a story. Take me, for example. I grew up in my family's trailer park, left home at eighteen, and moved to Birmingham without knowing a soul."

"What do you do?" Landon asked, pleased with Abi's candor.

"I'm a waitress."

Landon nodded, waiting for her to say more, suspecting that she would.

"I started off in pizza parlors, burger joints, coffee shops. But I've worked my way up to a rich people's restaurant over the mountain. I'm taking classes at the university, thanks to some government grants."

"So," Landon said, "a good story."

The sun was setting, washing the sky pink.

"Do you work?" Abi asked.

"I'm a psychologist. But I'm taking a few months off from my practice. I feel a bit distracted by my own troubles."

Abi nodded. "I guess all your friends want you to fix them without having to pay you."

Landon shrugged. "It's not so bad, and I usually don't mind. I hope I'm not keeping you from anything."

"I'm going for my run, but I wanted to meet you. Mr. Kasir told me you were moving in. He said I would like you. And I do, of course."

Abi grinned and hopped off the ledge. It was as if she understood that Landon wasn't ready to tell her story.

"We'll talk more," she said. "And if you need anything, just knock."

"Thank you," Landon replied, extending a hand.

Abi held it for a moment, staring straight into Landon's eyes. Then she nodded slowly, as if Landon had just told her everything.

ABI

"Get out of my fucking house!"

Abi woke with a start to the sound of Landon's voice screaming downstairs. She grabbed her phone and a hammer that had been forgotten some time ago on a nearby bookshelf. On her way down the steps, she dialed 911. When she got to the porch, Landon was running toward the sidewalk.

"What happened?" Abi called to her.

Landon whirled around. "There's a man in my house," she gasped.

"What's he doing?"

"He's just sitting in a chair. He's asleep or something."

"I've already called for help," Abi assured her, hustling to Landon's side and putting her arms around her. She pulled Landon close and whispered, "Don't worry. The precinct is only a few minutes from here. They'll be here soon. Just stay calm. I've got you."

"He's young," Landon told her. "He doesn't look like an intruder."

"But he is one," Abi said.

"He's got a sweater vest on. And nice trousers."

Within minutes, a police car arrived. A few neighbors had gathered in the yard. A cop jumped out of the car, holding his gun close at his hip. Abi pointed to Landon's door. Another officer emerged from the car and followed his partner inside.

When they came out, a young man was in handcuffs. He looked as though they'd roused him from a deep sleep.

"I think I know that guy," Abi said to Landon. "Three frat guys used to live in your place. Harmless, but always partying."

The neighbors formed a semicircle around Landon. They were full of apologies, telling her that this kind of thing never happened.

Jet arrived from across the way and asked Landon if she needed a Xanax.

Landon thanked her and said, "I'm okay. But give me a rain check. You never know."

"I'm sure he must have been a friend of those dudes," Abi said to Jet, who agreed.

"I bet he was all messed up and thought his buddies still lived there and it was okay just to walk in," Jet said. She was holding a glass of what looked like tomato juice, though Abi knew it was a Bloody Mary.

"I forgot to lock my door," Landon said.

In an effort to redirect Landon's attention, Abi introduced her to Jet, a night owl who hadn't yet changed from her typical goth gear into pajamas; Sam, the friendly neighborhood pot dealer; Roy, who was probably the closest to Landon's age and grew vegetables in his front yard; Tina, who often climbed out of her upstairs window and threatened to jump off her roof during parties she threw and then got wasted at; Sid, who subbed at a middle school and sold vitamin shakes on the side; and Nicole, a mousy bank teller who had once had a brief, ill-fated fling with Sid. Even though Abi knew Landon wouldn't remember any of them, she still felt obligated to introduce them all. They drew together as close as possible, like a football team huddled for the next play.

After a few minutes of camaraderie, they went back to their respective houses.

"I'm off to my folks' today," Abi told Landon, "but don't hesitate to let me know if you need anything." She wrote her phone number on a piece of paper and gave it to Landon, telling her to call her if she needed to. "I love your hair," Abi said, trying again to distract her new housemate, who was still trembling. "Let me French-braid it sometime."

Abi noticed that, despite the fact that the sun had yet to rise, Landon was already dressed in a long patchwork skirt and dangling earrings. She must have been up early, getting ready for the day, before discovering the passed-out frat boy in her living room. Even shaken, Landon was lovely.

"That's a really cute skirt," Abi said.

"Oh, thanks," Landon responded finally as she walked back toward her front door. "I'm just an old, foolish hippie. I still can't believe I left my door unlocked."

"Call me," Abi insisted.

Once she was back in her unit, Abi felt wide awake. The one bright side to the incident was that it had revved Abi up for the day ahead. She was going to visit her family at its compound of trailers.

She put on a short denim skirt and a T-shirt with "BITE ME" printed across the chest in large black letters. She was aiming to stun her relatives into silence, or at least to scare them enough so they wouldn't ask her about her dating life.

She slipped into her Volvo station wagon, which she had inherited when one of her uncles died. The car's odometer had long passed a hundred thousand miles, and it showed. She flipped on the radio and fished a half-smoked joint from inside the cellophane of her cigarette pack. She attached the joint to a roach clip and lit up. The hour's drive was always unnerving. Most of her relatives still lived in the trailer park. Rather than being proud of her for escaping it, they seemed judgmental and sullen whenever she visited. If somebody did mention her having moved to Birmingham, they prefaced it with, "Now that you're so uppity" or "Seeing as how you come from trailer trash, what makes you think . . . ?"

They could be downright mean.

Her daddy had cancer. That was the only reason she was going home.

She took the interstate to the Bessemer exit and followed the road that led home. She had a good buzz from the joint, so she rolled the window down and let the heady mix of industry and agriculture fill the car. The combination smelled a little like mothballs, but because it was so familiar, she didn't mind. She made the final turn onto the dirt road and pulled over to the side. Looking in the rearview mirror, she applied fresh lip gloss, sprayed some mint breath freshener onto her tongue, put Visine in her eyes, and ran her fingers through her hair. She braced herself.

A canopy of oak trees hung across the drive, their natural beauty almost stately. Still, only dilapidated trailers lay ahead.

She heard them before she saw them—a covey of rowdy kids she referred to as her nieces and nephews, though they were actually cousins of some kind or another. They stood in the middle of the dirt road, barely registering Abi's approach. She sat on the horn to herd them away from her car. That's when she saw two of the boys holding a cat by its legs, swinging it around.

"You little shits!" she hollered, throwing the car into park and raising a cloud of dust.

They dropped the cat, which crouched frozen where it landed. Abi scooped it up and gave the kids her most withering glare. She was so mad she didn't even think to soothe the cat, a calico. She climbed back into her car and laid it on the passenger seat.

One of the bigger girls yelled after her, "Don't tell Mama and them!"

Abi once used the phrase, too. She never quite understood who the *them* was, but she knew the word was pulled out when the situation was dire. When she bailed her cousin Petie out of jail, where he'd been held for public intoxication, the first thing he'd said was, "Don't tell Mama and them."

She drove up to her mama and daddy's double-wide and parked on the shady side. She grabbed her purse and the cat, knocked on the door, and walked in. Her daddy was on the scratchy old couch with the remote control in hand. A football game was on, but he turned it off immediately when he saw her.

"How's my baby?" he said, hopping to his feet to gather her and the cat in his arms. Her daddy was one of the few men she knew who was taller than she was.

"Hey, Daddy," she replied in the sweet voice reserved only for him.

"You got a new cat?"

"Yes," she said.

"What's its name?"

"Grits," she said off the top of her head. She wasn't sure why she didn't tell him the truth about the rescue that had just occurred. It wouldn't have surprised him one bit. She simply didn't want to cause a ruckus. She did know that she was taking this cat home with her. She set it on a chair and quickly peeped under its tail to see if it was female. Thank God, it was. Abi thought there were too many balls in the world already.

"Where's Mama?" Abi asked.

"Over at Aunt Sister's."

"Well, don't go get her," she said flatly.

Her daddy smiled and walked to the kitchen. Abi followed him.

"Your mother has redecorated," he said, gesturing like a *Price Is Right* model.

The motif, according to Mama, was Kountry Kitchen.

"Spelled with a *K*," he emphasized.

"Of course," Abi replied.

She knew that it wasn't right to love one parent more than the other, just like it wasn't right to love one kid more than the others. But for as long as she could remember, she and Daddy had this thing they shared—a way of coping with Mama that involved subtleties and sometimes, less subtly, laughing their heads off when she left a room after going on one of her rants about how country music had gone to hell or how black people were taking over America or, more recently, how upscale JCPenney was. Mama had started working part-time at the JCPenney to supplement Daddy's VA benefits and had taken to giving Abi lectures about fashion and dressing for success during their obligatory Sunday-afternoon phone calls.

Abi looked around the redecorated kitchen.

The backsplash tile was speckled and printed with a rooster under an apple tree. The oopsy daisy curtains were white with a pattern of tiny sliced limes. A tin sign nailed to the wall read, "I Kiss Better Than I Cook." A stack of resin shotgun-shell coasters was on the small peninsula, along with a magazine open to an article, "Magical ways to use Mason jars this Christmas." The refrigerator boasted magnets of snowmen and more roosters. The biggest magnet read, "It's My Party And I'll Fry If I Want To."

Abi fingered one of the resin coasters and laughed. Her daddy just shook his head.

"Want some tea?" he asked her. He pulled a pitcher from the refrigerator. It was new, too. More roosters.

"What's the deal with roosters?" she asked.

"You know, I quit trying to figure out your mother years ago."

He cracked an ice tray and dropped some cubes into two glasses, then poured the tea. Abi had always wondered why they needed ice if the tea was already cold. Just one of the many things the family did without much reason. Like how it put up Christmas lights even though the trailers were on a dead-end road and nobody would see them. Abi could hear Aunt Sister's reply: "Those lights are for us to enjoy." Around here, *us* was different from *them*. *Us* was everybody who called the trailer park home—Sister, Mama and Daddy, Abi's two uncles, several no-good cousins, and their offspring, that motley crew of cat torturers.

Grits had made herself comfortable, curling up and recovering nicely from the ordeal.

Abi and Daddy sat at the kitchen table. He took her hand.

"How are things in Birmingham?" he asked.

"Great, Daddy. I'm making lots of money just being nice to the people I serve. And," she said, cocking her head to the side, "I flirt a bit, too. There's one lawyer who comes in a couple times a month, and he leaves me a hundred-dollar bill every time."

"How about that," he replied.

"And you? How are you feeling?"

"I feel fine now. But the chemo begins in a couple of weeks." He tapped his fingers on the tabletop, and Abi could tell he wanted to say something else. "There's something I need to ask you about." He looked down into his glass of tea. "You know, the chemo is supposed to make you real nauseated. And everybody's saying that marijuana is good for that."

Before he could finish asking, Abi interrupted. "Of course I can get you some."

He smiled. "I don't know how much money to give you."

"Don't even think about that right now," Abi said, waving away the suggestion. "You know I'd do anything in the world for you, Daddy. And believe me, this is no problem at all. I can get it easy from one of my neighbors who runs a little mom-and-pop dealership out of his apartment."

That's when she heard her mama's voice at the door.

"Abigail!" Mama shouted. She knew Abi hated to be called by her full name. Even worse, when Abi was little and into something Mama didn't want her into, like making mud pies, she'd call to her, "Abigail Lynn!"

Mama walked into the kitchen. She was wearing pink capris and crimson slip-on shoes. Her shirt was printed in a potpourri of geometric designs that made Abi a little dizzy.

"Well, how do you like the new me?" Mama asked her, striking a pose.

"You look very nice," Abi lied.

"Well, it's plus-size, of course. But I get a 15 percent discount on anything I buy there. How do you like the new kitchen?" she asked, and kicked her shoes off. She sat at the table with Abi and her daddy.

"The kitchen is nice, too, just like your new outfit," Abi said.

"I can get you some great deals on clothes," she said, glancing at Abi's "BITE ME" T-shirt.

"Thanks, Mama, but I've got plenty right now."

Her mama lit a cigarette. "What does 'BITE ME' mean?"

"Oh, it's just a way to be funny."

Mama coughed and waved her cigarette smoke away from Daddy. "You know your daddy starts his treatments soon," she said.

"Yes, we were just talking about it."

Then, pleasantries and updates aside, Mama started headfirst into her usual questions. Was she seeing any nice boys? Was she making any money as a waitress? Shouldn't she drop out of school and go to work for the telephone company? Of course, Mama meant South Central Bell, which was surely not hiring, due to the fact that it no longer existed.

Abi was dying for a cigarette but didn't want to smoke in front of Daddy.

"Well," Mama went on, "are you dating anybody?"

"Not in particular," Abi replied.

"You know, all your cousins are married now except for you."

"Yes, seems that I knew that."

"I want me some grandchildren," she said. "Sister has so many now."

Abi wanted to say she'd seen the little tyrants when she got there, but she was interrupted by Grits, who jumped from the chair and walked toward Mama.

"Where did that thing come from?" Mama asked, clutching her hand to her neck like she was grabbing a string of pearls.

"Mama, that thing is a cat, and she's mine."

"Seems like in a place as big as Birmingham, there would be a lot of boys to pick from," she said, getting back to the subject at hand, the subject that drove Abi crazy. "Might not need another cat then."

Daddy sat silent, sipping his tea and reaching out to scratch behind Grits's ears.

Mama got up from the table, went to the bedroom, and returned with a JCPenney catalog. "Here," she said, "let me show you some things I'm considering for Christmas presents."

Abi looked at her daddy, who was hiding a smile. She knew that he knew she was in total misery.

Mama sat and scooted over next to Abi.

"Okay, look here. I'm sending cards this year."

"To whom?" Abi asked.

"I got friends," Mama said. "I got people I work with, and we got people—family—who don't live here. I've narrowed it down to three. Here's the reindeer with bells."

Abi noted the ornaments hanging from the antlers.

"And here is the simple winter print," Mama continued. "Look at all that snow. And here's the Three Kings, the Wise Men."

The Wise Men's beards curled up at the end, and the gifts they were carrying to baby Jesus were wrapped in contemporary paper with big bows on top.

"So, which one do you like the most?" Mama asked.

Abi searched for the least of three evils, finally settling on the simplest. "I think I'd go with the traditional winter print."

Mama looked at her, and Abi knew she'd chosen the wrong one.

"I kind of like the reindeers," Mama said.

Abi stood and stretched. She was going to slap her mother silly if she didn't get a cigarette soon, but it seemed cruel to light up in front of Daddy.

"Sit back down, Abigail," her mother demanded. "I'm not done."

Abi did as she was told.

"Now, here are the gifts. Look at the roulette drinking game."

"What does that mean?" Abi asked.

"I don't know, but there's another game here, see, called the Tic-Tac-Toe Drinking Game. See that board? And here are the glasses, some marked *X* and others marked *O*. I don't know if these drinking games are such a good idea around here. But Petie might like them."

"Mama, you don't give drinking games to an alcoholic."

"Why not? That's who they're made for."

She went on to show Abi a food grinder, processed meat pouring out of the mixer attachment, a hand-held vacuum cleaner, paisley melamine dinnerware, and finally a camo bedsheet set.

Mama leaned in and whispered to Abi, "I might get that for your daddy's bed, since he was a soldier."

Abi smelled the cigarette on her mother's breath, and her own lungs ached for smoke. "I need to get some fresh air," she said.

"One more thing and that's it," Mama promised. "Now, I'm showing you them because I might just get you one."

She pointed to a pink velour hoodie, then a gray fleece V-neck pull-over, a white boat-neck sweater with navy-blue piping, a long-sleeved sweatshirt—also pink—with a lace neck, and finally a short-sleeved polo-collar shirt dress.

"Don't get me that," Abi said, pointing to the dress.

"But it's Liz Claiborne," Mama argued.

Abi could bear it no longer. She leaned over and gave Mama a perfunctory hug. Mama's hands were still on the catalog. Abi noticed how swollen her fingers were and how her wedding ring looked like it might slice through the skin at any moment, it was so tight. No amount of soap and water could get that ring off.

"Listen, I'm gonna take a walk down to the pond."

"You're staying for dinner, aren't you?" Mama asked. Back home, everybody called lunch *dinner*.

"Maybe so," Abi said. She turned to her daddy. "Don't let the cat out, okay?"

He nodded and smiled at her.

"Aunt Sister is baking a hen," Mama went on.

It wouldn't do any good to remind her mother that she was a vegetarian. Either Mama couldn't remember it or didn't approve of it and therefore pretended not to understand.

"I'll be back in a few minutes," Abi said.

Once outside, she hurried to her car, grabbed her cigarettes from the dashboard and a beer from the cooler in the backseat. She headed down the footpath to the pond.

. . . .

Few members of Abi's family ever left the trailer park for good. One rare wing had done just that when Daddy's sister Nell married a tobacco farmer in Tennessee. When Abi was a little girl, her parents accepted an invitation to visit. They packed their old Chevy and headed north on Highway 31. It was August, and all the windows were rolled down. In the cornfields, the ears had tassled out and turned brown.

When they crossed the state line, her mama said quietly, "I never been out of Alabama before."

They arrived in late afternoon, in the high heat. The trip was a big deal for Mama and Daddy, Abi could tell. They gasped at the sight of Nell's home on a hill. Mama scooted across the bench seat closer to Daddy, like they were on a date.

Aunt Nell greeted them in the parking area at the back of the house, fly swatter in hand. She wore a sack dress and an apron with cross-stitching. Her gray hair was gathered into a bun, but a few ringlets framed her face.

"Come on in," she said, and hugged them one by one.

The kitchen was all white—white pantry, white cupboards, white cabinets, even white dishes. A big white table was full of freshly picked vegetables—tomatoes, yellow crookneck squash, okra, string beans, and honeydew melons.

"Excuse the mess," she said.

Mama started to wander. It seemed to Abi that, like her, Mama wasn't exactly sure what to do or where to plant herself.

Nell herded Abi and her parents toward a big gathering room with a pine floor, where a swarm of adults Abi didn't know or at least didn't recognize descended on them. Most were already drunk, she could tell that much. On the dining-room table was a huge platter of barbecue and fixings and a mess of empty beer cans.

"Let me get some more buns," Nell said, and went back to the kitchen.

Nell's husband, Uncle Mabry, pulled Abi aside and asked if she liked barbecue sandwiches.

"Yes," she told him shyly.

He lifted up her chin a bit. "You look like kin," he said tenderly.

Abi didn't know what to say.

"I just mean you're a sweet-looking, pretty girl."

He smiled at her, and she felt comfortable. He was a nice man.

Within an hour or so, Mama and Daddy were drunk like the rest of the relatives. Aunt Nell stood on the hearth of the fireplace and made an announcement: "Marcia is coming and bringing her boyfriend. I'm afraid she's been bitten by the love bug."

The love bug.

Abi froze. She had no idea what this meant, but it sounded bad. She set the white plate with her half-eaten barbecue sandwich on the table and clutched her bottle of ginger ale with both hands. She thought of mosquito bites, fire ants, wasps, hornets, spiders, red bugs, scorpions.

In the midst of Abi's fretting, Aunt Nell took her aside and said, "Let me show you where you'll sleep."

They went to the back porch to retrieve Abi's luggage. Abi grabbed the pink suitcase that Mama had bought special for the trip. Aunt Nell guided her upstairs to a line of closed doors and opened one of them.

"This is Marcia's old room," Aunt Nell said. "You'll be sharing a bed with her tonight, honey."

Abi sat on the bed, newly fearful of love bug germs getting on her. The bed wasn't particularly big, and she didn't even know Marcia. But she didn't want to seem rude, so she nodded and gave her aunt a smile.

Aunt Nell, as if sensing something in her, took Abi's hand in hers and said, "You're such a quiet girl. What a relief from all the ruffians downstairs. Marcia's a sweet girl like you, just older. She's in college."

Abi looked around the room at the dresser, cedar chest, and quilt stand. Everything felt old in a way that was comforting. Aunt Nell raised one of the small windows, allowing a slight breeze to kiss the eyelet curtains, and told Abi she could stay upstairs or come back down with her.

"I'll unpack," Abi told her.

Aunt Nell smiled and closed the door.

Abi heard Mabry's voice in the hallway, though she couldn't make out what he said. She heard Aunt Nell say to him, "I told you they were more than trailer trash."

It was the first time she had heard the term, but it was easy to understand the meaning. The words made a mark. Even after she grew up, moved to Birmingham, and made a life for herself, they were etched in her memory.

She went over to the window. The branches of an oak tree were so close they looked as if, given time, they might grow right into Marcia's bedroom. The cicadas buzzed away, more loudly than they did back home. *Love bugs*, Abi thought.

Marcia's vanity had three mirrors on hinges that gave Abi a fine look at herself. She sat on the small white bench in front of the mirrors and picked up an ivory brush with an M painted on it, then placed it gently back on the coverlet. In the drawer was a bottle of perfume. The fragrance was called *Ambush*. She took a whiff of it and pictured Marcia dabbing it behind her ears and on her wrists. She reached for a compact and, using the puff tucked inside, lightly applied powder to her cheeks.

Then she opened some lipstick. It smelled like peaches. The outer tube read, "Taste me." She put some on.

She heard a commotion downstairs and knew it must be Marcia. She wiped the lipstick off with the back of her hand, opened the bedroom door, and ran to the landing of the stairs. She saw her cousin in turquoise shorts and a crisp white blouse. Her curly chestnut hair, much like Abi's, was pulled back into a ponytail. Beside her was a suitcase with "AUBURN" written across it. A man stood next to her.

"This is Johnny," Marcia said.

Abi sat and watched the two of them through the posts of the staircase handrail. Johnny was shaking hands with the men. He was tall and handsome, holding a pair of sunglasses. Marcia was hugging the women. Everybody was abuzz with offerings of beer and barbecue, and soon the crowd moved out of sight. Abi got up and went back into the bedroom, put on her pajamas, and slipped into bed. She pulled the sheet up to her chin. It was way too hot for quilts. When she rolled over to face the window, she saw the moon and stars through the branches of the oak.

. . . .

Sometime during the night, Marcia must have crawled into bed because when dawn broke, she was there, warm next to Abi. She wore a white nightgown, and her hair was spread across the pillow.

Abi slipped quietly out of bed, put on her clothes, and went downstairs. She ate scrambled eggs and Virginia ham with gravy for breakfast. Aunt Nell and Mama had sliced a honeydew melon.

When Marcia emerged, she looked much different from the way she had the day before. She was wearing tight jeans and an orange T-shirt. Her curly hair was wild. To this day, Abi took to women who looked like they'd forgotten to fix their hair or simply didn't give a damn.

Marcia kissed Aunt Nell on the cheek and took a piece of honeydew melon. She got the orange juice from the icebox and drank a big swig straight from the bottle.

"Did Johnny go out to the fields?" she asked.

"He did indeed," Aunt Nell replied.

"Well," she said, and sat next to Abi. "Hello officially, Abi. Thanks for letting me share your bed. How about I take you to my favorite place on the farm?"

Abi smiled at her and whispered, "Thanks."

"If you're taking her to the pond, watch out for water moccasins," Aunt Nell said.

"She worries a lot," Marcia told Abi.

"I most certainly do," Aunt Nell agreed.

"I know what I'm doing," Marcia said to her.

"Be sure and wear your Keds," Aunt Nell went on.

Marcia held a leg up to show Aunt Nell she already had them on.

Soon, they were walking along a path that led away from the fields.

Marcia explained to Abi that it was harvest time for tobacco farmers. "When we were little, we had to pick hornworms from the plants all summer," she said.

Abi didn't ask what they were or what they looked like. She wanted to steer all conversation away from bugs.

"What do you like to do?" Marcia asked her.

"I like to read," Abi replied.

"Oh, so what do you like to read?"

"Biographies," she told her.

"What are you reading now?"

"The biography of Katharine Lee Bates. She wrote 'America the Beautiful.'"

Marcia reached up and gathered her curls. "It's hot already," she said. Then she began to sing, "'O beautiful for spacious skies, for amber waves of grain . . .'"

Marcia stopped, put her hands on Abi's shoulders, and turned her back to face the fields. "Around here, it's brown waves of tobacco," she said with a laugh.

They kept walking. The land rose and fell. At the crest of a particularly steep hill, Marcia pointed. "There it is."

It was a pond, but it didn't look like the muddy little one Abi knew from home. It was large and clear, more like a lake. The sunlight turned it a pleasing green. There was an island in the middle of the water where a weeping willow grew, its long and tender branches crying downward, brushing against the dark, wet earth. Abi understood why Marcia wanted her to see it.

They maneuvered through tangled vines and headed down to the water.

"Keep an eye out," Marcia told her. "If a pond is fringed by wetland, it provides a friendly habitat for frogs, turtles, and muskrats. The water looks green, and this means that algae is growing. It's a food source for the minnows, so you'll see lots of them. You see that canoe?"

"Yes."

"Have you ever been in one?"

"No."

Marcia helped Abi into the rusty aluminum canoe, then pushed it off the bank and jumped in. The little vessel lurched and rocked as it skidded into the pond. Soon, the ride calmed. The rhythmic movement of Marcia's paddling was smooth. Abi was a cautious kid, one prone to being skittish about adventures. But this was heaven.

"Like it?" Marcia asked.

"Oh, yes."

Marcia stopped paddling, and Abi turned around to face her.

"We'll stop here a minute," Marcia said.

A few stones were in the bottom of the canoe, and Marcia threw one in the water. A flurry of movement rose up around it.

"Look at all those dragonflies."

"Do they bite?" Abi asked her.

"No, they're here for our pleasure. Would you say they're emerald or blue or what?"

"I think they're blue-green."

"Like those pretty eyes of yours."

"Yours are pretty, too," Abi replied.

"Do you know you look exactly like I did at your age? We were talking about it last night. Can you see the resemblance?"

Abi blushed, hoping she'd look just like Marcia when she was older. "I wish I had sisters," Abi told her.

"I'll be your big sister. We can write letters to each other."

Marcia took off her shoes and wiggled her toes, and Abi followed suit. Abi felt that she and Marcia were right in the middle of something—not just the pond but something else. Time encompassed her. It was her friend. No need to look back or worry forward. And being surrounded by this assurance, she knew it was safe to ask the big question.

She hesitated. Then the words came forth of their own accord. "What's a love bug?"

Marcia threw her head back and laughed, causing the clasp to drop from her hair and into the water. She ducked a hand in after it but came up empty.

"Where did you hear about that?"

"Aunt Nell said one bit you."

"Oh, she's always in my business. Who did she tell this to?"

"All of us," Abi replied.

Marcia kept laughing. "I'm glad Johnny didn't hear that."

"He's your boyfriend," Abi said, as if to affirm.

"Yes, he's my boyfriend."

"Did he bite you?"

Marcia smiled at Abi. "That's just an old saying for when somebody has fallen in love."

"Why do people say *fall* in love, though?" Abi asked her.

"That's a good question. I truly don't know."

"Because it hurts? Like a bite?" Abi pressed on.

Marcia tried something new. "Know how it feels when you're playing on a swing set and you pump a few times with your legs until the swing is high, then you get butterflies in your stomach right when you start coming down?"

"Yes."

"Okay, that's falling, and it's a bit dangerous, but you love the way it feels, falling through the air. Because you understand that if you hold on tight, if you trust your hands, then you're home free, it's just you and the swing." She paused, then went on. "Sometimes, people fall in love the minute they meet somebody. It happens so quickly, like a bug bite."

Marcia looked wistfully into the water. Abi hoped she didn't mind telling her these kinds of things, teaching her a new language.

Marcia offered one last thought. "When somebody's in love, you can sometimes see it in their eyes. When they're looking at the person they love."

Abi kept her eyes downcast so Marcia wouldn't see them, because if she did she might see that, during their time on the pond, Abi had been bitten herself. She had fallen in love with Marcia.

Marcia picked up another stone and cast it sidelong into the water. The stone made ripples that caught the sunlight.

There would be many men—and women, too—whom Abi would love during the years ahead. But no matter who she was with, she always felt she was looking for the language of love that Marcia had taught her on the pond that day, years before.

LANDON

Landon leashed Alejandro and made sure to lock the door behind her. She was still a bit on edge from the break-in. She could walk down the street to where Cullom's renters gave way to homeowners. Or she could walk up the street, which would lead her past generic apartments, Vulcan Park, and ultimately to the top of Red Mountain. She looked up the street. She had been warned that Cullom got grittier the farther up you went. So she chose to walk down, even if it meant seeing the homeowners' places with their single mailboxes and well-tended gardens. They reminded her of what she had lost.

It was a perfect November day. The air was crisp. The sky was blue. The trees—oaks, maples, hickories—were big and old. Back in her suburb in Homewood, the trees hadn't been spared from construction.

Toward the bottom of the street, she noticed a house with a For Sale sign. It was a fixer-upper, to say the least. The weeds were growing wild and high. A fence was in need of repair. Alejandro sniffed around, interested in something. Landon hoped he was picking up a scent from a stray cat, rather than a squatter. You never knew what might be lurking in Southside. And yet, unexpectedly emboldened by the morning's adrenaline rush, she picked up Alejandro and headed for the porch. She peered inside cloudy windows. Then she tried the door, which wasn't locked. The curious scavenger inside her reared its head, excited by the possibility of discovery—maybe plates and cups, a ladder, Ball jars for canning, a microwave if she was lucky, a weed whacker that actually worked.

But when she walked in, she saw only a small fan and a box of nails. She put Alejandro down and unleashed him. He scurried down the hall to what turned out to be the kitchen—free of appliances—then around a corner into the living room. Landon followed him, and they came to a stop in front of a narrow staircase. He hesitated, so she gathered him up and made her way upstairs. In a closet in one of the bedrooms that yawned open from the landing, Landon finally found some treasure. She crept into the low-ceilinged walk-in and took note of papers that were strewn about, bundles of knotted Christmas lights. It wasn't exactly the find she had hoped for, but she couldn't resist. She discovered a box of garbage bags with a few bags still inside and stuffed the lights and the papers into one of them. She was particularly interested in what appeared to be letters—envelopes with handwritten addresses.

"Nobody but me would be doing this," she told Alejandro. "But I guess you're used to it."

Once they were back on the porch, she placed the bag by the door, leashed Alejandro, and continued down the street, hoping no one had noticed her trespass. The well-appointed windows of the neighboring houses stared back, unconcerned. At the bottom of the hill, she turned left. The houses began to change. Some had two entrances; others had lawns full of beat-up cars. Alejandro relieved himself in a patch of grass. It was then that she noticed pecans on the sidewalk. She looked up and saw the tree they had fallen from. Now, this was truly a treasure. Not today, but maybe tomorrow, she would wear her empty backpack and, assuming the residents weren't home, collect as many as it could hold. She had a nutcracker, one that had been her mother's, and could make herself a little feast.

She shouldn't feel guilty, she decided. After all, her women ancestors were gatherers who walked the ridges of mountains, collecting nuts and berries to keep their families alive. And if the people who lived here hadn't picked up the pecans, they apparently didn't want them.

She walked on, turned back westward and out of the rental district. The homeowners' lawns were immaculate. Though it was November, the crepe myrtles were still in bloom. The fall annuals—pansies, peri-winkle, and impatiens—were thriving, making every yard bright and colorful. But damn it if the homeowners hadn't all done the one thing she hated regarding gardening: they had trimmed the goldenrod, the nandina bushes, all the shrubs, with electric hedge cutters, shaping them into perfect squares or orbs. Nothing here was allowed to grow out of line, wild and graceful.

When Landon returned home, she remembered the bag of lights and letters she had left on the porch of the abandoned house. She let Alejandro into their apartment, filled his food bowl, then headed out to fetch her haul.

Back with her booty, she discovered that most of the envelopes contained merely bills, receipts, grocery lists, et cetera. Yet there was the occasional letter, handwritten on pink old-fashioned stationery. They all began the same way: "Don't toss this before you read it." The writer's name was Chelsea. The recipient was Brody. In the letters, she apologized profusely to Brody, explaining that she had changed, that she wanted to start over, that she wanted to have children: "I'm not the same girl as before" and "Please see me like the person I was when we first met" and "I'm begging you . . ."

Landon threw the letters away; she identified too much.

She walked to the window and drew the sheer curtains to one side. She felt the bad thing coming over her, the sadness of divorce. She wasn't Chelsea, though. Robbie had given her more than enough time to get help, and she hadn't. What finally compelled her to admit herself to the hospital was an intervention from her colleagues. They had noticed her ups and downs, as they called them delicately. Since they were all psychologists, they knew the language of her behavior. They reminded her that she was spinning like a top at times, frantically over-booking her patients. They noticed she was hungover many days and suggested she might be self-medicating.

She hadn't cried when they confronted her, but rather sat perfectly still, absorbing the knowledge that she was not as clever at keeping it together as she had hoped. She knew, of course, the symptoms of bipo-lar disorder. She treated patients with this diagnosis. How could she have missed it in herself? The stay in the hospital, the dual diagnosis of bipolar disorder and alcohol abuse—by the time Robbie asked for a divorce, she had been sober for a year, but it was too late.

Moments like this, running once again through the litany of mistakes that had led to the demise of her marriage—failure to recognize her illness, finances, infidelity, wanderlust—Landon wanted to toss her prescriptions along with Chelsea's letters. Overwhelmed by guilt and shame, she longed for the joy of mania.

ABI

Abi sipped on her beer and smoked a cigarette, staring out at her family's pond. Ever since her time with Marcia in Tennessee, she had been drawn to the muddy little pond, a short walk down a dirt trail from her mama and daddy's double-wide. Whenever she got out of school as a teenager, she went straight to the water without even dropping her backpack off in her bedroom. Now, she was grown. Her daddy had cancer. Her mama was working. It all seemed sad.

She heard footsteps moving through the tall weeds behind her. She turned. It was Daddy.

"Sorry about all this," she said, gesturing to the beer can and lit cigarette she was holding in her hands.

"No need to apologize," he said, and sat down next to her.

His eyes were fixed on the water. Neither of them said anything. She looked at his jeans and the sleeve of his flannel shirt. His hands were big and strong.

"Next time I come, I'll bring you the weed," Abi said, breaking their silence. "Let me smoke with you the first time because it isn't like it used to be. It's much more potent."

He patted her on the knee. "That's sweet of you."

"When was the last time you smoked?" she asked.

"Right after I came home from Nam."

"So how old were you?"

"Twenty-two."

It was then that she noticed something in his shirt pocket. At first, she thought it was a pack of cigarettes, but she realized it was a small book.

"What's that?"

He looked at her, studying her eyes like he was trying to decipher what to say.

"That's what I need to talk to you about." He took the book, a tiny New Testament, from his pocket. "I've been saved."

Abi's hand flew to her mouth. "Oh, no," she said without thinking.

"I would have told you sooner, but I knew it would scare you."

She wasn't sure what to say. Nobody in her family went to church. Certainly, nobody got saved. Growing up, she sometimes had tagged along to services with her friends, but that was only to see the boys. She was never comfortable with ceremonies. There was always an ingratiating, prolonged altar call at the end of the service, the congregation singing five or six verses of "Just As I Am." She'd watched a few friends walk to the altar, but she knew it was only because they'd just lost their virginity—or were at least to third base—and were feeling guilty. She couldn't for the life of her figure out why sex had so much to do with Jesus. When she lost her virginity, she felt emboldened and happy. Why would her girlfriends want to spoil it all by asking for forgiveness? Surely, that took away the thrill of it.

"Who did this to you?" she asked Daddy. "Some preacher?"

"No, no," he said. "I was just cleaning out some drawers a couple of weeks ago, and I found this." He looked down at the book, cradled it in his palm. "I've had it all my life. My parents got it for me when I was born. That was something people did back then. I started reading it and, I don't know, something came over me, something long forgotten."

Abi guessed this had something to do with his cancer.

Daddy put the Testament back in his shirt pocket. She was relieved. She was scared he might try to save her, and that was impossible. But then he pulled something from his jeans pocket—two nails welded together in the shape of a cross.

"I know you don't like this kind of talk . . . ," he began.

"That's right, I don't."

". . . but I wanted to ask you if you would carry this around with you. Think of it as a good luck charm or something. If you ever pray, you can hold it in your hand and think of me."

The knot in her throat made it hard to talk. "I don't pray, Daddy. I don't think I ever prayed." She remembered a single exception, when she thought she might be pregnant. And even then, it was only because she didn't want to hear Mama holler about a bastard child.

She looked around her, spotted a robin pecking the ground for worms. Two ring-necked doves were strutting together along the bank like newlyweds. She was always hoping to see a bluebird, but that was rare. She'd learned how to recognize birds and their songs from Daddy. She was particularly interested in mockingbirds, the way they lived by repeating what they heard. They had no song of their own. She looked at the sky. It was clear, without a trace of a cloud. It was pure blue.

She turned to Daddy. "I don't mind carrying the cross in my pocket," she told him. "For you, though. Not for Jesus."

He put it in her palm and closed his hand over hers. "Thank you. I know this isn't your cup of tea."

She thought of the towhees and their song, which he had taught her—*Drink your teaaaaa*—and managed a smile.

"Give me one of those cigarettes," he said.

"Oh, Daddy, don't start back now."

"What have I got to lose?" he asked her.

She gave him the pack, and he took one. She always liked the way he lit a cigarette with a match, drawing in hard, then letting the smoke out the corner of his mouth in a languid, thin line. They sat together by the pond, seeing who could make the best smoke rings, laughing at each other's failed attempts, until Mama called down to them from Sister's place, her voice splitting the air like an ax.

LANDON

L andon was spiraling.

A knock on the door saved her, snapping her out of it. She was thrilled when she opened the door and saw Abi.

"Come on in," Landon offered. "I haven't finished unpacking, as you can imagine, but this is my place."

"It's amazing," Abi said, looking around. "And you have a piano. Do you play?"

"I took lessons for twelve years, but I haven't played since college. I keep it around, though."

"Didn't you tell me you were a shrink?"

"No, but close. A psychologist."

"Oh, my God." Abi's face lit up. "Just what I need."

Landon tilted her head. "Why's that?"

"I just got back from visiting my family. I need professional help."

"Well, it's all free here."

Landon led her to the next room, which was less formal but still full of remnants from other lives—the old TV, stacks of vinyl, the blue leather couch and wingback wicker chair where Alejandro slept, her brother Nick's gold trumpet on the mantel alongside a framed photo of the two of them as children.

"That's me and my twin brother," Landon said, picking up the photo. "He was killed in a car accident when we were twenty-five."

"Oh, I'm so sorry," Abi said as Landon set the photo back on the mantel. "Look at your music," she continued after a beat, and walked over to the vinyls.

Landon was grateful for the change of subject, knowing she had some great albums for sure. Jazz and R&B, Janis Joplin, Joni Mitchell, the Beatles, and the Kinks. Her favorites and Nick's favorites, too.

"If you see one you like, it's yours," Landon offered.

"Oh, I couldn't!" Abi said.

"No, please. Take one. I appreciate your help this morning."

"It was my pleasure. I never pass up an opportunity to yell at a man. Have you met anybody else from the neighborhood yet?"

"Just the ones you introduced me to this morning, although I can hardly remember anyone."

Abi nodded an acknowledgment. Landon looked at her own hands, at the empty ring finger, at the light polish on her nails. She was waiting for Abi to tell her why this morning at her parents' had been so stressful. If she were in a clinical setting, she could and occasionally did say nothing at the onset of therapy, until the anxiety of silence finally forced the patient to say—or even shout—*something*.

Once when she herself was in therapy, she had a male psychotherapist do this to her. They sat in his office for thirty minutes in utter silence until she finally exploded, "You are just like my father!"

"How so?" he'd said.

"You're not talking to me. You don't care about me. I'm nothing to you."

She hated hearing herself because, of course, she knew that this was projection. Any man could have been sitting silent in the chair; any man she couldn't read became Daddy to her. And the fact that the silent treatment had worked made her feel like a scared child. She didn't like the technique, either as a therapist or a patient. And she certainly wasn't going to use it on Abi.

"Would you like a beer before you tell me what went down this morning with your parents?" Landon asked her.

"Yes, please," Abi replied. "You read my mind."

Landon went to the kitchen and got Abi a beer.

"None for you?" Abi asked when Landon returned with only one can.

"Oh, no, I'm sober. Can't mix booze with my meds."

"But you keep beer around?"

"For company," Landon answered.

Abi popped the top of the can and took a long sip. "I think I hate all of them except for my daddy. Is it okay to smoke in here? I can go outside."

"No, it's fine," Landon said. Abi gave her a quizzical look, so she continued. "It really is. I'd tell you if it bothered me."

"My daddy has cancer," Abi told her while lighting up.

"How long have you known?"

"About a week."

"Is it treatable?"

"Yes."

"Good. Still, it must be hard."

"Well, it's not just the cancer." She reached in the pocket of her denim skirt and pulled out the metal cross. "He's never been religious, but now he's saved. He asked me if I'd carry this around with me and pray for him." She leaned across the table and whispered, "I can't, Landon. I don't believe. What should I have told him?"

"What *did* you tell him?"

"I told him I would, but I don't intend to. But what if there is a God? What if praying for Daddy would help?" Abi paused and took a drag from her cigarette.

Landon nodded, gesturing for them to take a seat on the couch.

"You're a believer, aren't you?" Abi continued as she sank into the blue leather cushions. "When you were getting me the beer, I saw about ten Bibles all together on one shelf."

"Mostly inherited. Received as gifts or bequeathed to me. When my grandmothers died, my aunts, my parents. I couldn't throw them away." Landon felt it a sacrilege to toss anything that belonged to a family member who'd died. In fact, it was almost a superstition, if not quite OCD. She wasn't a counter or a checker, but she was a hoarder.

Landon stood to get the ashtray for Abi. Even that used to belong to her granddaddy. It was small and square, made of bubbled glass.

"Why did he have to ask for this?" Abi pleaded.

"Do you mind my asking what kind of cancer it is?"

"Kidney."

Landon reached out for Abi. Abi put her cigarette in the ashtray and let Landon hold her hands.

"Do they have a prognosis?"

"You mean, when will he die?"

"Well, sort of."

"We didn't talk about that. I don't want to know that because I can't believe he's going to die. If he dies, there will be no one I'll ever speak to again in my family. But he's not going to die."

Grief and fear of dying were not Landon's expertise, clinically speaking.

Abi leaned in closer. "I have to lie to him, don't I? I have to tell him I'm praying for him. I hate it when people say that because they don't mean it." She lit another cigarette. "Like, on Facebook, somebody will post, 'Sitting in my car, afraid to go into the store,' and people will comment, 'Praying for you.' I mean, really! Or 'Burnt my casserole in the oven,' and somebody comments, 'Give it to Jesus.' Like he likes it that way—burnt."

Landon smiled, understanding exactly what Abi meant.

"So, tell me," Abi continued, "do you believe any of it?"

"Yes," Landon replied after a pause. "But I'm not one for public religion. In fact, I'm not one for religion, period. I don't go to church. But things have happened to me that make me believe we're either humans trying to be spiritual or spirits trying to be human. No, no, that's not any kind of answer. Just . . . mystical things have happened to me."

"Like what?"

"I've just felt it."

"Felt what?"

"The spirit," Landon replied.

Abi got up, and Landon was afraid she was leaving. But instead, she walked around the room smoking her cigarette, letting the ashes fall where they may. She looked up at the ceiling, then back at Landon.

"You know, I don't have a clue what you're talking about," Abi said.

"I know."

"So do you believe some people are going to hell?"

"No, I don't believe in hell. Sometimes, I think this is hell, with all the shit we go through."

Abi nodded in appreciation.

"I once heard a progressive pastor say that going to heaven was like going to a symphony," Landon continued. "Some people will have studied God, and I don't mean just read their Bibles, but they've seen God in nature, have tried to love instead of hate, have been open to people's differences. So when they get to the symphony, the music will be familiar to them. Others might not recognize the music at first, but they will in time. The thing being, we're all going to the symphony."

"I like that, Landon, even though it's a stretch."

"It's a nice metaphor . . . or it's bullshit," Landon replied.

"But I went to church a few times with friends, and didn't Jesus say that nobody was going to heaven unless they believed in him?"

"Yes, but he was quite a young man when he said it. We're all a little self-involved in our twenties and thirties. Maybe if he'd lived longer, he would have thought better of it."

Abi sat back down and rolled her cigarette in the ashtray until the burning end was a fine point. She took a deep breath. "What do you know? I actually feel better about everything. I mean, I really do. Listen, I know you don't know anybody in the neighborhood, so I was wondering if you would walk to Sam's place with me. Just two houses up."

"Sure," Landon replied.

"But I need to tell you something first. Well, let me start by saying that Sam is a good guy—from Greene County, one of the biggest extended black families in Alabama, or so he says. Both his parents were schoolteachers. And he is studying engineering. But he does sell a little weed. It's more of a bartering business. For example, I'm a waitress. Sometimes, I bring him nice dinners from the restaurant, and he gives me some weed from his drawer." She paused and put her hand to her mouth. "I'm sorry. I didn't even ask if you get high."

"Not in about twenty years," Landon said.

"Well, if you ever want to, let me know. I'm gonna smoke with Daddy because it's been awhile for him, too."

The idea of smoking weed didn't seem so far-fetched to Landon. She remembered those early days when she and Robbie—conspiratorial and tender—shared joints at home, in the park, in the car, at the beach, in bed after sex.

"Okay," Abi said, "want to come?"

"You will think this is silly," Landon began, "but I have to tell Alejandro that I'm leaving and I'll be back soon. I read this in a book by some Tibetan monks, about how to make your animal feel safe—that you should tell your pet that you're coming back."

Abi laughed. "Go ahead."

When they stepped outside, a man's voice rang out from across the street. "Hey, there, girls!"

Abi turned to Landon, "That's Roy."

He hollered, "How's it going, new girl?"

"She is fine," Abi shouted back, "considering the frat boy who helped welcome her to the neighborhood this morning."

"I'm picking the last of the okra and tomatoes. I'll bring y'all some in the morning."

Abi waved to Roy and took Landon by the elbow. "Walk faster," she whispered. "He'll talk for an hour if you let him."

"Later, Roy," Abi called over her shoulder.

Landon followed suit, waving goodbye to Roy and walking swiftly with Abi.

SAM

Abi had texted to say she was bringing the new tenant over, so Sam grabbed a big plastic bag and quickly started emptying ashtrays filled with lipstick-stained cigarette butts. In the kitchen, the counters were stacked full of dirty takeout containers. He stuffed them into the trash bag. Then he stood on the high porch of his upstairs unit overlooking the alley and tossed the bag into the open dumpster right below. He knew that if his girlfriend were there, she would have given him a talking to about carrying the bags downstairs and doing it the right way. But his method was so tempting, and he never missed.

Although he had met Landon earlier, after the break-in, he was uncertain how she might feel about his lifestyle. She was, he thought, old enough to be his mother, and he knew what his own mom would think of his business. He patted down the cushions of his lumpy couch. It had seen too many parties.

He heard Abi's knock. Always the same—five long knocks spaced apart, followed by two quick ones. He opened the door.

"Sorry," he said, waving it all away—his apartment.

Abi stepped inside and administered her usual chest bump. Sam was always amazed at Abi, how different she was from all the other women he knew.

"It's not messy," Abi said, then turned to Landon, who had followed her inside. "Isn't he beautiful? Doesn't he make you want to fall into his arms while you tell the sad, sordid story of your life? High-school quarterback, this one."

"Have a seat, ladies," he said, gesturing to the couch.

Landon sat, but Abi headed for his kitchen, calling back, "Can I get something to drink, Sam?"

"I wouldn't go near the milk or orange juice," he said. "I need to do some tossing out today."

"What about the Dr Pepper? There's only one left. Can I have it?"

"Help yourself."

Abi returned, head up high like a preacher. "Mark my word, guys," she said. "Pot will be legalized after this next election. And Obama will be our next president."

Sam leaned back in his chair, bemused. "Ah, are you crazy, girl?" he asked. "You think all you white folks are gonna vote for a black man who used to do coke, who is the son of a white woman and an African man? Don't get your hopes up."

"Hope is the whole point," Abi said. "*The Audacity of Hope*—that's his book, you know? Jet lent it to me."

"Well, he is pretty audacious to talk about the audacity of anything."

"I'm just saying."

Sam stood and retrieved the bong from his bedroom.

"Whoa," Landon said. "That's so much bigger than the ones I remember from my smoking days."

"Show her everything," Abi said.

He began pulling out pipes of all sizes in a kaleidoscope of colors, then a tiny Ziploc bag with two buds the size of lemon drops. Most of his stash was hidden away in the hall closet. He kept only small bags lying around.

"All these pipes . . . ," Landon said. "Don't people still use empty toilet-paper rolls and aluminum foil?"

"Just old people," he said, then patted her shoulder. "I'm kidding."

He put one of the tiny buds in the water bong and asked Landon if she wanted to smoke. He suspected this must be a big deal for her.

Landon looked at the bong with a hint of trepidation. "Not to offend," she said. "My uncle—the oldest living relative I have—warned me, 'You live in Southside, you're gonna be living next door to a drug dealer.' I guess he had it right, but the dealer is a few houses up, not next door."

Abi and Sam laughed. Then they explained to her what to do. She took a hit and coughed most of the smoke back up. Abi and Sam both took their turns.

"Things have changed," Landon told them, still coughing. She took another hit. "That's it for me."

Abi was all over her with questions. How did it taste? How did it feel? Was it really different from the stuff she smoked in the seventies? Landon told them how a lid or an ounce once cost twenty-five dollars. Sam told her that the two tiny buds they were smoking were worth about that much.

"Oh, but let me tell you . . . ," Landon said, and put one hand on Abi's knee, the other on Sam's. He could tell she was buzzed. "During the summer of 1975, the movie *Stay Hungry* was shot in Birmingham. All the Hollywood people brought this super weed to town. Acapulco Gold. My husband, a topographer, was also involved with local theater. They gave him the job of lining up extras. So he got cozy with the stars and started buying some of this Hollywood weed, which was expensive but worth it." She told them, "I saw Sally Field get high."

Sam laughed. "Yeah, buddy."

Abi looked impressed. "Who else?" she asked.

"Jeff Bridges."

Sam leaned forward, "Wait a minute, wait a minute. Wasn't Arnold Schwarzenegger in that movie?"

"How did you know that?" Landon asked him. "You weren't even born yet."

"Unc had that on video. He was an extra."

"Who is Unc?" Landon asked.

"He's Sam's uncle," Abi said. "Unc. Uncle."

"Yeah," Sam said. "They filmed a lot of it in Mountain Brook. The country club. Or maybe it was Birmingham Country Club. And it was Schwarzenegger's debut. And the fellow who wrote the book was from here, too, right?"

"You got it," Landon replied.

"Sam," Abi said, "Landon has quite a collection of old vinyls."

"You got any Sly and the Family Stone?" he asked.

"I do, actually. I do," Landon said. "I'm going to get that album for you."

"Landon's a regular vinyl soup kitchen," Abi said. "She's going to end up giving all her records away. So don't bring your homeboys over and let them choose one, or that girl of yours. This is strictly a Mr. Kasir's neighborhood thing."

"It's all good," Sam said.

"What does that mean?" Landon asked him.

"What does what mean?"

"I mean, when somebody says, 'It's all good,' it's not that everything is good, right?" she asked. "Just the moment at hand, right?"

Sam reached over and put a hand on her shoulder. "You're stoned, girl."

"She's a psychotherapist," Abi said. "Or was one. Got to analyze it all."

Sam stood, and Abi, too. Sam knew what she was going to do. She did it often.

Standing chest to chest with Sam, she said, "Landon, this is the only man I know, other than my daddy, who's taller than me." Abi kissed his forehead.

"I'm gonna grab a beer," Sam said. "Anyone else? Landon?"

"No thanks," she replied.

On his way to the kitchen, Sam raised the window shade. The sunset was spectacular. It threw its light along Cullom Street. Sam saw Roy gathering up the last of his garden vegetables, looking like more than an ordinary man. He was Adam, and this was Eden. Paradise.

Damn good bud, Sam thought. He'd forgotten why he'd gotten up in the first place.

"Sam, my daddy has cancer," Abi said abruptly.

He whirled back around. "Aw, babe, I'm so sorry to hear that."

"He wants—he needs—some stuff to help with the nausea when his treatments begin. I know you don't keep a lot around, but I was wondering if you could talk to Unc about getting some extra."

"No problem," he said. "It's all good."

JET

As Christmas neared, the neighbors attempted to decorate their places with homemade materials. Jet, for her part, decided to make a tree out of the bamboo stalks that grew near the alley behind her unit. She cut them down, gathered them up at the base, and braced them in an urn she'd pilfered from her mother's house when she left. She attached beer tabs to paper clips and hung them from the stalks like ornaments.

The next morning, she threw on some jeans and black heels with dark red soles, grabbed a Mountain Dew, and went to the front porch for a smoke. She stared at Sam's place across the street. His girlfriend's car was parked at the curb. Jet bristled. She would often run across the street to buy a few buds and spend all day smoking them with Sam on his couch, just to be near him. Once, she had held tight to him when saying goodbye, trying to communicate what she wanted from him, trying to see if he wanted it, too, but he had slowly disentangled from her. He wasn't interested.

"I'm over it," she said, though nobody was there to hear her.

Landon passed by with her dog. Jet hadn't yet had a real conversation with her, just an occasional wave and a "Doing all right?" shouted across the street. She knew from Sam that Landon was cool, and that she was a therapist. Probably a good friend to make.

"Hey, Landon!"

Landon looked up and waved. Jet guessed that Landon might be her mother's age, but she sure didn't dress like her mother. Landon wore jeans or long embroidered skirts. Her hair wasn't short and teased up in the back like most of the older women Jet knew. From a distance, Landon looked comfortable and relaxed but still pretty.

"Jet?" Landon said, pausing at the walkway. "That's your name, right?"

"How could you forget it?" Jet laughed. "Come on over, if you have the time."

"Let me put my dog inside."

While she waited for Landon, Jet surveyed the porch that she shared with Tina for evidence of a recent rager she'd thrown. Tina liked to climb out her window and sit on the roof, or sometimes threaten to throw herself off of it. Jet decided she wouldn't tell Landon about Tina. She noted the empty beer cans Tina had left on the porch, the open grill that needed to be cleaned, leaves that needed to be swept, the glider covered in dust. Their porch was always like this, but damn if Jet was going to do something about it. She wouldn't clean up a mess that wasn't hers.

When Landon returned, Jet decided not to invite her in right away. She preferred to be outside, felt safer for some reason, meeting somebody for the first time, especially a person old enough to be her parent.

"I'm so glad we're finally meeting," Landon said.

The two women shook hands.

"Marlboro Reds," Jet said, holding up her pack of cigarettes. "Same brand that our next president smokes. Do you like him?"

"Who?"

"Obama."

"Yes, of course. Who wouldn't?"

"Most of Birmingham," Jet said.

"Well, I bet Cullom Street is mostly blue."

Jet agreed. "Even the lawyers who own those big houses down the street," she said. "They are bleeding-heart liberals. Otherwise, they wouldn't be caught dead in Southside, among people like us. You want to come inside?"

"Sure."

Jet's place had two big rooms that could be closed off by pocket doors. Behind those two rooms was her bedroom.

"I like your Christmas tree," Landon said, gesturing toward the bedecked bamboo.

"We make do with what we've got," Jet said. "If you don't mind, let's go to my room. These other two rooms are full of furniture my mother sent me. I'm not exactly comfortable with her selections. Just like her, stuffy and hysterical."

Jet's bedroom was much different from the rest of her apartment. Two big, black beanbag chairs were on the floor. Her bedspread and pillowcases were deep indigo. The curtains were crimson and let in no light.

"Have a seat," Jet said, gesturing to the beanbags.

"Thanks," Landon replied, sinking into the black corduroy.

Jet sat in the other one and took off her stilettos. "These kill my feet, but I'm wearing them for Sam."

"Is he your boyfriend?"

"No." She hesitated. "Well, he could be. I wish he was."

A beat passed between them. Jet noticed Landon looking a little uncomfortable, taking in the room.

"Do you have kids?" Jet asked.

"I do. Two daughters, probably around your age."

"I bet you were a good mother."

"Well, you'd have to ask my daughters about that."

Jet paused, then lit a cigarette, wondering whether or not to tell Landon the truth about herself. After all, Landon was older, and from what Abi had told her, she'd been a therapist. And her eyes were gentle and welcoming, as if she'd be wide open to any conversation Jet might choose to have with her.

"I like the neighborhood," Landon said.

"We're a family around here."

"And what brought you here? Are you a student?"

"I already graduated with a double major—history and philosophy. That's why I work at a bookstore that pays minimum wage."

Jet stood to grab an ashtray from the dresser and light a black candle. The only reason she didn't have to run to work this morning was because she'd volunteered to work Christmas, and the store had given her a day off in return.

"My dad died when I was eighteen," Jet told her.

"That must have been awful, losing him."

Jet sank back down into the beanbag chair, cigarette in hand. "Yes, it was bad. But the really bad thing is that my mother, for whatever reason, chose that time to tell me I was adopted." Jet inhaled sharply on her cigarette, exhaling with her words as she continued. "My birth mother was my aunt. Turns out, she gave me to her sister, who adopted me. So I grew up thinking that my adopted mother was my real mother, and her sister was my aunt."

"That must have been very difficult," Landon said.

Jet nodded, silent for a moment while she thought about just how difficult it had been.

"One thing that really hurt was that my birth mother had another daughter a couple of years later and kept her." She took another drag on her cigarette. "So I thought this kid was my cousin when she was really my sister. I lived this lie all my life until my dad died. Maybe he was the one who told my mother and aunt not to tell me the truth. I forgot to ask you if you need anything to drink."

"No, I'm fine," Landon said.

Jet swallowed the last of her Mountain Dew.

"So what did you do?" Landon asked.

"Hell, I packed up my clothes and took the bus to Birmingham. I spent my first few nights at the YWCA, then learned of a women's shelter downtown. The women had a place to sleep at night in the church basement and a breakfast to eat in the morning. During the day, they had to leave the shelter and seek work. A lot of the women were prostitutes." Jet paused, taking a deep breath. "They helped me learn."

Jet glanced over at Landon to see how that augured. Knowing that Landon was a shrink made it easier to open up. Surely, she had heard it all over the years. Landon's face was still, free of judgment. She said nothing, only smiled slightly, so Jet prodded her.

"Don't you think my mother should have told me the truth from the get-go?"

"The truth is always best," Landon replied.

Jet leaned forward, her long black hair falling like a curtain. "Are you sorry I invited you in?" she asked Landon. "People must do this to you all the time—free therapy."

"I'm just listening," Landon replied. "I'm interested."

Jet wanted to believe this. She looked at the candle. The wax was melting down the sides. She reached over Landon to her bookshelf and took down two books: William Blake's *Songs of Innocence and of Experience* and Sylvia Plath's *Ariel*.

"My favorite books," she told Landon.

Landon smiled and nodded. "I read them somewhere along the way," she said.

Jet set them in her lap, mindlessly stroking the worn spines.

"One day, a car pulled up at the curb of the shelter. A man got out; he was wearing a collar. Somebody whispered, 'Priest,' like he was a cop or something. He walked over to us and asked me if I felt like talking to him. I guess he picked me because I was the youngest. Father Patrick. He put me up in his parish's transitional apartments. He showed me their soup kitchen, a free lunch. He hooked me up with a parishioner named Trish who helped me apply for college, and all the scholarships and loans. Then he set me up with Mr. Kasir, who had this place here up for rent. They were so nice and expected nothing in return."

"Let me ask you something," Landon said, touching Jet's arm gently. "Is Jet your given name?"

"Almost," Jet said with a laugh. "It's Jenette. I used to babysit, and the kids couldn't say it—it always came out 'Jet, Jet.' I liked it, so I started calling myself Jet and never looked back."

"Good for you," Landon said. "It is a great name. Very evocative. You know, makes people want to know what you're all about."

"Now, you tell me your story," Jet said.

"I have daughters about your age. One is in the military and will deploy to Iraq soon. I'm divorced. Currently unemployed. I like it here. I like Mr. Kasir. Do you?"

"I love that man," Jet replied.

Landon stretched her legs. Her long broomstick skirt was light blue. She was wearing sandals even though it was December.

"So, tell me about Sam. How do you feel about him?"

Jet shook her head. "I don't know, I don't know. There's just something about him. When I'm over there, I want him to pick me up like a baby and put me to bed in his room. I can't figure out what it's about." Then she quickly changed the subject. "I want you to meet Father Patrick. Why don't you go with me to midnight mass on Christmas Eve? I invited Abi, too. She hates church, but she's been like a big sister to me."

Landon hesitated. "It's been awhile since I've been to church."

"You'll like it," Jet assured her. "They're really nice. Episcopalians, very liberal."

ABI

Abi woke up early to run. It was going to be a warm day for December. She had asked Landon to go with her to see her parents. She did her stretching, then started jogging slowly in the direction of the Vulcan Trail. The trail was relatively new. Once an abandoned rail bed that was used for dumping, the surface was paved for runners in 1997, around the time Abi moved to Birmingham.

Today, she began her run in the alley behind Green Springs Avenue, just a block from Cullom Street. This would take her to the trail. Abi didn't like to wear headphones. She wanted to hear what nature had to offer.

She wondered if she would have become a runner had it not been for her proximity to the Vulcan Trail. It was such a refuge, a small piece of nature she could enjoy while still inside the city limits. In summer, the tree-lined trail offered a respite from the heat. In winter, the bare trees yielded a view of the city. All of the red, yellow, and orange autumn leaves were gone, leaving only shadows on the pavement.

She had made runners out of her previous boyfriend, Scott, and Celeste, her partner after him. They could never keep up. She often wondered if they were still running, if she'd cross paths with either of them one morning. But she was all right being alone. She didn't miss them. She didn't miss anything when she was running. She felt most alive when her legs were moving, endorphins enacting a chemical change in her body that could be better than drinking or drugs or sex. Her favorite moment was when she felt a second wind, her body aching but also craving the pain. When she ran, she pushed past her limitations. It was therapy. If only she could have been a runner as a kid, a teenager. The closest she came to soothing herself back then was to sit by the pond.

At the end of her run, Abi cooled down by walking between Green Springs and Cullom. Landon had agreed to go with her to give her daddy the starter kit she'd gotten from Sam—an eighth of mid-grade and a small pipe. They were leaving at noon, so she still had enough time to wash up and study. She had a sociology exam coming up.

Abi paused for a minute on the porch and wiped her face with her shirt, then took the stairs up to her place. The cats were asleep on her bed. She had been afraid Cinderella might not like the new member of the family, Grits. But so far, so good.

Abi flung herself across the bed so they might cozy up to her, but they couldn't be bothered. With her right hand, she petted Cinderella; with her left, Grits. After a few minutes, she got up and drew a warm bath. She stepped in and slid down so that everything but her face was underwater. She lathered up, using her bar of lavender soap, then tilted her head back, lifted it, and washed her hair with the same soap. The first time Abi had set foot into Landon's bathroom downstairs, she was amazed by all the various soaps, shampoos, conditioners, bubble baths, and body washes that lined her tub.

One night, she and Landon had been sitting outside on the swing. Abi was pulling her hair up and twisting it into a bun. The street lamp lit up the porch. She remembered something from her teenage years.

"I used to pull my hair out," Abi said. "I mean, there were actually bald patches underneath my curls."

Landon leaned forward, her face bright. "Trichotillomania," she said with a little relish.

"What?"

"That's what it's called, when somebody pulls their hair out. You don't do it anymore, do you?" Landon asked, reaching up to touch a curl that had fallen free from Abi's bun.

"No. But I did when I was fourteen or so. I remember sitting in math class, unable to work a problem. I'd stare out the window to the school-yard and take a strand with my fingers, first playing with it, then pulling it out. It wasn't like I grabbed a handful and jerked it out. It was one strand at a time."

"Were you also a cutter or a burner?" Landon asked.

"How did you know that?"

"A clinical guess. It's all stress related."

"Look," Abi said, opening her hand to show Landon the scar where she had once put out a cigarette in her palm.

Landon had taken her hand and kissed the scar.

Abi lay in the tub, thinking of that sweet gesture.

After her bath, she put on a pair of jeans and an Auburn War Eagle T-shirt. She had no interest in football whatsoever, but her family was a bunch of Alabama fans, and she had bought it to needle them. She shook her head to give her hair a bit of drying, then left it to its own devices.

Her sociology textbook was an oversized paperback with a group of cartoon people screaming on the cover. Like a crowd of fans, they held up a sign that read, "The Real World."

Abi loved the social sciences. To her, they shone a little light on why people did the things they did. She ran her finger along the chapter titles she needed to study, under the heading of "Framing Social Life": "Cultural Crossroads," "The Self and Interaction," "Life in Groups," and "Deviance"—the last being, of course, the most interesting to her.

If things went right, she should get her BA a year from now. Then she was going to get a master's in social work. Landon had told her that once she had her master's, she could be a therapist.

It was maddening that nobody back home ever asked her about school. It was all about her not finding the right boy. But school was much more interesting to her than romance. The cats were enough to cuddle with at night. And she had friends, Landon being the newest.

After a few hours of studying, Abi gave Grits and Cinderella one last petting. She grabbed the paraphernalia that Sam had given her and a daily devotional from Mr. Kasir and stuffed them into her purse. She hesitated, then reached into Sam's baggie and broke off a bit of the weed for herself, for later on. She didn't feel guilty; it was like getting a tip at work.

She called Landon and asked if she was ready. She was.

"Be sure and wear those cross earrings of yours, okay? My daddy will love them."

Landon did exactly as she was told. They got into Abi's car and rolled down the windows a bit because of the unseasonably warm weather. As they drove, the wind whipped their hair into a frenzy.

"I need a bandana," Landon said.

"Oh, we want to look like the wild and scary city women that we are."

Abi had never taken anybody to the compound. It was her secret. But now that her daddy had cancer, everything was different. And she felt that Landon was the perfect person—a bit older, kind, nice to look at—to present even to the judgiest of her family members.

Abi drove her usual route—from Cullom to Green Springs to I-65—and veered left to get on I-59. They passed the steel mills that had birthed the city.

"I finally had a long conversation with Jet the other day," Landon told her.

"Oh, really," Abi said, pulling her eyes from the road for a moment to look at Landon. "What did you think?"

"I like her."

"Oh, you like everybody," Abi said.

"No, she seems to have gotten her life together. After where she's been, it's pretty impressive."

Abi eased up. "You're right. She is so young, and has such problems with men. I've sat with her many nights while she cried over her past and relationships gone bad. I think we both need to reassure her that we're here for her. She's not old enough yet to see that it's your women friends, not your male lovers, who will save you."

"She asked me to go to midnight mass with her."

"Are you going?"

"I think so. I told her yes. Are you?"

Abi shook her head.

"Well," Landon said, sounding worried, "you still have to help me get dressed."

"Of course! Just don't get saved."

"I don't think Episcopalians have to get saved," Landon replied.

The interstate carried them out of the city. When Abi took her exit, the landscape changed. There were fields, now plowed under and empty for the winter. Pine trees lined the road, their needles bright against the otherwise dormant roadside. Horses were behind wooden fencing. The houses were far apart, so unlike the city. They passed a girl hanging sheets on a clothesline. An older woman sat in a chair watching—still, like the horses. They flashed by a solitary cow, an aging truck, and piles of wood. Abi lit a cigarette and hung her arm out the window.

"Who was the first person you were ever in love with?" Landon asked out of the blue.

"One of my cousins," Abi replied.

"Let's hear it for the South!" Landon exclaimed. "What did you like about him?"

"Her."

"Like I said, let's hear it for the South!"

"Her name was Marcia. She was from my Tennessee family. A lot older than me, and in love with her boyfriend. I just had a crush on her—it's not like we ever kissed or anything. She taught me some things. About love."

"What did she say?"

"We were out on the pond, and I asked her things about love, and she answered them. I was young. It was just a fascination, an infatuation. But I still carry it around with me. I'm always looking for her."

"My wedding anniversary is coming up," Landon said. "The day before Christmas."

"On Christmas Eve?"

"We were hippies," Landon said. "We didn't want to make a big deal out of it. We always went to a restaurant in Bessemer on our anniversary. The Bright Star. I'm sorry."

"Why?"

"I don't want to be one of those women who talks about her divorce all the time."

Abi touched Landon's shoulder. "You hardly talk about it at all."

Abi pulled onto the dirt road that led to her family's compound and sat on the horn.

"What are you doing?" Landon asked her.

"It's a warning so all the brats will get out of my way."

And sure enough, when the trailers came into view, a gaggle of kids ran alongside the car.

"You stole our cat!" one of the boys shouted.

They scurried around in front of the car, trying to block Abi from driving any farther. They threw handfuls of dirt. Then the oldest of the boys launched a rock that hit her tire.

"Bitch!"

"Sorry," Abi said to Landon.

Maybe she hadn't thought this through. Maybe she shouldn't have brought Landon. What if Landon stopped liking her when she saw what kind of place she came from? She didn't want her to think that she'd once behaved like this.

The boys didn't let up. Finally, Abi stopped the car and got out. One of the girls copied her brother and threw a rock her way.

"Listen, you little motherfuckers," Abi hissed, walking toward them. She didn't want Landon to hear her. "You go home right now. If you don't, I'm getting back in the car and I'm gonna run over you. All of you. You will be flat as pancakes. Then I'll toss your mangled bodies into the pond."

"Mama, Mama!" they yelled, scattering. "Abi's gonna kill us!"

She got back in the car, trying to look composed. "And people wonder why I don't have kids," she said.

Once they reached the double-wide, Abi saw Daddy sitting outside on the stoop. When he spotted Abi, he stood, a smile crossing his face. She parked and jumped from the car.

"Daddy!" Abi said as she threw her arms around his neck. Hearing Landon exit the car behind her, she unraveled herself from her father to make the introduction. "Daddy this is my new neighbor, Landon. And Landon, this is my daddy."

"Hello, Daddy," Landon said. "You two look just alike."

"My name is Will," he said, "but you can call me Daddy if you want to." He gave Landon a sideways hug.

Daddy looked at Abi's War Eagle shirt and smiled. "Can't resist making everybody down here crazy, can you?"

Abi smiled at him.

"I have good news for you," Daddy said in his deep baritone.

"What's that?"

"Your mother isn't here. She got called in to work."

Abi looked up at the sky and raised her palms, as if acknowledging the God she didn't believe in. "A Christmas miracle!"

LANDON

Landon sat at the vanity and looked at her reflection in triplicate. All the furniture in her bedroom was from her parents' marriage suite—the vanity, bed, chest of drawers, night table, and lamp.

In a few minutes, Abi would be coming in to help her get ready for mass with Jet. Landon had been thinking about Abi's father. He was a handsome man, probably only ten years older than she. She thought of the way he ran his hand down her arm after he hugged her. But he was a friend's daddy, and the gesture was hard to assimilate.

Landon felt that no matter how rough growing up in a trailer park had been on Abi, she had a father who loved her. The longing, the yearning for the kind of paternal love that Landon had been denied was fresh on her mind. Nobody in the neighborhood knew anything about her yet. Not really.

A few times, she had mentioned Nick in passing to people who noticed their photograph. Nick had been born five minutes before her. Life began at the same time for them, so they moved through the years on the same course. Nick was beautiful. He had a head full of soft curls, blue eyes, and a perfect physique for baseball, which was his passion. He had played in the minor leagues before the accident. He was a catcher. Landon still pictured him with that mitt in place, his balance, his guts. It was a dangerous position to play.

She spent her childhood sitting in the bleachers with her mother.

Her father didn't come to the games.

They lived in a subdivision of Birmingham. There, the men worked in foundries. They made things such as valves and pipe fittings and ball bearings. The steel mills, the plants, the industries—all unregulated at the time—threw smoke and sometimes fire into the sky, which was never blue. The factory families were part of the new industrial South and lived in modest houses built so close together they could see right into their next-door neighbors' dens if the venetian blinds were raised. They heard each other's fights, witnessed stolen kisses, and saw what was playing on the neighbors' black-and-white TV sets.

Growing up, kids from the block had played whiffle ball in Landon's backyard. The trees were aligned in such a way as to form the perfect first, second, and third bases. The next-door neighbors had a chain-link fence that offered the opportunity for a home run. During the summer, the gnats were so bad that the children wore swimming goggles to keep the bugs out of their eyes.

When Nick started Little League, he kept playing whiffle ball with the younger kids. He encouraged them, gave them gentle pointers, and was genuinely excited when they landed a hit, even when they were playing on the opposite side. He was the kindest person Landon had ever known.

Nick had the gift of being both a good catcher and a good hitter. When they were twelve years old, their father finally came to one of Nick's Little League games. Their mother was aglow with pride over her intact family. Their father bought Landon a sno-cone and even had one himself. He was a different person.

But Nick didn't have a good night.

Maybe he was anxious because their father was there. But he missed some pitches. He struck out twice. Landon's heart raced. She watched her father's face turn angry—the way the vein along his temple pulsed. He became again the man she knew. Her mother's happiness turned frantic.

During the ride home, they were all mute. Their mother, Nick, and Landon were too scared to say a word. They knew what was about to happen.

Their father pulled into the carport, and they got out of the car—it was a new Chevy, and he was proud of it. They quickly went inside and scurried to their bedrooms. Landon's hands were shaking.

Before she had time to change into her pajamas, her father's voice roared through the lion's den they called home: "Landon, come here."

He was in Nick's room. Once she sat next to Nick on the bed, their father took off his belt. He yelled at Nick. "Get those phony baseball clothes off. Strip down to your underwear. Now," he growled. "Hustle it!"

Landon turned her head the other way. She was already crying. So was Nick.

Then their father told Nick to face the wall.

"Now, watch carefully, Landon. Watch my hands, and stop crying those crocodile tears. You stop it, too," he said to Nick.

Mother's voice from the hallway was shrill. "Don't do this to him, Frank. I will leave you if you do this."

Her father turned to Landon. "Don't listen to her. She's not going anywhere. You people can't survive without me."

You people.

"Stand up, Landon."

He put the belt in her hand and stood behind her with his arms guiding her, as if he were a golf coach teaching a youngster how to hold the club and how to swing.

"Now, here we go," he said smoothly.

His hands were over hers, and together they delivered the first blow. It hit the middle of Nick's spine. Immediately, the place on his back turned pink.

"You aren't even trying to cooperate!" he yelled at her. "Here we go again."

Another blow. She knew this one would be sharper and deeper because her father was squeezing his hands so tightly over hers.

"Okay, now you've got the gist of it." He moved away from her. "Now, do it by yourself. Don't be a weakling. The softer you hit, the more hits, until you do it right. We'll stay here till midnight if it takes that long."

Landon looked back into her father's face. His brown eyes were demonic, his face puffy and red, though he didn't drink. In a way, it would have been better if he were drunk. But he was stone-cold sober, and this made it horrific. She knew in that moment that she hated him. And that he likely hated her, hated the whole family. She knew Nick was hurting as much for her as he was for himself. That's how Nick was. He knew the last thing in the world she wanted to do was hurt him.

"Give that to me," her father said, snatching the belt back from Landon. "You think if you don't hit him, it's over? We haven't even started yet. Now, see this?" he said, and pointed to the buckle. "If you can't do it right, you're gonna have to do it so the buckle gets him. You understand me, Landon?"

She nodded.

"Wipe those tears off your face," he said.

He stood behind her once again. He squeezed her hands. "Go."

He still was doing all the work. Her hands were trembling; she couldn't do what was being asked of her. He stepped away again.

"Now," he said, "I'll say it once again. If you don't hit hard, this thing could go on for hours."

"Please, Daddy," she begged, "whip me instead."

"Why would I do that? You weren't on that baseball field. You didn't play a miserable game. Humiliate your whole family."

"I don't care. Hit me instead."

"Oh, so you want Nick to hit you?"

"No, I want *you* to."

"Not happening!" he yelled.

Nick whispered to her, "Just do it."

With that, Landon began hitting Nick. She pretended he was their father. She vowed never to speak to that man again. She promised God this was the last time she'd hit a child, her own or anyone's. She tried to land her blows low, so her brother's underwear could absorb them, but her father saw through that.

"Quit it. I know what you're doing."

Landon felt numb—not just her hands but her whole body. She hit her brother over and over, harder and harder. Finally, her father took the belt and delivered a last blow. It drew blood.

That's what their father was after: the blood of his son.

. . . .

Abi's voice cut the memory short.

"Landon, I'm here."

"Come on back," Landon called.

She didn't get up from the vanity. She brushed the tears away and stared at herself in the mirror.

"Are you all right?" Abi asked as she came to stand behind her.

"Yes. Fine."

"Oh, I'm so excited," Abi said, as if she could sense Landon wanted to move on. "Let's make you beautiful, even though you already are. You have great hair." Abi ran the brush across Landon's mane. "Ever had anybody French-braid it? I can't believe it's so lustrous."

"That's because I've never done anything to it—no dye, no blow-dryer, no highlights."

Abi stopped brushing. "You're kidding me."

"No, I swear. It's the truth." Landon was proud of this fact and was happy to share it. She had worn her hair the same since she was thirteen years old—bangs, a bit long, turned under, and often pulled back with barrettes. It was light brown and soft. Gray had appeared at her temples years ago, but she didn't mind.

Abi began the process of pulling strands together, starting at the top and working her way downward. Landon closed her eyes. She hadn't been fretted over in a tender way for a long time.

When Abi finished, Landon pulled the side mirrors inward to get a better look. She smiled.

"Okay," Abi said. "Now, let's see what you're gonna be wearing. I can't believe Jet roped you into this."

"I've never been to an Episcopal church. I was raised Baptist—took a long time to get over that."

Abi was surveying Landon's closet. "All these long skirts. Do you even own a short skirt?"

"Just the denim one, and I'm not wearing that."

"Well, here," Abi said, and took out an aqua blouse with a few tiny, tasteful sequins around the neck that caught the light.

Landon stood and retrieved a long black skirt that fit nicely—certainly the dressiest thing she owned.

"Jewelry?" Abi asked.

Landon opened the top drawer of the dresser and brought out four jewelry boxes.

"Jesus Christ," Abi said. "Where did you get all this?"

"Most of it is costume, from my grandmother, my aunt, and my mother."

"Costume jewelry sells like hotcakes on eBay now, did you know that? If you ever need some cash, let me know, and I'll help you set it up online."

For tonight, they agreed on an opal necklace Landon's mother had given her. The opal fell perfectly inside the V-neck of her blouse.

Abi was searching the closet. "Where are your heels?"

"I don't wear heels," Landon confessed. "I don't even own a pair."

"Well, that's okay," Abi said, pulling out a pair of simple black ballet flats. "Tonight, you'll just be hippy *élégante*."

Landon brushed a bit of powder over her face and applied mascara, then a smear of the coral lipstick she'd owned for nearly a decade. She had never liked dressing up, always preferred dressing down, like her mother. When her mother died, the funeral director had asked for a recent photograph to give to the mortician. In it, her mother was wearing shorts and waving with a gardening glove still on. When the funeral home opened the coffin for the family viewing, however, they found her in scarlet lipstick and painted fingernails, her hair teased and sprayed into a webby poof. Landon started laughing and couldn't stop. Apparently, there had been a mix-up. A wealthy Episcopal woman had also just died. It got Landon through the funeral, laughing inwardly as she imagined the other woman—a real lady—laid out in the neighboring parlor without her polish or bright lipstick.

"All right," Abi said "You look great. Nobody will ever guess you're unemployed, divorced, scared, and out of place."

Landon laughed and felt her nerves lessen. She thanked Abi, and they headed to the front room to wait in two matching antique chairs for Jet.

. . . .

St. Andrew's was within walking distance. It was an old brownstone on the corner of Eleventh and Cullom. Whenever Landon had passed it on her walks, she'd noted the gardens. Something was always blooming, even in December.

Before she and Jet went inside, Jet showed her the tiny columbarium. Landon shuddered.

Father Patrick was dressed for midnight mass, in satin robes and gold vestments. Jet pointed him out to Landon as he stood at the entrance greeting people. Landon didn't know if she should shake his hand or what. Even though it was dark, she saw that he had kind eyes.

He hugged Jet.

Jet introduced Landon as "our newest tenant on Cullom Street."

"Nice neighborhood," Father Patrick said, extending a hand to Landon. "We're all in this together."

"I've never been to midnight mass," she told him.

"Have you been to an Episcopal church, to the Eucharist?"

"No. I grew up Baptist."

"Don't feel like you have to kneel, genuflect, make the sign of the cross, or anything. If you have been baptized at any time, in any church, then feel free to participate in the Eucharist."

Landon was sure she'd do that; she'd heard from Jet that they served up real wine here, not Welch's grape juice like the Baptists did. She'd take a big swig of it.

As they walked into the narthex, Landon shook her head. "I can't believe I'm doing this."

"Doing what?" Jet asked as she reached into her purse for some lipstick to paint her lips even darker.

Landon told her that they had to sit in the back because she was claustrophobic and might need to dash out, in the throes of a bona fide panic attack.

Once they sat, the organ brought up the music—a cue to rise—and the service began with a processional. First came the two acolytes, to light the candles. Then the priests in their colorful robes. One was waving incense. The smell was strong, like the incense Landon and her friends once used to mask the stench of pot. But this was different. It was like pixie dust being disseminated among the parishioners, permeating every part of the church like magic.

Goose bumps ran down her body. Maybe she was here for a reason.

The choir followed. They were singing "O Come All Ye Faithful."

Landon wondered if she was one of the faithful. Her life was a mess. But she wanted the words of the hymn to include her. She wanted to belong. In fact, she had to belong. Maybe she'd return to this church. Maybe she'd be able to let her guard down with these Episcopalians. They had a reputation of being accepting. She wanted that, too—to be a person of interest, a stranger taken in, no questions asked.

Landon noticed that not everybody was dressed up. A few men wore jeans. Across the aisle, a couple of girls were holding hands. She wanted to believe they were partners. Perhaps this was for her, if she could get past this place where she was stuck in life. She recalled the scripture that called believers "the fellowship of the mystery." Landon imagined how they might get together to ponder what they didn't understand and, through that pondering, become able to transcend.

One of the priests started speaking words she didn't know. She glanced down at the program. This was the Collect for Purity. Everybody sang the "Gloria," a hymn of praise. She couldn't find a hymnal, only *The Book of Common Prayer.* The congregation was singing from memory. The priest prayed. He read from the Old Testament. For the New Testament reading, another priest walked down the aisle toward the center of the church.

"Praise be to God," the parishioners said in unison.

When it was time, she followed Jet to the front to partake of the bread and wine.

"Take, eat: This is my body, which is given for you."

Then, "Drink this, all of you. This is my blood of the new covenant, which is shed for you."

Landon wasn't sure she was fit to participate in the Eucharist. She was sinful. She was lost. As she accepted the wafer, she tried to tell the priest with her eyes how sad she was, how alone. He made eye contact with her. She thought she noticed a slight nod, as if he did indeed know who she was, what she needed, where she might find it. She was caught off-guard, confronting not just where she was but who she was—a woman with no compass, no star to guide her, no destination. The past was behind her, gone.

For so long, Christmas Eve had been her wedding anniversary. No longer. There was nothing to celebrate. There was simply this mass. Its history. Experienced by people all over the world.

By the end of it, they were all on their knees, including the priests. The idea that they, too, made mistakes, were mortals like the rest of humanity, got to Landon. When Father Patrick took a knee, she wanted to cry. She had seen Christmas pageants. But this wasn't pageantry. This was real. The saints were almost palpable. The dead—her mother, father, and brother, who had long since left this earth. Everyone there, all in one place, all of one accord.

Landon thought she might return to this church. She looked ahead in *The Book of Common Prayer* to see what came after Christmas. The

Epiphany, when the Magi beheld Christ and knew who he was. They recognized him.

Something deep within Landon understood this. The Magi—the Wise Men—were simply a few pagan astrologers from the east who saw a star that didn't jive with the night sky as they knew it. They wanted to check it out, and they did. And that was what Landon was doing now.

Landon told Jet all this when they got back in her car.

"I like that, too," Jet said. "I'm not saying I believe it, but I like the part about them being astrologers." She was checking her phone for messages as they talked. "Sam was supposed to fucking call me."

Jet put her phone back in her purse but didn't start the car.

"You know I was a history and philosophy major," she said. "And with Father Patrick and all, I've read a lot of the Bible. There was another Epiphany, when John the Baptist was going about his business baptizing people in the name of a man he'd never met. Jesus came to be baptized, and suddenly John knew who he was. 'Behold the lamb of God, who taketh away the sin of the world.' Remember that part? I'm sure you do if you were a Baptist. It wasn't of interest to me until I met Father Patrick and he pointed out that both the Magi and John the Baptist were part of the Epiphany because they recognized Jesus. Like all you have to do is see. Pretty cool, if you think about it."

Jet started the car. Landon was taken aback by what Jet knew and the ease with which she talked about it. Of course, just because she talked about it didn't mean she believed it.

Jet began to drive, then reached over and bumped Landon's arm with a soft fist. "Did you like Father Patrick?"

"Oh, yes."

"You think he's hot, don't you?"

"What makes you think that?" Landon asked.

"I'm just observant," she replied.

They were heading up Cullom Street by then.

"Do you think he is?" Landon asked.

"If he weren't a priest, I might think so."

Landon shrugged. That he was a priest was the very reason he might appeal to her. He was an impossibility. During her manic periods, she would have thought it an enticing challenge—to bring a man of the cloth to his knees, not at midnight mass, but alone.

MR. KASIR

Mr. Kasir always woke up early, around four. He would put on his jacket and head outside, where he sat in a patio chair to look at Venus. He liked to think of it as the morning star, even though he knew it was a planet.

He knew scripture that spoke of Jesus as the bright and morning star, in Revelation. And then, of course, there was the mythology surrounding the planet—Venus, the Roman goddess of love, beauty, fertility, and desire. When visible, it was the most brilliant planet in the sky. On winter mornings, Mr. Kasir could make it out clearly.

It was Christmas morning, and desire, not reverence, was driving Mr. Kasir's thoughts. When he had put an extra lock on Landon Cooper's door after the break-in, he noticed a photograph of her when she was younger. In it, she looked just like a girl he had known. Not just known but loved. *Carissa.*

He wanted to see the picture again, maybe even to tell Landon about Carissa, about whom he'd never before told anyone. He was going to find a way to drive to Cullom Street that day. Since he and Mrs. Kasir entertained their grown grandchildren on Christmas night, he had most of the day free. He feared that Landon might have nowhere to go, nobody to see.

He looked at his watch. Mrs. Kasir would be getting up around six o'clock. He started to think of reasons, excuses to tell his wife. Perhaps he needed to warn his tenants that a cold wave was coming, to leave their faucets trickling so as to avoid frozen pipes. But the front was still several days away.

He went back inside to the kitchen and retrieved his notebooks from where he kept them in a cabinet above the washer and dryer. He set them on the kitchen table. Every tenant had his or her own file. They were ledgers where he recorded rental payments, but they also held details about repairs made, as well as general comments.

He got some coffee started and sat down. Then he pulled Landon's notebook from the stack.

When Mrs. Kasir walked into the kitchen—a bit after six, as he knew she would—Mr. Kasir looked at her face and realized he need not feel guilty or make up a lie about where he was going. His wife was kind and would likely be distracted by Christmas planning.

She fixed pancakes.

While they were eating, he mentioned Landon. "She has no family here," he told her.

"Well, should you go see her?" she asked, putting her fork down.

It was so sweet and direct a question, he wanted to cry. He had kept his secret from her and carried the weight of guilt all these years, burying his thoughts of love lost under the everyday trials of marriage and business. But now, Mrs. Kasir was making it easy, making it aboveboard—the idea that he wanted to see Landon's photograph, to think of Carissa.

"And you can take her one of those banana nut loaves I baked."

He reached for her hand and squeezed it.

"Have you been up thinking about Abe Jr.?" she asked.

Their son had caused so much pain over the years. Even after he got out of prison and started doing light construction, he never came home to be with his parents. Christmas had become a particularly sad time for the Kasirs. Abe Jr.'s absence left its handprints all over the holiday.

"No," Mr. Kasir said firmly. "I'm not thinking of him."

"Good," she said.

Mr. Kasir helped his wife with the dishes, then went to the den to watch TV. All of the local channels were overrun by Christmas—ways to make the holidays better, what airports were closed, what was delayed, all reported by news anchors who must have been miserable.

Finally, at eight o'clock sharp, Mr. Kasir reached for his phone. He reasoned that by then it wasn't too early to call. He prayed she'd answer.

And she did.

"Landon?"

"Hi, Mr. Kasir."

"How did you know it was me?"

"Caller ID."

He just couldn't wrap his brain around anything the least bit technological. Nothing was private anymore. He didn't know what Facebook was, he hardly knew what online meant, and yet all of his tenants asked him for his email. Mrs. Kasir operated an email address for both of them. He worried about identify theft. He didn't understand that either, but it was a phrase that bothered him.

"Mrs. Kasir has baked you a loaf of banana nut bread, and I wanted to bring it by, unless you're busy."

"I'm not busy at all," she said. "It's just me and Alejandro. I've made some hot apple cider, and there's nobody to drink it but me. Come on over."

He put on his jacket and his gloves. Mrs. Kasir wrapped the bread in aluminum foil and was about to hand it to him but stopped.

"Abe, it's cold out there. You've got to wear a scarf and a cap of some kind. Here, wear one of these." She reached for two toboggans.

Once he was fully insulated, she handed him the bread and asked him to call her if he was going to be longer than a couple of hours. He kissed her on the cheek, then the lips.

"Something's wrong with your head today," she said.

He wondered why she wasn't bothered by his need to see Landon. Then again, when you were married as long as they had been, were as old as they were, things like that didn't enter your mind.

His gloves made it hard to grip his cane, and holding the bread didn't help. Once he was on the truck's running board, he tossed the bread across to the passenger side and hoisted himself up into his seat.

There was no traffic. His neighborhood was quiet. Younger families had moved in and, as a result, the homes were decorated with lights on the eaves, wreaths on the doors, and plastic Santas in the yards. He knew the children in those homes were all busy opening gifts, tossing wrapping paper here and there, trying to ride their new skateboards inside. But they had yet to bring things outdoors. When he returned, the streets would be buzzing with bicycles, fathers putting on training wheels, boys breaking in footballs, girls jumping up and down on pogo sticks or dancing with hula hoops.

When Abe Jr. was young, they had spoiled him on Christmas. One year, they even gave him a much-coveted Radio Flyer sled, even though it snowed only once in a blue moon in Alabama. Abe Jr. still believed in Santa long after his friends had given up, and one day got into a fight over it, tussling in the yard with a schoolmate. There was no way of knowing then that he would never stop fighting. When he returned from Vietnam, still a young man, he was already drinking heavily, with the drugs not far behind. Mr. Kasir did all he could to help his son, but after Abe Jr.'s war, he was too far gone.

He took Highway 31 rather than the interstate from Vestavia, where he lived, then on through Homewood, where Landon used to live, and then down the crest of Red Mountain just a bit, down Cullom Street to Landon's house. He parked right in front of her place, took the bread in one hand, and—trying to avoid using his cane—slid down from his seat to the running board, then to the curb.

Landon appeared at the door as if she'd been watching and waiting. "Merry Christmas, Mr. Kasir."

"And the same to you," he replied as they went inside.

He handed her the bread. She peeled back one end of the foil and inhaled.

"I love the way homemade bread smells," she said with a smile. "Just sit there at the table and . . ." She paused. "You aren't using your cane!"

"I'm trying to grow young," he told her.

"Good luck," she said. "So am I. You sit here, and I'll bring you some cider. I'll cut a few slices of the bread, too."

When she left the room, he got back up, went to the mantel, retrieved the photograph that reminded him of his girl, and set it on the table. He got the piece of shrapnel from his pocket and put it beside the picture. No need to be coy about any of this; he was determined to tell her today.

When she returned to the parlor with the cider and bread, she picked up the photo.

"Christmas was never good at our house when I was growing up,"

Landon said. "My father used it as a threat with Nick—my brother, here—always telling him that Santa wouldn't come because he was such a bad boy. It hung over us like a dark cloud."

Mr. Kasir sat quietly next to her, sensing she had more to say.

"My father never told me or anyone that he was sorry. He didn't say much other than what he yelled at my brother. But a few days before he died, when he was heavily sedated, he told me a war story."

Mr. Kasir nodded. He knew how war could change a man, make him hard.

"By then, I was grown up," Landon continued. "Degreed and practicing. I was sitting in his hospital room, and he told me that, on Christmas Eve 1944, his ship was on a shakedown cruise from Seattle to San Diego. The crew docked in the harbor. He was an ensign fresh from midshipman's school, and this was his first Christmas away from home. The war in Europe was winding down, but not in the Pacific. He had been assigned to an attack transport ship whose purpose was to load boats to evacuate casualties, if I remember correctly. And to deliver marines and army infantrymen to invade islands. The men would spend Christmas Eve and Christmas day in San Diego, then on the twenty-sixth they would sail into the Pacific. He told me there was a veteran officer twice his age who invited him over for Christmas Eve dinner. He was so moved by that invitation, that gesture of kindness. I wanted to ask him why he never extended that kindness to his own son, but I didn't. What would his answer matter? My brother was gone. The damage had been done at that point."

Mr. Kasir noticed for the first time since he arrived that, aside from Landon's red sweater, nothing in her home spoke of Christmas. She offered him a piece of the banana bread and took one for herself.

"I fought in that war, too," he told her.

"What branch?"

"Army. My generation believed there would never be another war. We thought we'd won the worst of them. But then there was Korea. And Vietnam came along and took my son with it. He survived, but it did something to him. He can't hold a job, spends any money he makes on drugs."

Mr. Kasir looked at Landon. She furrowed her brow, and he felt embarrassed.

"I assure you he will never be your landlord. All my properties eventually will go to my grandson, Jason. He's nothing like his father."

"He's a good boy like you, isn't he?" Landon asked.

The morning light fell gently, blanketing the dining-room table, the buffet, the china cabinet, the piano. And he knew it was time to talk.

"This photograph, of you and your brother."

She nodded. "We were seventeen, I think."

"I want to tell you . . ." Mr. Kasir took a deep breath, mustering his courage. "You remind me of a girl I met."

"Tell me," Landon said, leaning back into her chair and fixing her eyes on him. Her gaze was gentle, and he felt reassured. *This must be how her patients feel,* he thought.

"I was sitting outside a field hospital in France," he began. "The shrapnel had been removed from my leg. I was recovering from my own injury as I took care of my wounded men. My head was in my hands, not knowing how they would fare. I know I was looking down because it was her feet I saw first. She was wearing sandals. I didn't look up. I didn't want a villager to see me like this. I wanted to be a brave American. She was wearing a dress, a white cotton dress."

Landon nodded, and he knew it was all right to say more.

"Her hands . . . ," he began, and then his voice broke.

Landon touched his shoulder. "It's all right."

"She gave me a sip of water. I didn't know any French other than oui and merci. She didn't know English. We had to talk with our eyes. For a minute, I thought I was hallucinating. I'd heard of some soldiers . . . The mind and body can take only so much, you know? And some men snap. Maybe that's what happened to your father."

Landon flinched, then reached for his cup. "Want more cider?"

"Thank you. But no, I'm fine."

He waited, worried that he'd upset her.

"Keep going," she urged.

"Carissa. She was just an ordinary girl being kind to a soldier. Every day, she'd meet me at the hospital and take me home with her. I met her family. Sometimes, we'd lie under a tree, and I kept feeling like she wanted to ask me something. She was speaking French, but there was urgency in her face."

Landon put her hands over his. "Maybe we can figure out what her question was."

"Maybe so."

. . . .

On the way home, Mr. Kasir left the car windows open. He hadn't felt this way in a long time. He felt connected. He drove up the hill, then turned right to cross the mountain.

When he got home, Mrs. Kasir was in the kitchen cooking his favorite meal: chicken and dumplings, mashed potatoes, and squash casserole. He liked the warm comfort of these foods together. Plus, they were easy on his teeth.

She was at the stove. Her back was to him.

"How is Landon?"

She had an apron on. He stood behind her and put his arms around her waist.

"Have you lost your mind, Abe?" she asked, not even turning from the stove.

Since he was no longer alone with his secret, Mr. Kasir felt unburdened. He was filled with appreciation for his wife, the meal she was cooking for him, the strength she had when they were going through those years with Abe Jr. It made him love her all the more, something he didn't quite understand but most definitely felt. It fell over him like a blanket.

SAM

S am was stepping out of the shower when he heard a knock on his door. He threw on some jeans and a T-shirt and looked through the peephole. It was Landon and Jet. His grandfather, Poppy, had taught him about hospitality. If friends came to see you, no matter who or when, you should welcome them.

Jet made him nervous, so he was glad that Landon was with her. He opened the door and invited them in.

"You look like the Wicked Witch of the West, girl," Sam said upon taking in Jet's ensemble. "Those boots in particular."

She bent to unlace them at the top, which revealed black stockings.

"You should take that coat thing off, too."

She stared at him. "You mean my cape?"

But taking off her cape didn't help. Underneath it, she wore a sheer top, blood-red. Sam scratched his head and looked at Landon.

"This is starting to remind me of Joe Cocker's 'You Can Leave Your Hat On,'" Landon said.

"True that."

Sam figured Jet was there to get high, though he wasn't sure about

Landon. He gave her a look-over, as he had when he first met her. She was older, but he was certain Unc would go for her.

Landon reached into the back pocket of her jeans and retrieved a hundred-dollar bill. "This is to pay for Abi's daddy, whatever he needs next," she said. "She said you can't just give her what it's gonna take. You're too generous as it is."

A remark like this coming from a woman his mother's age made him feel good. He had spent a lot of time as a boy feeling bad.

"Y'all want to get high?" he asked Jet.

"Not really," Jet said, and this set him back a bit.

Sam suspected Jet had a thing for him, but he was spoken for. Not uninterested, just unavailable. Plus, she always looked like an angel of death.

He stared at the bill Landon had handed him. Ben Franklin stared back at him. He could sense the two women also staring at him. Feeling awkward, he offered up his favorite party trick.

"I can do something not many people can. I can tell you who's got their faces on currency."

This was something his grandfather had taught him when he was growing up, working in the family's country store back home.

"Oh, yeah?" Landon asked. "That seems pretty easy."

Sam smiled. "That's what they all say. Try it."

"Well, Ben Franklin," Landon said, gesturing toward the bill in his hands. "Jackson on the twenty. Hamilton on the ten."

"Washington on the one," Jet piped in. "Lincoln on the five."

"And?" he asked the two women.

"And?" Landon said, "Did we forget something?"

"Grant on the fifty."

"Oh, the fifty!" Landon said, slapping her hands together.

"Everybody always forgets something. My granddaddy taught me that. Would y'all like to sit?"

The two women sat next to each other on the sofa by the door. Sam sat in a dining chair that he pulled up to the coffee table. He reached for a nearby baggie and pulled out a purple and green bud.

"Sure you girls don't want to smoke?"

"No thanks," Jet repeated.

"Tell me about your family, Sam," Landon said.

"You're not going to analyze me, are you?"

She laughed. "Only if you want me to."

"Well, I was raised by my mom and my granddaddy," Sam said. "My daddy died of a heart attack when I was five. Mama was a schoolteacher, so it was Poppy—that's what I call him—who took care of me. Poppy is what you would call a pillar of the community—businessman, lay pastor. And he was one of the Tuskegee Airmen."

"That's incredible," Landon said.

Jet leaned forward dramatically. "Sam," she said, sounding aggravated or excited—Sam couldn't tell. "You never told me this! I was a history major!"

He didn't know.

"I can't believe you're kin to an Airman. Their success is what made it possible for Truman to integrate the military. They paved the way for the civil rights movement. Speaking of which," she went on, "I have those Obama yard signs in the back of my car, if you want one."

"You better ask Mr. Kasir before you put up signs in our yards," he said. "It's his property, after all. Don't you think she should, Landon?"

"Yes, but I'm sure he'll be fine with it. I'd love a sign, Jet."

Sam couldn't for the life of him understand why these two women believed a black man had a chance at becoming president. It was always the white folks who thought so, which was odd. In all their excitement, there was no way to explain it to them. White folks were going to have a hard time handling it when Obama lost. Black folks, on the other hand, knew better than to get their hopes up. Nobody back home was putting signs in their yards. The men who gathered to talk shop at Poppy's store didn't mention it. Nobody, including Poppy, preached it from the pulpit. They had all seen too much, gotten their hopes up too many times.

Growing up, Sam never really knew a white person. His community was made up largely of extended family. White folks were mostly referred to in hushed tones. The men at the store would keep an eye on the white deliverymen who came in with boxes of sandwich bread or cartons of milk. Most of them had lived through it all—the violence, the bombing of Sixteenth Street Baptist Church, the cross burnings, the dogs and fire hoses. Some of them had participated in the bus boycotts and joined the march in Selma. To these men, white folks were foreign.

That's why Sam was shocked when he moved to Birmingham for school and suddenly white girls were all over him. He had hardly shared space with whites, much less touched them, talked to them, flirted with them. Sometimes, he wondered if they—even Jet and Landon—were going out of their way to prove their colorblindness by being so friendly with him.

Thank God for Tanya, his girlfriend. Whenever anybody asked who she was, he'd reply, "Tanya's my girl, my girl."

He was glad to be going to the university, studying engineering. It kept him focused. And contrary to what people probably thought, he never went to class high. But when he walked home from school every day and turned the corner onto Cullom Street, there they'd be, waiting outside his apartment—a gathering of blond girls with Obama '08 buttons on their shirts and pipes in the pockets of their designer jeans.

He was glad they came in groups. Being alone with a white girl made him anxious because they tried so hard. The things they said, the way they struggled to find the right word for black made him feel embarrassed for them, and for himself. Poppy would say, "'Do unto others as you would have them do unto you.'" What he wanted them to do unto him was to chill. And so, thus far, he had maintained a cool reserve.

He wished Jet understood all this.

She was still talking about the Airmen.

"They started flight training in the army's PT-17 Stearman biplane. They were an experiment to see if black men could be trained to fly combat aircraft," she said.

Sam looked at her. He was surprised she knew all this. "You should be a teacher," he told Jet as she and Landon got up to leave.

She shrank back when he said it. It was endearing, the way the compliment embarrassed her.

"I mean," he said, "couldn't you work on getting your teaching certificate and keep your job at the bookstore?"

"I guess so," she said quietly.

"You guess so?" he pressed.

"I've thought about it."

He smiled at her, and she looked down at the carpet.

"I'm serious, Jet. You need to be a teacher."

"Like your mama?"

"Yes, just like her."

He put a finger under her chin to lift her face, to look her straight in the eye. All of his fears about getting close to her vanished. He felt like Poppy—as if it were his responsibility to practice the gift of exhortation.

After they left, he went to his bedroom, which Tanya had recently redecorated. No matter how nasty his apartment got, he always tried to keep the bedroom nice and inviting, for only the two of them. There was a king-sized bed with ivory sheets and a dark blue comforter and pillowcases. The bed took up most of the room, but Tanya had brought in a glass-topped bedside table from her mother's place. Sometimes, Tanya stayed overnight, and she'd set her jewelry on the table, probably like her mother had done.

Tanya had a job as a legal secretary and made good money. She had no use for his business or the white girls that it serviced, and occasionally she threatened to leave him if he didn't stop. He had made it clear to his clients that if her SUV was there, they were not to come knocking, so she was a mystery to most in the neighborhood. He liked it that way.

This afternoon, he and Tanya were headed to his family's place for Christmas. Tanya was a city girl, Birmingham born and raised. Her skin was darker than Sam's, probably because her ancestors, unlike his, had not been slaves at the mercy of white planters. People in Greene County used the term *high yellow*, and though Sam never liked when folks commented on his light skin, he at least preferred that terminology to *mulatto*, which made his skin crawl. He hated the sound of it.

He thought about Jet and her Obama signs. Obama, with his Kenyan father and Kansas mother. Did he really have a shot? He wondered if anyone would mention it today. Some of his family were Hillary supporters. They had an affinity for the Clintons that puzzled him, even referred to Bill Clinton as "the first black president." He couldn't wrap his mind around it, but it made more sense than the thought of Obama getting sworn in next year.

. . . .

When they got to Greene County, Tanya went straight to the kitchen. That's the way it was at family gatherings—the women hung together around the simmering pots, and if it was warm enough, the men gathered outside, huddled in groups of two or three, smoking cigars and talking about who was the best bet for the Super Bowl. Sam headed outside and found Poppy sitting on the porch swing. He sat next to him.

Sam wasn't interested in letting the women fawn over him—how tall he was, how educated he was going to be, when was he going to marry Tanya.

Poppy put an arm around Sam. "How's my boy?"

Sam shook his head and grinned. He looked at the old trees, the mess of cars parked haphazardly in the yard, his uncles, his younger cousins playing a game of tag football. He knew Poppy had been waiting for him and was eager to discuss things deeper than sports.

After a period of comforting silence, Sam took a leap. "You like Obama for president?" It was worded that way to mean, *Do you think Obama can win?* Like sports fans placing a bet.

"What do you think?" Poppy asked.

"I don't think he can," Sam replied.

Poppy grinned and looked at Sam. His eyes were penetrating. They always had been, which was one reason he was such an effective pastor. The irises and pupils were slightly opaque now, the whites populated with thin red lines like tiny road maps. Still, they demanded attention. Sam waited for him to answer.

"Are you registered to vote?" Poppy asked.

"No."

"Well, there's your answer. If folks don't turn out, he won't win."

Sam nodded. Poppy always made everything seem so simple, so obvious.

"So, what is the mood where you live?" his granddaddy continued. "That neighborhood is mostly white, right?"

"Oh, they're all about Obama. And love to tell me that."

"You need to register."

"I will, Poppy. I will."

Poppy closed his eyes briefly, then stretched out his arms and studied his hands. Sam recognized this as the prelude to one of Poppy's opinions of great import.

"Everybody's got their job to do," his granddaddy told him. "My job is not so much to elect him as it is to keep him alive. So when I get on my knees at night, I pray for his safety. And for the safety of his wife. And for the safety of his children. I hear they got extra protection for him from the Secret Service, but you know your history. Every time I see him on the TV, I can hardly pay attention to what he's saying, I'm so busy worrying about who might have a gun in those big crowds he draws. This is what God has put on my heart—to pray for his safety during this campaign. I know you can't believe he will win. Neither can I, or any of us gathered here at this blessed homeplace to celebrate the fellowship of the mystery which is in Christ. I put this election in his hands so I can fold my own in prayer. And you, your job is to vote."

Sam looked down at the concrete, at his own Nikes and Poppy's torn-up old orthopedic house shoes. Sam wanted to give this moment the sanctity that it warranted. He remembered how Poppy took him as a young boy to Eutaw, the county seat, to watch him vote. They still had the old-fashioned booths with folding curtains then. He watched Poppy's hands pull the levers. On their way out of the polling place, Poppy reminded him that it had been only a few years back that black folks were given the right to vote. Sam hadn't really understood what that meant to his granddaddy, but he tucked it away to resurface at moments like this.

The women began streaming out the door. Dinner was served.

"Poppy, one more thing," Sam said. "I learned in my Spanish class that the word for Jesus is *El Señor*—'The Man.'"

Poppy looked around at all the menfolk putting out their cigars and gathering on the porch to go inside.

"Yeah, buddy," Poppy said. "'The Man' indeed. That's what he is."

JET

The day after Christmas, Jet drove to BookWorld, where she had been working for almost three years. The place was wacko with bright lights and sidelines galore. The café inside was a gathering place for college kids who were too young to drink. Jet never saw a book in their hands. The magazines and papers were next to the café, but few people flipped through them. Everyone got their news online. The travel section was full of plush, bright turquoise chairs so people could relax as they browsed books they'd never buy about places they'd never go. The card and gift section was the only one highlighted by a neon sign. Among the most popular products—not just in the gift section but the whole store—were charm bracelets featuring the work of famous artists such as Frieda Kahlo and Salvador Dali.

Jet was in charge of the children's department. It was even more heavily sidelined with arts and crafts, dolls, stuffed animals, puzzles, kinetic sandbox sets, easels, beads, stamps and stickers, board games. It was difficult to find a book in the tornado of primary colors, especially as frenzied children ping-ponged among the toys.

One of Jet's priorities as department manager was to make her story-time alcove free from distraction. A rainforest motif hung over-head, its green paper flora out of reach of sticky hands. Three small blond wood benches were arranged in a semicircle around the old-fashioned rocker where Jet sat to read during story time. When it wasn't story time, the rare bookish kid would often use it as a hiding place.

Jet started her morning ritual by putting the books back into their correct places, running a finger across the spines to check the titles. She paused at *The Runaway Bunny*. As much as she hated her mother right now, she still remembered her hushed voice at night, when she lay in bed with Jet and read to her. It had been so soothing. It shocked Jet, when she began working at the store, to learn that the author of her favorite childhood books, Margaret Wise Brown, was bipolar and led a wild life full of lovers, both male and female; that she spent her first royalty check on an entire cart of flowers; that she never settled down and died an early death. At her home in Maine, Brown had constructed an outdoor boudoir with a table, nightstand, and mirror nailed to a tree. In the stream nearby, she kept bottles of wine cool. Brown hadn't particularly liked children, and yet her words had comforted more of them than anyone would ever know.

This morning, Jet felt the familiar sadness, the anger that still accompanied her parents' deception. It tainted everything, even Jet's sweeter memories. She wished her aunt Stephanie, her biological mother, had been more like the Runaway Bunny's mother—there to save her at every misstep. Jet hadn't seen or spoken to either of her mothers since learning the truth. Only when she was a bit tipsy or stoned would she allow herself to picture Stephanie. It made her wonder how she could have missed it, who her father might be, if he was why the two sisters had decided to raise Jet in a lie.

Lenny arrived just in time to drag Jet out of her bad mood before it overtook her. He was impeccably dressed in slim khaki pants and a cornflower-blue sweater. His blond hair was brushed over to one side and fell soft and lovely over his left eyebrow. Jet was jealous of the way Lenny managed to make looking good seem so easy.

"How's it going?" he asked, joining her at the shelves.

Jet shrugged.

"Breakfast?"

Jet followed Lenny over to the café. It opened thirty minutes early to serve the employees. They each ordered a cappuccino and a Danish—one hour of their minimum-wage paychecks spent. Then they headed to the setup of chairs between the coffee counter and the front window.

Lenny jumped right into telling her about his weekend. He had his eye on the bartender at The Quest—Lenny's bar of choice.

"He's not really my type," he said, and reached for his napkin. "He's just a tad too soft. And you know me."

"Right," she replied. "You want a straight guy to turn."

Lenny smiled.

Jet looked at Lenny's hands. He had studied classical piano for twelve years, and his fingers were long and nimble. He'd make a good surgeon—he was premed at the university and had just been accepted to medical school. His days working at the bookstore were numbered. He was a few years younger than Jet, but she considered him a peer and was envious of the men he attracted. The children's department wasn't an ideal place to meet men, but occasionally a cute guy—flying solo—would linger too long, stealing glances at Lenny.

"How's Sam?" he asked.

"Tanya—you know, his girlfriend I've told you about—she drove him to see his family on Christmas day. He's got eyes only for Tanya. He told me once he could never date a white girl. But I bet you I'm not even white. Look how dark my skin is compared to yours."

Lenny smiled. "Don't say that around Sam."

"I know, I know."

They watched the other staff members filter in. She and Lenny were a country unto themselves in the children's department. They were tight as ticks and weren't interested in being friends with the people who worked in adult literature or science or travel or self-help or any of the other worlds in the store.

"Don't you think," he began, "that it's time you talked to your mother? Like, your actual mother, Stephanie?"

"I guess."

"I just don't think you'll find peace until you do."

She reached over and touched his hand. "What am I going to do without you?"

"And I love you, too, baby," Lenny said. "That's why I'm hoping you can take the initiative. I mean, I wonder how she felt when your mom told her that you knew. Don't you think she feels guilty? And maybe she'll tell who your father is."

"And why my skin is darker than the rest of you white folks."

"And we're back to Sam."

Jet sighed and nodded.

"You know what you need to do?" Lenny said. "You need to get one of those kits where you can swab your cheek for DNA and send it off and learn what you have in you."

"It's too expensive."

"Start saving. Look, I'll bring a thermos of coffee to work every day and pick up some cheap donuts at the gas station. That will save you almost seven dollars a day."

She smiled. Lenny was without doubt her best friend right now.

"I want you to meet Sam, and I think maybe it's time you met Landon, too. She's like everyone's surrogate mom. And you need one."

She was right about this. Lenny had come out to his parents after church one Sunday, and his mother had gone berserk. The punishment was severe. He wasn't to darken the door of their house until he got well. All financial help was cut off, including tuition payments. Suddenly, Lenny was in need of a job. He applied at the bookstore and met Jet, who was in the middle of her own big change—calling off her wedding to Lenny's predecessor in the children's department, a man who knew nothing about Jet's life on the street and, Jet realized, nothing about who she really was. Jet had fallen into a comfortable relationship with him when they started working together, had kept it simple because she wanted something simple. But it had gone too far, and she finally ended it. She wanted someone who knew her. And then came Lenny.

"Five minutes till showtime," Lenny said, checking his phone. "Tonight's the Iowa Caucus results."

Lenny worked only half days because he had classes or labs in the afternoon. They agreed that he would come by her place after she got off at six and at least have a beer. They finished their breakfasts, then ducked through the rainforest canopy that heralded the children's department.

Jet was already worried about what Lenny would think of Sam.

. . . .

When she got home from work, Jet went to her bedroom and stripped naked. She looked at her body in the mirror. She knew she was too thin for Sam, but she couldn't do anything about it. She had been slight all her life—only five foot one and always hovering around a hundred pounds. Sam could so easily pick her up—if he wanted—and carry her to bed.

She covered her breasts with her hands, wishing they were bigger, though she liked her dark nipples. She sat on the edge of the bed and put on her black stockings. She always started with those. She slipped on the black heels with the red soles that Sam had once said he liked. Tonight, she was going to wear her new brocaded corset for the first time. It had bronze detailing, crisscrossed leatherwork, a front zipper, and side chains. She finagled her way into it and looked again into the mirror. Nobody would see the corset, and this was sad. Maybe she'd lift her shirt and show it to Landon—or Lenny, for that matter. He might find it interesting. Next, she pulled her long hair back and put on her earrings—black onyx in the first holes and silver studs in all the others that ran up the sides of her ears. Finally, a simple black skirt and soft black jersey top with pink satin ribbon along the hem—a hint of innocence.

She flipped on the radio and reached high in her closet for the box that held her family photos. She took out an old videotape of her and her half sister, Caroline, playing on a Slip 'N Slide during summer. She put it in her ancient VCR and watched the two of them taking turns running, then belly-flopping on the slick surface before sliding gleefully to the end. Her daddy—her adopted father—must have been at the camera because there were shots of her mother, Ann, and her aunt Stephanie. They were stretched out in lawn chairs talking. On the video, Stephanie sat with her thin legs crossed and her dark hair falling down her back just like Jet's. She dressed like a gypsy, in a mix of embroidered fabric and gold jewelry. Maybe that's what they were—gypsies.

Jet thought about who her real father might be. She had never seen Stephanie with a man. She was a wanderer and moved from place to place with her other daughter. For some reason, Stephanie and Caroline disappeared during Jet's adolescence. Jet never asked about them because by then she was in high school—a cheerleader, a gymnast, a straight-A student. She was voted Most Likely to Succeed. Even now, she laughed at how wrong her classmates had been.

She rummaged through the photos and found one of the sisters as young girls, not quite teenagers yet. Stephanie was brooding. Ann wore a smile that was undoubtedly fake; it was big and forced. At the bottom of the box was a piece of paper with Stephanie's phone number, which her mother had given her the day she told Jet the truth. It was after her father's service and burial. The kitchen was full of flowers her mother had saved from the funeral and put into vases with water.

"I have something I need to tell you," her mother said, her voice trembling from what Jet at the time assumed was grief, though now she knew it was fear.

Jet braced herself. Her mother's words were unsettling, the kind of preface people gave when they were about to divulge a dark secret.

"When Aunt Stephanie was seventeen years old, she had a baby."

"And?" Jet said. She looked at her mother, who was staring at the floor. "Aunt Steph had a baby and . . . ?"

"Well, it was you," her mother whispered, as if the room were filled with witnesses.

The morning sun poured over everything. The funeral flowers suddenly felt wrong. Jet couldn't process what her mother had said, so she thought about the flowers. They were probably from people who hadn't wanted to come to the service and took the easy way out.

Jet started crying. Her mom was crying, too.

"Why?" Jet said, crouching and covering her face. "Why, why, why?"

"Your father and I couldn't conceive, and Stephanie . . ."

At her mother's silence, Jet was filled with hatred.

"Why are you telling me this?"

"I thought you'd want to know the truth."

Jet stared at her mother, angry at everything about her. She was irritated by her coiffed beauty-parlor hair, her frumpy clothes and boxy shoes. She had always looked and acted older than the other moms.

Jet wasn't thinking, *How could Aunt Stephanie have given me away?*

She was thinking, *How could my mom take me and never tell me?*

Then she realized her daddy wasn't her real father either. That morning, she had buried him, and now he was dead all over again.

"Who is my daddy, then?"

"Honestly, Jet," her mother said, looking tired, "I have no idea. But I'm going to give you Stephanie's new number. You should call her."

Jet didn't call her aunt—her mother. Instead, she waited until her mother—her adoptive mother—fell asleep, and then she packed up and left home. Skipped out on a job interview and ran off. The rest was history. And now, all these years later, Jet still had that number in her box of photos. She pulled it out this evening and put it in her wallet. She didn't know why. Maybe it was time.

Jet put the box away and looked at herself once more in the mirror. Fully dressed, she felt untouchable. She felt invincible, unless she thought about Sam. If she thought about Sam, she melted like candle wax.

She got a beer from the fridge and called Lenny.

"You're still coming, aren't you?"

"Look out the window," he said.

There he was in the parking area, checking his hair, getting out of his car. He pulled a six-pack from the passenger seat. She stood and ran to the front door, so happy to see him. During the holidays, neither of them had a home to go home to.

"Oh, my God, Jet. You look like Morticia Addams."

Jet swatted playfully at his face.

"You do," he kept on.

Then he must have sensed something in her and changed his tune. "You look fantastic," he said. "I wish all those suckers at the store could see you."

"You've got to see my corset," she said, and lifted her shirt so he could.

"Jesus, what is that?"

"A corset."

"A what?"

"Quit acting like a man. You know what a corset is."

"I've never seen one up close, though. It's terrifying," he said. "Kind of hot, though."

"Now that you're here, I'm gonna text Sam."

Afterward, she turned back to Lenny. "When we see him, act like you're my boyfriend."

Lenny shook his head. "If he knows I'm faking for his benefit, won't that make it worse?"

"Straight guys never pick up on that stuff."

"You think?"

Jet ignored Lenny, applying an extra layer of lipstick before leading him out the door.

SAM

Sam put on jeans and a gray hoodie. He brushed his teeth and picked up the bottle of cologne Tanya had given him for Christmas. He didn't know what to do with it, where to dab it on his skin. So he reconsidered and left it alone. He put a pipe in his pocket and dropped a few buds into one of his tiny Ziploc bags. He generally tried to avoid walking around with weed on him, but he was only going down the street.

His TV was on. He was ready to go to Landon's place but lingered awhile, listening to the pundits. It was clear that this was going to be close. He wondered if Poppy was watching. He pictured him in his old chair, fully dressed but wearing a robe all the same because, as he aged, he had a hard time feeling warm enough. Sam thought of Poppy's house shoes, how far they'd walked. He guessed Poppy's house would be quiet except for the occasional sound of distant trains or stray dogs howling at the moon.

Sam longed for that quiet, and to get inside Poppy's head. He wasn't afraid of growing old—he wanted to be wise, to know how to pray and believe there was a God. Sam had spent his boyhood in church and was proud of Poppy whenever he was called on to preach. But he never heard the words, not like he knew he was supposed to. He would fidget with his buddies, going through the hymnal and silently scribbling "in Bed" at the end of each hymn's title, trembling with inaudible laughter. "I Surrender All . . . in Bed." "How Great Thou Art . . . in Bed." "Jesus Paid It All . . . in Bed."

He didn't know why the hymnals were even there. The choir had its own music, and it was the only part of church that held Sam's attention. As the singers grew louder, Sam would get swept up, clap along with them, and move. He could have sworn he learned to dance in church. Or at least it was where he learned rhythm.

At church, the women always arrived looking serious, but by the time the music started they were sweating, swaying, and waving their hands, their faces all big, open smiles and closed eyes.

The first time Sam took Tanya to church, she came to life in a way he had never seen. Generally reserved and prim, she dove right into the music, reaching for the ceiling as if to make way for the sky, the sun, the universe. When he witnessed the desire and passion she had inside, he couldn't help wondering if he was good enough for her. Even though his family was big and respected in Greene County, it didn't have the city money that Tanya's family had. And he certainly wasn't making what Tanya was making. He knew she didn't like his dealing, but she hadn't left him over it.

Tonight, he walked to Landon and Abi's house alone. Landon greeted him at the door. He followed her to the kitchen and accepted the beer she handed him. Abi, Jet, and Lenny were laughing, and he guessed maybe they'd had a few already.

"Lenny, this is Sam. Sam, Lenny."

They shook hands.

"This is important," Jet said to Sam. "The Iowa Caucus is always important."

He sat beside Jet on the couch. Lenny was in the lounge chair. Abi was in the wingback wicker and Landon on the ottoman. Jet looked relaxed, if a little stiff around the middle. It looked to him like she might have a back brace on, and he wondered if that's why she always wore her weird clothes—to distract. When she leaned against his shoulder, Sam didn't shrug away.

The exit poll results were coming in, and it looked good for Obama. The commentators kept mentioning the youth vote.

"Those TV anchors are really pulling for him, aren't they?" Sam asked no one in particular.

Jet was popping her knuckles. Sam stared at her hands, so fragile and tiny—like a child's hands. He put his hand over hers.

"It's all gonna be good," he assured her.

If Obama didn't take Iowa, Sam had his own concession speech for his white friends. He was going to be like Poppy, strong and conciliatory. He still didn't believe Obama would pull this off, but he was starting to notice the excitement around him.

The pizza man arrived, and Landon paid him. But nobody was hungry for food yet; they were hungry for a sign in the form of a victory. Sam offered to pack a bowl, but no one wanted to smoke until the results were in.

He looked around at the strange group. Lenny, who Sam sensed might have been apolitical—or at least not starry-eyed—until this moment. Abi, mindlessly petting Alejandro as he lay curled in her lap while she stared intently at the screen. He watched Landon put the pizza boxes on the table and arrange the napkins and plates she had set out, always keeping her eye on the TV.

At the commercial break, everyone was quiet. In that moment, Sam allowed himself to, as Poppy would say, "'be still and know that I am God.'"

"We are ready to call for Iowa," the anchor announced, cutting off the end of a commercial for an ED medication.

And there he was. Obama's black face appeared, a light turning on, and suddenly Sam believed. The others jumped up like their asses were on fire and started screaming and hugging each other. They cheered with beer bottles, passed around Sam's pipe, broke into the pizza. To Sam, everything was a blur. He felt the stirrings of something brand new—the idea that he was a part of this.

When Obama started speaking, the apartment grew silent once again.

"They said it couldn't be done," he began. Sam felt like Obama was talking directly to him. His words made sense. And when he got to the part about hope, Sam welled up inside. "Hope is what led a band of colonists to rise up against an empire. What led the greatest of generations to free a continent and heal a nation." He was talking about Poppy. "What led young women and young men to sit at lunch counters and brave fire hoses and march through Selma and Montgomery for freedom's cause." He was talking about Sam's mother, all his relatives who had marched. "Hope is what led me here today. With a father from Kenya and a mother from Kansas and a story that could only happen in the United States of America. Hope is the bedrock of this nation. The belief that our destiny will not be written for us, but by us, by all those men and women who are not content to settle for the world as it is, who have the courage to remake the world as it should be." He was talking to Sam now. "We are not a collection of red states and blue states. We are the United States of America. And in this moment, in this election, we are ready to believe again."

"This is a moment, isn't it?" Sam asked the room as Obama concluded his remarks.

Everyone had their cell phones out. Landon was trying to call her daughters. Lenny and Jet were quietly, furiously texting.

Abi was screaming into her phone. "Daddy! Are you watching?" she said, pulling the metal cross out of her pocket.

Sam thought of calling Poppy, but it was late, and whatever he needed to say could wait until morning. Still, this reminded him of the altar calls after the sermon, when people surrendered their fear and pride and knelt near Poppy's feet as he quoted his favorite scripture: "'And now being surrounded by so great a cloud of witnesses, let us lay aside all the weight that doth beset us and run with patience the race that is set before us.'"

JASON

Jason Kasir got the phone call at dawn. He thought before he answered that it must be Granddad wanting him to help out with a tenant dilemma—moving a piece of heavy furniture or sawing a dead limb from a tree.

But it wasn't his granddad. It was his father.

"Jason," he said. "I got bad news, buddy. I'm bummed."

Jason sat up straight. Anxiety ran like fire ants in his chest and down his arms. He hated what he already knew, what his father was going to tell him.

"I'm in the county jail."

It wasn't the first time. And yet every time, instead of calling one of Jason's older sisters, his father called him. Jason wondered if it was because he was closer to his father's parents, who wouldn't answer calls from Abe Jr. anymore.

Jason threw on some jeans and a sweater. He looked out the window and saw a light snow falling. Ordinarily, this would be a great day, since it so rarely snowed in Alabama. He got online and checked out the forecast. Little accumulation was expected. Still, it would have been—without his father's phone call—an exciting day. Jason would have called his girlfriend, Carly, whom he'd met at Alateen, and gone over to her place to watch the snow from under her comforter. The two were now twenty-one, but they had bonded quickly at meetings when they were teenagers over shared experiences with messed-up parents.

But instead of a day of keeping warm with Carly, Jason would be forced to bail out his father. Again.

Jason drove downtown to the Northside. He parked in the deck and took the crossover to the jail. The sheriff's deputy at the front desk looked as bad as the guys in the tank—eyes swollen, face red, as if he were nursing his own hangover. Jason showed him his ID.

"I'm here for Abe Kasir Jr."

The deputy looked at him. "That an Iraqi name or what?"

"We're Lebanese," Jason replied.

"Oh, really? Sounds Muslim to me."

Jason felt a kind of anger rise but tried to keep cool. "We're Christians," he said.

The deputy stood and got a file from the cabinet, sat back down, thumbed through it, and said, "This is your daddy we're holding?"

"Yes, sir."

"Looks to me like this isn't his first time around. He's got a thick chart here. Not his first time around, is it?"

"Could I see him, please?" Jason didn't know if he wanted to cry or yell.

The deputy directed Jason to the visitation room, where he'd wait until his father emerged, handcuffed. Jason had been through this before.

After nearly thirty minutes, Abe Jr. appeared through a blue metal door. He had bruises on his face and a cut over his right eyebrow. He looked old, as old as Granddad. He was dressed in what looked like brown operating-room scrubs. He sat down at the table across from his son, smiling weakly.

Jason checked his father's arms to see if they showed any track marks or collapsed veins. He didn't see any. This meant his dad was taking Oxycontin right now, rather than shooting heroin.

Jason resented the knowledge he carried about classifications of drugs, painkillers in particular. He wanted to be normal. Carly's mother was an alcoholic. Though he knew addiction was addiction, opiates seemed so much more shameful than booze.

"I need to get out of here," his father said.

"What's the charge?"

"Possession with intent to sell."

Jason felt the despair creeping up on him. Then he closed his eyes, silently recalling the Serenity Prayer, which he had learned in Alateen: *God, grant me the serenity to accept the things I cannot change, the courage to change the things I can change, and the wisdom to know the difference.*

"Jason, man? Hello?"

Jason opened his eyes and stared at his father. He was grateful that he had learned his father's disease wasn't his. "Don't ask, don't talk, don't feel," they'd say in Alateen, reciting the old rules of their messed-up homes.

"I said I need to get out of here," his father repeated.

"How much?" Jason asked calmly.

"You need to ask the deputy," his father told him.

Jason knew that his father wasn't going to rehab again. He had no intention of long-term recovery. Why should he if he knew that Grand-dad, once Jason told him what had happened, would pay to get him out?

And sure enough, his next words were, "Go tell Pops I need him to come down here and get me out."

"I don't want to bother him with this," Jason said.

His father slammed his hand on the tabletop that separated them. "Goddammit, son!" he yelled. "I'm not getting no bondsman, if that's what you're thinking. We're family, damn it."

The deputy appeared at the door and motioned for Jason to rise. "Time's up," he said. He gestured for Jason to leave, nodding toward the door. Then—with no small effort—he took Abe Jr. by the arm and led him back behind the bars.

Jason sat in the parking lot, gripping the wheel tightly, trying to breathe. He wanted to call Carly, but it was too early.

He drove back home, made some coffee, and sat on the couch, leaving his coat on. He was shivering even though it was warm inside. He looked around his apartment, at the posters on his wall, his laptop, the framed maps his grandmom had given him, the things he'd carried with him into adulthood—his old baseball cards, a globe, Harry Potter books, a Swiss Army knife.

His place was one that his granddad owned, so he didn't have to pay rent. He knew that in many ways, he was lucky. But not in other ways.

Jason knew he would have to tell his grandparents. They wouldn't like his keeping it from them. But it wasn't even seven o'clock.

He pondered the idea of not telling them. After all, his father had used his one phone call on Jason, and the information was Jason's to share. If he didn't tell his grandparents, then maybe he could break the chain of enabling. If he kept his father's incarceration to himself—telling only Carly and his group at Alateen—then maybe he would be doing the healthy thing.

Jason thought about his father sweating out the withdrawal on his cell floor. The county wouldn't intervene. Then maybe his father would finally hit rock bottom, feel that pain, get some humility, have nobody to turn to but himself, or maybe a higher power.

But what if he died in there?

The conversation Jason was having with himself wasn't new. The pattern was always the same: his father was thrown in jail; he called Jason, who went to see him; then Jason delivered the message to Grand-dad, who—despite his grandmom's interventions—inevitably rushed to get up the bail money. Grandmom had been to Al-Anon, so she wanted no part of Abe Jr.'s cycle.

Jason knew he wasn't free from the sickness. He felt compelled to tell his grandparents because he knew it would hurt Granddad not to help, to learn only later that his son was locked up.

Jason decided he'd wait awhile before going over to his grandparents'. At least his father would have to suffer through some suspense.

He went to the bathroom and stared at himself in the mirror. He was nothing like Abe Jr., with one exception. Jason had inherited his father's eyes. Dark as the Warrior River, where they used to go fishing together.

Jason had borne the brunt of his father's addiction. His sisters married young and got the hell away from Abe Jr. His mother's career was taking care of her addicted husband. Jason got lost in the shuffle. When he turned twelve, he went to live with his grandparents. Now, he was in college on a music scholarship and doing well. Jason didn't play an instrument. His voice was his instrument. He sang in the choir at the Ka-sirs' church, often soloing, and had on occasion even made some money singing at weddings and funerals.

Jason sent Carly a text: "Call me."

Back in his bedroom, he lay in bed with his phone in his hand. Finally, it rang.

"Hey, babe, what's up?"

Jason told Carly that his dad was in jail. She asked if he wanted to come over. He told her he had to go see his grandparents first.

"Just talk to me for a while," he said.

She understood that need, and told him a red cardinal was perched on the ledge of her porch, so beautiful against the tiny flakes that were falling.

He closed his eyes and listened to her voice, feeling calmer with her every word.

"Just keep talking," he said.

MR. KASIR

When Mr. Kasir's phone rang, he was in the kitchen, sipping coffee and watching Mrs. Kasir. The breakfast dishes were washed. She was taking off her apron. He answered. It would be one of his tenants, he knew.

"Hi, Mr. Kasir. It's Landon Cooper."

"Hello, Landon." Mr. Kasir put his free hand to his chest. "How are you doing? You've been on my mind."

This was an understatement; he so wanted to tell her more about Carissa. Mrs. Kasir patted his shoulder and left the room.

"So, I've been nominated to call you and ask if some of us can put up Obama signs in our yards."

"It's fine by me," he replied. "The yards are yours."

He stood and walked to his window, peeking out at his lawn. A few flakes of snow were blowing, but they disappeared before they hit the grass. Although real snow had been forecast, nobody in Birmingham wanted to get their hopes up.

"Is it snowing there?" he asked her.

"Let me check," she said.

He pictured her walking over to the window and pulling the sheer curtains back.

"Yes, it is! It is!"

"I know you and Abi must agree on the signs, but are Jet and Sam in agreement? And there is Roy Manley across the street from you, and Nicole, who lives upstairs from him. And Jesse, in the bungalow. And Tina. Sid. Frankly, I've never been in this position. I wonder if you should ask them."

"Of course," Landon said.

Mr. Kasir reconsidered. "No," he decided. "It's easier to get forgiveness than permission."

He offered to help plant the stakes. Landon tried to dissuade him, but he insisted.

"This snow won't stick," Mr. Kasir said. "And even if it does, the truck has four-wheel drive."

"I do have something to give you," Landon said.

"I'll be over soon."

He took a deep breath and walked past Mrs. Kasir, who sat by the fireplace knitting. Good, he thought. She hadn't looked out the window yet at the light snowfall. She would have put her foot down about his going anywhere.

Once outside, he saw that the children on his street were starting to appear, toting sleds as if there was something actually to slide on. He turned the heater on and headed over the mountain.

When he got to Landon's house, he saw the signs on her porch. Before he could knock, she was there at the door, a warm smile on her face.

"Come in, Mr. Kasir," she said.

"Don't you want to get to it?"

"We don't have to put those signs up right now. You need to warm up first, and the coffee is already made."

Just as it had during his previous visits, Landon's apartment felt like a holy place. She brought him the coffee in the same good china and sat down. Then, bless her, she got up, went to the secretary, and retrieved a copy of the photograph of her and her brother.

"Here," she said. "I made a copy for you, so you can look at it whenever you want to."

It was as if she knew how important this was to him.

Landon's home was alive with plants, light, and hope. What if she had not rented from him? Now that she was in his life, he hardly recalled what it had been like without her, when he had nobody to hear him out, to say her name to—*Carissa*. It wasn't a secret now.

"You have to remember," Mr. Kasir said, "that we had spent months training for the invasion—fastening splints, winding bandages, making tourniquets. It wasn't fear so much as anticipation. We knew we wouldn't have sterile dressing rooms like we did in our rehearsals; we'd be working in the sand on a beach. We had seen drawings on blackboards of what the invasion was to be like. We were all wondering, would we drown? Would we be able to save anyone? We were expecting—and we found—gaping shrapnel wounds, loss of limbs, men blinded and knocked unconscious. When we were in the throes of it, everything was so loud and fast, you couldn't focus on any one thing. There were ships, tanks, men—and women, too—doctors, nurses, drivers. It was so big, so big a fight. After a few hours, I started to think I was dreaming, like I was seeing myself outside of myself."

"Depersonalization," Landon said, setting her coffee cup down gently.

"That so?" he asked.

"Yes, but go on."

"After the worst of it was over and men were divided into the living and the dead, I walked over to the water's edge, barely feeling my leg. So many things had washed ashore."

"Like what?" Landon asked him.

"I recall a tennis racket, a banjo, a football, some glistening oranges floating in the water—things that soldiers had brought with them. Once we were up on the bluff, we could see the big picture—the war. But it was those peculiar personal items that stayed with me."

"Then you met Carissa," she said. "Tell me more about her."

"I'd like to." He picked up the photograph of Landon at seventeen. "I just can't tell you how much this reminds me of her."

He told Landon that Carissa came to him every day, right outside the field hospital. She ran to him like he was a long-lost friend and embraced him when he stood to meet her. *Kasir*, she called him, and his name sounded foreign and lovely in her mouth. He was aware, always, of the language barrier. And how to break it.

Mr. Kasir sipped his coffee and paused, wondering what was appropriate to tell a woman. He remembered that it was summer. The countryside was lush. Butterflies were everywhere. There were green hedgerows on either side of the dusty road they walked along. Pecan trees and apple orchards. Cows grazing here and there. Carissa took his hand, and they walked together down a side road that ended in a covey surrounded by long, hanging tree limbs, away from the road. Red flowers grew everywhere; he later learned these were geraniums. She lay on the grass. So he did the same. They were under the tree, looking up at the sky. She pressed his hand to her cheek. He turned to lie on his side to look at her. She turned her face to let him see her eyes.

"We were looking at each other," he told Landon. "Her eyes, they were full of concern, and her brow was wrinkled with that unspoken question. She didn't understand English, but I thought it seemed she wanted me to talk to her about what I'd seen. And so I started talking, then I started crying. And she held me. I started shivering—not because I was cold but because I had never loved a girl like I loved her, in that moment. Are you all right with what I'm telling you, Landon?"

"Of course," she replied.

Her little dog, Alejandro, was begging to be held. She put him on her lap.

"I realized that this battle was right next to her village. She must also have been frightened. Maybe she felt safe with an American soldier, I don't know. But one thing was for certain: we were both caught up in something that was too much for a young boy and girl to comprehend. But there was something, something she was trying to tell me."

"A question, perhaps," Landon said. "A question she wanted to ask you."

"Yes," he replied. What he didn't tell Landon, because he thought it inappropriate, was that she had kissed him, and the question was in the kiss—slow and beseeching.

He looked again at Landon to make sure she was still with him.

"That night, she took me home with her like she always did. Her father prayed over the food before we ate. They bowed their heads, and he said my name. I guess they were grateful to me, to us, for saving their country."

She smiled. "What a story, Mr. Kasir. What a story you've carried."

Just as it had been with Carissa, words were not always necessary. Mr. Kasir sat in silence with Landon, lost in his thoughts of France. Finally, he told her that he needed to be getting home, that they ought to put up the signs in the yards before the weather got worse.

When they stepped out onto the porch, Landon kissed his cheek and snowflakes danced in the wind.

JASON

When Jason pulled up to his grandparents' house, he saw that his granddad's truck wasn't there.

He knocked, then entered without waiting for a response. His grandmom was sitting at the table drinking orange juice and eating a biscuit. She was ageless, Jason thought. Her skin wasn't like other old people's. It was nearly flawless.

A smile broke across her face at the sight of him. She got up from the table and hugged him tight. Then she backed up. He could tell that she suspected something was amiss. He knew he must look distraught.

"Dad's in jail," he said flatly.

She absorbed this with a brief furrow of her brow, then turned to fetch a couple of biscuits for him.

"Drugs?" she asked calmly, retrieving a jar of strawberry jam from the refrigerator.

"Of course," Jason said. "It never stops with him. Where's Granddad?"

"He had to run over to see one of his renters. I didn't know it was snowing or I would have put my foot down."

"It's not sticking," he told her.

His grandmom sat and reached for his hand. "Did you go see him?" she asked, looking tenderly into his eyes.

Jason nodded.

She didn't push for more information. They quietly ate the biscuits she had made from scratch. She made everything from scratch, even the jam that Jason had spread across his biscuits with abandon.

"He told me to ask Granddad to come see him."

"To post bail," she affirmed.

"Of course."

That's when he heard his granddad's truck pulling into the carport.

"That's him now," Grandmom said.

When his granddad entered the kitchen, Jason rose to give him a hug.

"Jason! What brings us the happiness of a visit?"

Jason looked at Grandmom. He almost didn't have it in him to repeat what he had just told her.

"It's not good news, Abe," she said.

"What, what is it?"

Grandmom stood to collect Granddad's coat and hat from him, then headed toward the hall closet. Jason stared down at the tabletop, unable to speak.

When she returned and sat back down at the table, Grandmom said, "Abe Jr. is in the county jail."

Jason looked at Granddad. "It's drugs again," he told him, knowing how much it would hurt to hear. He saw the familiar despair descend over his granddad, like lights going out in the middle of a storm, quick and all consuming. "He called me," Jason said.

Granddad slapped his hand on the table. "Why didn't he call *me* instead of *you*?" he roared. "He's a coward, that's why. Has to drop bad news on his boy, rather than call his father. I don't even want to know the details."

Jason knew his granddad was mad at his father, not him, but he felt guilty all the same. Grandmom must have sensed it because she reached across the table and squeezed his hand.

"He wants bail money," Jason said.

"Well, he's not getting it from us," Grandmom said, though both she and Jason knew that wasn't true. Granddad was the pushover, the enabler, the father who wouldn't—or couldn't—hold firm, who, Jason knew, was likely already working out in his head if he had enough in his checking account or would need to go into savings.

They must have spent thousands on his father, Jason thought, including the cost of more than one stint in rehab.

"I just don't get it," Granddad said, starting his usual lament. "How many times do we do this? And if this thing Abe Jr. has is a disease, like the rehab doctor told us, then why didn't it get cured? I don't understand. I just don't get it. That doctor said the only thing that has ever worked is to go to meetings. If it's a medical disease, how on earth can it be cured in the basement of a church, sitting around with a bunch of other junkies, swapping stories? Nothing will heal him but going back in time, keeping him away from Vietnam."

Jason had heard this speech before.

"Don't make excuses for him, Abe," Grandmom said. "You were a soldier, too."

"Maybe it was the Agent Orange," he said.

"I'm not buying that," she replied. "His troubles are his own, and blaming anything else won't help him."

Granddad folded his arms on the table and dropped his head.

"Granddad?" Jason asked. "Are you okay? I'm sorry. I didn't want to upset you."

He lifted his head. "Oh, no, my boy," he said. "You did the right thing, coming to us. I'm so glad you knew where to go."

Grandmom was already taking pots and pans from the cabinet to fix a meal. She believed that eating a good supper was the only way to feel better. Or maybe, Jason thought, she was thinking of herself; maybe it helped her to be doing something with her hands.

"Do you know what he's charged with?" she asked from the stove.

"He was selling," Jason told her. "Oxy, probably. I guess to support his own habit."

"What's that?" she asked.

"Oxycontin. They call it 'hillbilly heroin' because so many guys switch to it to save money."

"And what is it?"

"Real strong painkillers."

"Did he tell you," Granddad interjected, "what his bond was set for?"

Grandmom whirled around. "Abe, you are not going to bail him out again. Let him call some of his cronies, if he has any left. We are not spending one more penny on him. We're not going to enable him."

Yes, Jason thought. Grandmom had been to Al-Anon. She knew the lingo, and she knew the hard facts.

Granddad got up and disappeared into the living room. Jason followed and watched him pull the sea-green curtains aside.

Jason was surprised to see the snow that was collecting in the front yard and on the gazebo. He sat on the couch. Granddad put some logs in the fireplace, then got that morning's newspaper and a handful of small wood to use for kindling. He got a long match from a drawer and lit the kindling, then poked at the flames as they began to catch.

"I'm changing my will," Granddad said, turning to Jason. "I'm giving you *all* of the properties. When Grandmom and I die, you will inherit them . . . and the people. Your father will get nothing. And your grandmother is right. We aren't going to bail him out this time. He can spend some time in the Jefferson County Jail. He might have to go to prison again, but nobody is going to save him. All those times I drove to Montgomery to visit him at Kilby, buying cigarettes for him and giving him cash for the canteen, I thought I was helping. I thought I was protecting him."

"Let him hit bottom," Jason interrupted. "The only way he can go from there is up."

Jason stood and walked back into the kitchen, where Grandmom was slicing onions, peppers, okra, and garlic. He suspected she was going to make chicken and sausage gumbo for him. She knew it was his favorite meal.

"We're not going to bail him out," Granddad called from the living room. "Not this time."

Grandmom made the sign of the cross and smiled at Jason.

His granddad walked back to the kitchen.

"If he tries to call you, Jason," he said, holding Jason's shoulders and looking right into his eyes, "don't answer. If it's going to be hard for you to resist answering, we will get you a new phone, and he won't know the number. All that matters to me is you, son. *Your* future, *your* peace of mind."

Jason gave his granddad a hug. "Can I have a smartphone?"

"You can have whatever you want," Granddad said, pulling back from the hug and smiling at Jason. "But what is a smartphone?"

Granddad didn't wait for an answer. Instead, he turned toward the back door.

"Where are you going, Abe?" Grandmom asked.

"I left something in my truck."

He returned with what looked like a photograph. Jason watched as his granddad retrieved a notebook bearing the name *Landon Cooper*. Granddad tucked the photograph into the side pocket, face down. Jason had no idea what that was about but figured he would someday.

"*Resolve*," his granddad said. "I want you to look up a word for me, Jason. In the dictionary."

"Granddad, nobody uses a real dictionary anymore," Jason responded as he followed his granddad back into the living room. "It's all online."

But he looked it up anyway. "'*Resolve*,'" Jason said. "'To find an answer or solution, to settle something, to reach a firm decision about, to declare, to decide, and to progress from dissonance to consonance.'"

"Now, tell me what those last two words mean," Granddad said, using his cane to get situated comfortably in his chair.

"Well, in music, dissonance means lack of harmony, and consonance means in harmony. There's actually a whole musical lesson contained in those two words, but I won't go into that now. Let's just say that dissonance means conflict, in-fighting, disagreement. And consonance means agreement. Resolve, I guess, is that point at which dissonance moves to consonance. We want that in our lives—right now, today, at this moment—and the only way to get it is to break ties with my daddy."

"I'm so proud you have that music scholarship," Grandmom interjected. She appeared from the kitchen, wiping her hands with an old gingham towel.

"Those words make sense to me," Granddad said. "That is what I feel. I have *resolved* that we will not bail him out. I have *resolved* that all the property will be yours. But I don't want you to think of being a landlord as your fate, your job. You keep studying whatever it is you want to be. Just remember that the monthly rental payments from the tenants will always provide income for you. You understand what I mean?"

"I do," Jason said. "And I hope you know how much I appreciate it."

"You'll do a good job. I will make all of this official."

"He's so young, Abe," his grandmom said.

"I'm twenty-one," Jason said. "I can have a drink in a bar now, Grandmom."

"Well, I'm not planning on dying soon," Granddad said. "But let me go ahead and show you how I keep up with the renters." He held out

Landon's notebook. "Here's what I do. There is a notebook for every dwelling, every renter. I keep them like journals. See how I've written when they paid for each month, and if they had a problem getting up the money? I've written the things we did to avoid eviction. We are fortunate because we own the houses. We've been blessed, and it's our responsibility to help others less fortunate."

"Your granddad is being kind," Grandmom chimed in. "But remember that he worked hard to get these properties. He's made a name of Kasir. Having a good name is as important as anything in a man's life."

"That's right, son," Granddad said.

He stood and walked toward the laundry room with Landon Cooper's notebook.

With her husband out of the room, Grandmom turned to Jason. "You don't have to keep those notebooks," she whispered. "All you need is a ledger."

"I want to do it like Granddad does it."

She returned to the kitchen to work on her dark roux. When it was coffee brown, she would turn the heat to low, finish chopping vegetables, and render the sausage. The house was already fragrant, and Jason thought about how good it would smell once she added all the right spices.

JET

Jet was in her bedroom, packing for the concert in Destin. This would be the first time she went to a concert alone. But she could make the trip with her eyes closed. She knew Highway 331. The road to the Gulf Coast began in Montgomery, about a hundred miles south of Birmingham. Even though Highway 231 was quicker, 331 was more scenic. Sure, it was rough going fifty-five on a two-lane road. But Jet didn't mind. It was a never-ending Alabama controversy—which highway was a better path to the Florida Panhandle, 231 or 331. Almost as controversial as which team you pulled for in football, Alabama or Auburn.

She was wearing jeans and a Widespread Panic T-shirt she'd bought at the band's last area concert. In her backpack were a second pair of jeans, another T-shirt, panties, and a travel-sized shampoo. In her purse were her wallet, a baggie from Sam, and a one-hitter shaped and painted up to look like a cigarette. She had no hotel reservation for the night. Since everything in the Panhandle was probably booked, she would just get back on 331 when the concert was over and look for a place in south Alabama, like Opp.

At the last possible moment, Lenny called and told her he could go with her after all. She hadn't seen him since he quit the bookstore to work at an emergency clinic. "Just to get my feet wet," he'd said. Though she was thrilled to have Lenny, some part of her was disappointed. Going it alone had started to sound exciting.

Picking up Lenny was easy, since he was on the way. Jet got on 65 and took the exit to his place in Hoover, a white-flight suburb outside the Birmingham city limits. She wound her way around his apartment complex, which looked like every other apartment complex, and wondered why he hadn't moved to Southside yet. She was betting that he would, once medical school began.

She pulled up to his building and called him on her cell. "I'm right outside your door."

"On my way down," he replied.

He was wearing jeans and a pale blue dress shirt. He also had a backpack with what Jet assumed was his change of clothes. He carried a Styrofoam cooler that Jet suspected had beer inside. He put his things in the backseat.

"What's with the shirt?" she asked him.

"I knew you'd say that. Can't a boy look nice?"

She laughed. "Oh, baby, you look gorgeous in anything."

"If only the boys thought that," he replied. "Road beer?"

"Not yet. Not until after Montgomery."

"Have they replaced me at the store yet?" he wanted to know.

"Of course not. I'm working with no help. The corporation loves it that way."

They passed through Alabaster and Calera.

"I met somebody," he said.

"Oh, yeah?"

"At Starbucks." He got a beer from the cooler. "See, this doesn't begin in a bar, and that's a good sign, isn't it? I was having a cappuccino, studying slash daydreaming. I was by the window, and he was outside at a table under the awning. When I noticed him, he was already staring at me. He had his dog with him—a golden retriever, just like me. He didn't look away when I made eye contact. We just kept staring at each other until he finally came inside. Left his dog tied to a pole. But then he went to the counter and got a croissant. Like, what?"

"Go on, go on," Jet said, and switched the car into cruise control.

"So, finally, he walked up to me, and we started talking. His name is

Brett. He's in law school. We went out for sushi the next night, then back to his apartment, where we just talked. We didn't even do anything. Just held hands," he said, and took a big swig of his beer.

"You're lying," Jet said.

"About what?"

"You didn't even kiss?"

"Believe me, I wanted to."

"So, then what?"

"Well, we've either seen each other or talked on the phone every day since then. And yes, we have kissed, but that is it. He is not a tail chaser. I think he wants to go slow."

"You've only kissed?" she said. "Well, aren't you just the poster child for abstinence."

He laughed. "Where are your dreary duds, Morticia?"

"I'm not sure they're right for the Panic crowd. Now, hand me a beer. We're past Montgomery."

Once they were on 331, they settled in. Like only close friends can, they were silent at times, then deep in conversation. They listened to music and occasionally rolled their windows down to smell the rich farmland. They passed through the tiny towns of Snowdoun, Ada, and Highland Home before reaching Luverne, which called itself "the Friendliest City in the South" and was home to "the World's Largest Peanut Boil." They passed Brantley, "Front Porch Capital of the South." The old plantation homes were white with big wraparound porches and gingerbread latticework. Muscadine vines grew in the yards. The next stop was Opp, "the City of Opportunity."

Jet glanced over at Lenny. "Thinking about Brett?"

"Yep."

"How sweet," she said. "And now, I think it's time for me to get high. Can you get the one-hitter out of my purse? It's already loaded."

They reached Florala and crossed the state line.

And that's when it happened.

Looking back on it, Jet would see that it was inevitable, or at least probable. She wasn't careful enough.

The patrol car's blue light flashed. It was county. She immediately threw the one-hitter in the console and put the tiny Ziploc in her jeans, right below the belt line. It was a quick decision, but she figured—without having time to think it out—that the officer wouldn't search her.

Her heart was racing, but she tried to stay calm for Lenny's sake. "It's just a checkpoint," she told him. "I can handle this."

"You don't want to have anything on you, do you?" Lenny asked, sounding frantic.

"They can't frisk me if there isn't a female to do it," she explained.

Inside, she was also frantic. In the past, she had been pulled over for speeding and running a stop sign, but not with pot in the car, and not with stuff that smelled so strong. If she had just waited to get high. Or done it in Opp in the little forested area right in back of the Dairy Queen. But not in the car.

She pulled over. The deputy was already walking in the direction of her car.

"Hi, ma'am. I'm Deputy Franks. Can I see your driver's license, proof of insurance, and car registration?"

Jet already had these ready to show him.

He leaned in closer and put his nose in the air. "What's that smell?"

Jet smiled at him and shrugged, but she could tell he wasn't going to be easy. In general, she could talk her way out of anything. But this Deputy Franks wasn't even making eye contact with her.

He went back to his car.

"Just don't freak out," she said to Lenny. "Nothing's going to happen to you. And if it happens to me, it's my problem, not yours, okay?"

The deputy came back and asked, "Y'all been drinking?"

"Just my passenger," she replied. "Not me until we get there."

He was sniffing again. Jet knew that he knew she'd been smoking. But she waited. She was trying to remember what cops were allowed to do during a stop.

"Okay, so let me see you get out of the car."

She did as she was told. For a moment, he turned his attention to Lenny to ask where they were going. In that instant, Jet got the tiny Ziploc of buds out of her pant waist, flipped it to the ground, and stood on it, trying to make it look like just a part of the dirt. The sun was going down, and the road was getting dark. She hoped this might save her.

Deputy Franks took his time. His blue lights were still flashing. A few cars slowed down. Jet imagined she was in one of them, curious, happy she wasn't the one pulled over.

"Come stand over here, fella," Franks said to Lenny.

Jet kept quiet and still.

The deputy scratched his head and looked back down the road. "Can I look around in your car?" he asked.

Jet didn't know he had called the department, but sure enough, another car arrived and a female deputy got out.

Franks said to her, "I'm asking them if I can search the car."

"I don't think you can do that," Jet stated.

"Who was driving?" the female asked.

"She was," Franks said, gesturing to Jet. "Put your hands up against your car, facing away from us." Then, to the woman, he said, "Search her for me, would you?"

"I'm Deputy Mason," the woman said to Jet. "I have to put you in cuffs for now, so just put your arms behind your back. You've never been in any trouble, have you?"

"No," Jet said, starting to panic.

Mason leaned close to Jet's ear. "I know the cuffs are uncomfortable. I'll get you out of them as soon as I can. Don't give Deputy Franks any trouble. This will be over, one way or the other, as quickly as possible."

Jet nodded. She tried to glance to the place where she had tossed the pot. When she did, Franks leaned down and picked it up. Jet's heart sank.

He held it up for Mason and Jet to see. "This was right beside the car door," Franks said to Mason, then turned to Jet. "So, this is how the thing will work. We're going to take you in. This fella here, well, let me see your driver's license, too."

Jet caught a glimpse of Lenny's shaking hand as he pulled the wallet from his jeans pocket.

An eternity passed before the deputy returned and gave Lenny his ID back. "Okay, you're good," he said to Lenny. Then he turned to Jet. "This car is yours. Do you give this gentleman permission to drive it home or wherever you were going?"

"Yes, I do."

Franks gave Lenny the keys.

"May I say something to him?" Jet asked.

Franks gestured for her to go ahead and speak.

"Don't try to go to the concert," she told Lenny. "Just drive it back to Birmingham and park it at your place. I will call you."

Lenny's blue eyes were wild in the headlights. "Can I say something to her?" he asked Franks.

"Go ahead."

"Don't I need to stay nearby?"

"Don't worry about me," she said firmly. "I can manage. Trust me, Lenny."

Lenny took Jet's keys in his hand. Jet could tell he was a wreck. Lenny didn't have a stomach for things like this. But she wasn't about to let him get involved or try to help at this point.

When Lenny left, Deputy Mason helped Jet get into her car, rather than Deputy Franks's. She turned the ignition and pulled into the road.

"We're taking you to the county jail in DeFuniak Springs," she said. "You had just crossed the state line, though. So, as we speak, we are officially in Florida. DeFuniak Springs is the county seat of Walton County. Are you confused about any of that?"

Jet could see her dark, braided hair through the grate.

"You understand what I'm saying, hon?" she asked, looking in the rearview mirror.

"Yes, ma'am," Jet replied.

"Are your hands hurting from the cuffs?"

"Yes, ma'am."

"Okay, I'm pulling over, and I'll take them off. I don't think you're a flight risk."

"Hardly," Jet replied. "My car's on the way back to Birmingham."

"Birmingham," Mason said. "That where you're from?"

"That's where I live, yes, ma'am."

"The big city . . . ," Mason said, trailing off.

DeFuniak Springs.

When Jet was growing up, she knew DeFuniak Springs meant she was getting close to the beach. Her family went every year, first week of June.

Now, here she was in a cop car.

For the rest of the drive, they were silent. Jet was pissed at herself for trying to toss the weed. They hadn't even searched the console or her purse. And if she had just left it tucked into her jeans, she wasn't sure Deputy Mason would have found it.

The police car pulled up at what felt like a garage entrance or the drop-off of an emergency room. Deputy Franks was waiting for them under an awning that stretched from the building to the grass on the other side. Jet stayed in the car and watched Deputy Mason get out, walk inside the big glass doors, and stand at a counter. Deputy Franks followed her. They stood casually, leaning their elbows on the counter, as if placing an order for burgers. They even laughed at one point. Jet couldn't hear the conversation, but her eyes were glued to them.

They came to Deputy Mason's car and opened the back door.

Deputy Franks said to Jet, "I'm arresting you for possession of marijuana. You have the right to remain silent when questioned. Anything you say or do may be used against you in a court of law. You have the right to consult an attorney before speaking to the police and to have an attorney present during questioning now or in the future. If you cannot afford an attorney, one will be appointed for you before any questioning, if you wish. If you decide to answer any questions now, without an attorney present, you will still have the right to stop answering at any time until you talk to an attorney. Knowing and understanding your rights as I have explained them to you, are you willing to answer my questions without an attorney present?"

Jet glanced over at Deputy Mason, who nodded slightly and kind of smiled, as if to say, or so Jet hoped, *This will be resolved.*

But when they took her inside, Deputy Mason disappeared. The night shift was sparse. A piece of paper taped to the wall read, "Intake and Booking." There was a coffee machine and a candy machine. Jet saw only two other people, both of whom were working behind the counter. One appeared to be a guard. The other, a woman, wasn't uniformed, so Jet figured maybe she was clerical. This wasn't the first time she'd been in trouble. When she was tricking, she was held once. But it never got this far. They'd let her go with a lecture and some numbers for counselors because of her young age.

Deputy Franks went behind the counter. "Empty your pockets," he said.

He put her purse and wallet in a box. Jet felt like she was having a bad dream: the mug shot, the fingerprinting, the danger in his voice when he said, "Come with me." He directed her to a small room. There was nothing inside except a bench and a metal sink and toilet. The fluorescent lights cast a green glow over everything, adding to the nightmare she was in. The door had a small window, which Jet noticed only when Deputy Franks closed the door behind her.

First, she sat on the bench. Then she got up and tried to see what, if anything, was happening on the other side of the window.

After an hour or so, another girl was brought into the room. She was fucked up for sure. Jet guessed it was a DUI. She could smell the liquor.

"This is the pits, isn't it?" Jet said, hoping to establish herself as friendly.

"Not my first rodeo," the girl replied.

"I was on my way to the Panic show," Jet told her. "You, too?"

"Well, I'm as drunk as a rat," the girl said, and started moving toward Jet. She had a menacing look on her face. Jet backed up, but the girl got closer. She reached out like she was going to either touch or hit Jet. Then she laughed. "Scared the shit out of you, didn't I? Are you a debutante or something?"

"No. I work at a bookstore."

"Oh, so you're a smart bitch, right? Not so smart, though. You still got arrested."

Jet sat back down on the bench. She had no use for drunks. Back when she was hooking, she hated it when her johns were plastered. They tasted bad. They were sloppy. Sometimes, they couldn't get it up and blamed it on her.

Jet waited, keeping an eye on the girl, who eventually passed out.

Finally, a guard came in and led her out of the room. "Okay," he said. "One call. And I mean only one."

There was a sign with a list of bondsmen and their prices. It was like a menu where nothing looked good. She asked for her wallet. She knew what she had to do.

When the guard brought it to her, Jet fished out the scrap of paper with Aunt Stephanie's cell number. Steph and her other daughter, Caroline, lived in Seagrove Beach, which was close.

Jet dialed the number and held her breath.

"Hello?"

"Aunt Steph? This is Jenette."

"Jet!" Stephanie sounded surprised. "How are you? Where are you?"

The guard was standing close to her. He jingled some coins in his pockets. Then he yawned and looked down the hallway. "Long night," he said to the woman behind the counter.

Jet tried to sound calm. "Actually, Aunt Steph, I'm in the Walton County Jail."

"Oh," Stephanie said. "Are you all right?"

"I've been arrested for possession. Some pot. You're my one phone call."

"Listen," Stephanie said, "I'm thirty miles away, maybe a forty-five-minute drive. Caroline is here. We'll get in the car as soon as we hang up. Can you make it another hour?" She didn't wait for Jet to answer. "Don't worry, I have enough money. I'm glad you didn't call a bondsman. That was smart. And listen, I know lawyers. We'll take care of this, one way or another. Just sit tight and know that you will be out of there soon."

Somewhere along the way, Jet had started crying. She couldn't speak, and instead made a choking noise as she swallowed a mouthful of air.

"Oh, angel. You don't need to say anything else now. Just wait on us."

Jet hung up the phone and handed her wallet back to the guard. She was overcome by Stephanie's reaction. She seemed like she had been down this road before.

Back in the cell, Jet wished like hell that she had a watch or a clock to look at. She tried counting seconds: "One Mississippi, two Mississippi, three Mississippi." But by the time she got to sixty, she was weary of her attempt to make time speed up. It seemed to have the opposite effect.

The other girl in the cell was lying on the floor. The guard came by to offer her a phone call, and she raised a sweaty palm and waved him away. Jet wondered how she was going to get out, then quickly dismissed the thought. It wasn't her problem. She sat on the bench and waited.

An eternity went by. Finally, a guard appeared at the door.

"Jenette," the guard said. "Time to go."

"Does that mean I can come out?"

"That's what it means," he replied, and she thought she saw an affectionate smile cross his face. She had, after all, been a good inmate for this brief time. She guessed he probably had seen and heard a lot.

He led her down the hallway. She saw Stephanie and Caroline before they saw her. They were on the other side of the counter. Jet walked faster and was about to fall into Steph's arms when the guard held his hand up, blocking her from moving farther.

"You will need to sign some papers," he said.

Jet signed without reading them. She just wanted out of this place. Stephanie still wore her hair long, just like Jet. For a brief instant, Jet felt she was seeing Stephanie for the first time. Her mother. How could she have missed it?

Caroline's smile was big. She and her mother seemed so glad to see Jet. Stephanie paid the bail money with a stack of twenty-dollar bills. After counting the money, the woman behind the counter gave

Stephanie a piece of paper, the date of Jet's court appearance.

Once they were in the parking lot under the streetlights, both Stephanie and Caroline hugged her.

"If it wasn't you, it would have been me," Caroline joked.

Jet was relieved. She felt safe with these two women, her family.

They got into Stephanie's car and headed to Seagrove.

"There is no way I can ever, ever—"

Stephanie interrupted. "Ever thank us for this, right? Not to worry."

"Mom's been down some back roads," Caroline said.

Then Jet said what had been on her mind for the hour of waiting. "Have you called my mother?" She flinched as she said *mother*.

"Are you kidding me?" Stephanie said. "Judge Judy? Of course not."

Jet knew the secret was out. She knew that Stephanie was her mother, Caroline her sister. And she knew that they must know she knew. She longed to talk about this with both of them, but it was a conversation for the next day. For tonight, the mood was unexpectedly pleasant—goofy, almost celebratory, without a hint of judgment. Jet thought of how long ago her mother had given her Steph's number, and how glad she was to have waited until this night to call.

. . . .

Stephanie's house was a few blocks from the beach. Jet took it all in, looking for clues as to the life she could have led.

The kitchen was sleek and modern—nothing like her mother's, which was ordinary. In the living room, the furniture had a raised leaf pattern. It was simple but elegant.

"This is called Cabana Banana," Stephanie told her, "which sounds absurd for how pretty it is."

"I like it," Jet said, running her hands across the material.

"In there is a Florida room."

Jet turned her head to see.

"Some people call it a sunroom, but I think Florida room sounds much more interesting."

Jet saw that the furniture was white wicker—a wingback, rocker, and sofa. Everything was perfect. It all felt friendly and comforting.

"I know what you're thinking, and I'll admit I didn't pay for any of this," Stephanie said.

She didn't say who did, but Jet reasoned it was either Caroline's father or perhaps some older man Steph had dated. She did have a way with men, as Jet's mother had told her in a somewhat condescending tone.

Caroline's cell rang, and she disappeared into another part of the house.

"She has a new boyfriend," Stephanie explained.

"I wish I did," Jet said.

"How about a glass of white wine?" Stephanie asked. "I'm sure you could use a drink. It's technically morning, but white wine is technically juice."

Jet hesitated, then said, "Yeah, why not?"

Stephanie poured two glasses of wine and then led Jet to the Florida room. Jet sat on the wicker sofa, Steph in a whitewashed rocker.

"Where were you going, anyway?" Stephanie asked.

"To a concert in Destin."

"That explains it," Stephanie joked.

Jet smiled. "The thing is, I didn't have the pot on me. I had it stuffed in my jeans at the waist. When the deputy looked away, I flipped it to the ground. But he found it later. And, I don't know, I guess weed proximity was enough of a reason to arrest me. Plus, I'm sure the car reeked."

Steph leaned over and patted her leg. "Like I said, I know lawyers."

Neither knew how to begin the conversation they needed to have, so they sat quietly. In the end, Stephanie suggested they walk to the beach.

"Caroline will be on the phone for hours. And anyway, we need some time alone."

She put the bottle of wine in a cloth bag, along with a couple of plastic wineglasses.

When they reached the beach, they took off their shoes and Stephanie put a towel down. The moon was almost full, reflected in the white sand of the beach. The stars, too, were bright and alive. Occasionally, a cloud drifted across the sky, casting blue over everything. The waves crashed against the shore in white swells. Jet dug her feet into the sand.

When she was a kid, Jet had wanted to make her parents disappear, just long enough that she could walk alone on the shoreline, searching for shells and maybe a piece of driftwood. But her parents were always coaxing her to come back, to keep away from the water. Jet realized that this was the first time she had ever been to the beach without them. Being here with Stephanie, she felt that she'd finally come home.

The two women sat quietly sipping their wine, watching the stars overhead.

"Jet," Stephanie said finally, "it's a long story. I'll tell you if you want to hear it."

"Please," Jet whispered.

Stephanie freshened their wineglasses. She rolled her jeans up. Jet saw that she was wearing an anklet. It caught the light from the moon. It was the color of champagne.

"Ann, your mom, couldn't have children," she began. "I was dating this Italian guy, Arnold, a total womanizer—not that I believed the rumors. When I got pregnant, he told me he was on board. A few months passed, things got real, and he was gone. I moved in with your parents. Your father, your adoptive father, was the person who suggested that I give my baby to him and your mom. They were established. They'd take good care of you. And I couldn't argue with that. They had taken me in when your birth father left. I was entirely dependent on your parents. But for a while, I thought I'd keep you. I thought I could do it. It wasn't until those final weeks that I relented. I felt overwhelmed. I was young, scared. Your parents told me I would still get to see you whenever I wanted." Stephanie paused. "I can't tell you how many times I've rehearsed this story, but I'm not telling it right. I want you to know that I did want you. But I was convinced that the right thing to do was let them raise you. I figured I might have other children someday. I was seventeen, just a girl myself. I was selfish. And in a way, I was mad at you. I thought I'd still be with Arnie if I hadn't gotten pregnant. I heard he had run off to New Orleans, and I wanted to go and find him. I just . . . I've prayed for years that you wouldn't inherit my tendency to fall in love with bad men."

"I did inherit it, Aunt Steph," Jet said.

"I hate that. I'm sorry. Says a lot about nature versus nurture, doesn't it?"

With each break, the waves were inching closer to Jet and Stephanie.

"I never had your mother's sense. Your father, he was a good man. And she was a virgin when they married. I was nothing like her. She wanted a traditional life. I didn't. I didn't have it in me. I was born under a wandering star. Your mother wanted to stay put. I was a nomad."

"I get that," Jet said. She wasn't sure what she was feeling. Peaceful and destroyed all at once.

"I want you to understand one thing, Jet. I thought they were going to tell you the truth from the get-go. But the years went by. I traveled a lot. Whenever I came home, I saw you, but it wasn't enough. Then I got pregnant with Caroline. Her father was much older, and he wanted a family. I thought maybe I was getting a second chance to do it right. We got married and moved here, and things were okay for a while, until I filed for divorce. You know why? Because he was a good man, and I can't take a good man."

"God," Jet said. "I'm just like you."

Stephanie sighed. "I'm sorry, so, so sorry."

"I remember your visits," Jet said. "You and Caroline, when I was a kid. I have an old videotape of me and Caroline playing on my Slip 'N Slide. I remember that day. I miss those days—all of us together."

"The day your mom called to tell me she had told you the truth, I was so scared. I felt like a failure. I didn't think you'd ever speak to me again. And who could blame you? I know that you don't believe this, but we all had your best interest at heart."

"I know," Jet said.

"The road to hell . . . ," Stephanie said as she reached for the wine bottle.

Jet finished her glass. A breeze had picked up, and the very edge of the horizon was starting to warm.

She looked over at Stephanie. "I'm not mad at you," Jet said. "That is the truth. I get it. It was so easy for me to understand why you gave me up. Secretly, I think I always wished you were my mom. I wanted a cool mother like you."

"It has its drawbacks. Just ask Caroline."

"So, where do we go from here?" Jet asked.

"Well, tomorrow, we'll talk about how to proceed with your court appearance. I'll call one of my lawyer friends. What will you do about work? I mean, I'm assuming that you'll need to stay here for at least a few days or maybe a week."

"I'll call and say I have the flu. My boss is a real germophobe. Maybe he'll actually hire an assistant department manager so I can stop doing everything all by myself."

On the walk back to Stephanie's house, Jet felt lightheaded. And it wasn't the wine. For the first time in years, she felt like herself. Her honest self. She knew she had a legal battle ahead of her. But at least for a time, there was nothing she needed to escape from. Not even the past.

LANDON

Landon sat at her bedroom vanity and carefully put on her ancient Charles of the Ritz foundation, powder, eyeliner, and lipstick. She usually opted for a bare—or almost bare—face, harking back to her bra-burning days. But today, she would wear it all. She'd even purchased new mascara that felt like she was coating her lashes in wax. She used her fingers to make her damp shoulder-length hair turn under a bit. And when that was all done, she searched the vanity drawers for some nail polish. She wasn't sure she even had any, but she discovered a bottle called Sunset Gloss. The pigment had separated from the glue, and the bottle looked more like a Tequila Sunrise than a sunset. She shook it and twisted it open, which took some effort.

After her nails were dry, she put on her favorite skirt, the long purple one with a lace overlay; a white embroidered blouse; and her only pair of dress shoes, the black flats. She didn't want to wear the cross earrings because it might rankle Abi. Instead, she chose tiny opal ones that were barely visible, lost in her hair.

She wasn't sure, or didn't want to admit, why she was girling it up.

"Landon!" Abi's big voice rang out from down the hall.

"I'm here. I'm ready," Landon said, and walked into the parlor where Abi stood.

"You look so beautiful," Abi told her. "Did you dress up for Daddy?"

Landon grinned and waved the question away. She knelt to pet Alejandro, causing her skirt to spread across the floor. "Don't worry, little man," Landon told her dog. "I'll be back soon. I'm just going to meet with Abi's daddy to talk about his treatment plan. But then I'll come right home to you."

"That's so sweet how you tell him when you're leaving," Abi said. "It's funny. It's so . . . so you."

. . . .

When they arrived, Landon spotted Will at a booth. The seats were burgundy vinyl, and the table was set for three. He stood and hugged Abi, then Landon.

"How are you feeling, Will?" Landon asked him.

"I'm good, all things considered," he replied.

"I know one of the waitresses here," Abi said. "She's behind the bar. I need to go say hello. Be right back."

Once she was out of sight, Landon and Will slid into the booth, sitting across from one another. Landon put her napkin in her lap and started to open the menu. Will put his hand on the table and let his baby finger brush against hers. For just an instant. But Landon felt it all over. Then, knowing herself too well, she attempted to rearrange her reaction in her mind. He had barely brushed her skin. Surely, it was by accident.

Abi returned to the table with a glass of wine.

"It's good to see you girls," Will said.

"It's good to see you, too, Daddy," Abi replied.

He looked at Abi, then at Landon—right in her eyes. She didn't think he was a womanizer. That's not what she was picking up on at all. She guessed his life was pretty isolated in that trailer park. Maybe he never saw any women, period, other than Abi's mama and Aunt Sister.

Abi nursed her wine as all three of them turned their focus to the menu. Then Abi asked Will if he had brought the instructions. He reached down to the seat and retrieved a packet. He gave it to Abi, and she in turn placed it on the tabletop so Landon could also see it.

On the first page was a sequence of questions: "How does chemotherapy work?" "What does chemotherapy do?" "How is chemotherapy used?" "How does my doctor decide which chemotherapy to use?" "Where do I go for chemotherapy?" "How is it given?"

After they ordered, Will explained what he knew about each of the questions. Their conversation while they ate turned away from cancer, to Abi's job, Landon's garden, the election.

Abi waited until they finished eating before she started making plans.

"Since you're doing one week of treatment followed by three weeks of rest, I want you to stay with me during the week you're in treatment."

Landon put her fork down and waited for his reaction, hoping for Abi's sake that he wouldn't balk at this. But if he did, that's why she was here. She assumed.

"Now, you know your mama won't like this," Will said. "But I won't know my prognosis until after a few rounds. But let's just say I have only a year or two."

"Daddy, stop!"

"No, no, don't worry. I've actually thought this out. I was hoping you'd want me to stay with you."

Will put his hand over Abi's. Landon felt the familiar pang of envy over this show of fatherly love.

"I just mean this'll be part of what I'll say to your mama. I'll say I don't know how long I've got, and she's got to let me make my own decisions. Because they say it's important to my chances of beating this thing if I take it into my own hands."

"That's true," Landon interjected. "The feeling of empowerment affects the outcome of treatment, be it in a psychological sense or a physical. It can make a difference. Feeling powerless is unhealthy."

"That's why I brought a psychologist with me," Abi said. "Don't you just love her?"

"I love whoever you love, sweetie," Will said. "You know that."

The waitress came by to ask for dessert requests.

"What do you have?" Landon asked her.

"Lots of pie—lemon icebox, peanut butter, chocolate, coconut cream, and pineapple cheese."

"Anybody want to split one with me?" she asked.

"Bring a slice of lemon icebox," Abi said, "with three forks."

After the waitress left, Landon told Will and Abi about a conference she went to once in Boston. "When the dessert arrived, I glanced over at the man sitting next to me and realized his choice was better than mine. So I asked him if I could have a bite. He was dumbstruck. Now, you know if he'd been from here, he would have said, 'Sure, darling. Here, take half of it.' "

Will laughed. He held her gaze.

When the waitress came back with the piece of pie, they all took bites, careful not to be greedy.

"Communion," Landon said, lifting her forkful of cool lemon custard.

" 'Do this in remembrance of me,' " Will said.

Abi stopped eating and put her napkin to her face. Through the paper, Landon heard her take a deep, shuddering breath. But she composed herself quickly.

"Let's not say *remembrance*," Abi said. "Like it's right around the corner. I mean, hell . . . I don't know what I mean."

"I know what you meant," Will said. "Don't worry. I'm not on my deathbed. In fact, I haven't felt this good in years, sitting here with you girls. I'm sure I'll be staying with you in Birmingham, Abi, no matter what your mama has to say about it. It took cancer to make me realize I need to make my own decisions. The Bible says, 'Wives, submit to your husbands.' That's something I've never seen in all my life. Women run the family. Not that I mind."

"So glad I'm not married," Abi said.

"Me, too," Landon replied. And at that moment, she meant it.

"So, now that we've gotten religion out of the way," Abi said, "on to politics. Where do you vote, Daddy?"

"At the old schoolhouse."

Abi turned to Landon. "Where I went to elementary school." Then, to her daddy, "You will vote for Obama, won't you? Just for me?"

"We'll do anything for our kids, won't we?" Will said, smiling at Landon. "Absolutely." Then, gesturing to Abi, "This kid in particular."

Landon picked up the tab, and Abi left the waitress a big tip.

Outside, the chill in the air was weaker than it had been a few weeks before. It was January. By next month, the daffodils would be blooming.

How depressing, Landon thought. Winter ended so suddenly in the South, from one day to the next. Time for Landon's depression to begin.

She loved the look of winter. In the winter, she could see the lay of the land, the way tree branches, bereft of leaves, formed patterns against the sky. Plus, the onslaught of people with seasonal affective disorder made her feel less alone in her melancholy.

In the spring, the pollen, the heat, the too-bright sun—it was all too much for Landon, and everyone else seemed so happy about it. The signs of new life didn't comfort her.

Landon knew this was all part of the complexity of her bipolar disorder. If she stayed on her meds, the spring would be bearable. But that was easier said than done.

There was, of course, the campaign to keep her going—more caucuses and primaries, and before she knew it, the election.

ABI

When Abi arrived to pick up her father, Mama was standing outside the trailer with her arms crossed, wearing what appeared to be a snakeskin jumpsuit with a blazer over it. When she got out of the car, Abi saw that her mama had on a new pair of boots, too—all from JCPenney, no doubt.

"Hey, Mama," Abi said. "You look great."

"Don't try to make this all right by complimenting me."

"Is Daddy ready to go?"

"I'm not happy about this," she said.

Abi tried again. "Isn't that snakeskin you're wearing? I love it."

"Well," Mama said, softening, "I like it." She tugged on the hem of her blazer. "You're early, aren't you? Your daddy is still in the shower. Since you're here, you might as well come in. Don't be surprised; I've changed the kitchen a bit. Christmas is over, and Valentine's Day is right about the corner, so I've spruced the place up."

Abi wished Landon were with her to witness the kitchen. Her mother had left no kitsch unpurchased. The oopsy daisy curtains had been replaced by scarlet strips of material. The new table runner looked like a treasured heirloom dotted with embroidered hearts, but Abi was certain it was polyester. The set of plates stacked on the table had pink hearts painted along the edges. The matching cups were tiny—fake demitasse with tiny saucers the color of apricots. There were thick plastic highball tumblers with "Love Me Right" stamped on them. A piece of metalwork was attached to the wall—a steaming cup of coffee with "Love" painted in cursive, slanting to the right in the middle of the steam. A string of red lights stretched from one side of the room to the other. There was a red curtain on the pantry door. On the wall were tinsel hearts with arrows, red paper lanterns, heart-shaped hanging paper decorations, Cupid cutouts, white heart silhouettes, and decals with "Happy Valentine's Day" or "I Love You" on them. An unopened decorating kit on the table advertised itself as a twenty-eight-piece set. Mason jars full of red M&M's were on the counter. And there were new pink and red heart-shaped refrigerator magnets.

"These have a warning on the back," her mama said, plucking one of the magnets from the refrigerator door. "'Choking hazard. Not for children under three years.' I figured since we don't have any kids that young around here, they were safe. Unless one of your cousins comes in here dead drunk and tries to eat one."

"Yes, I think they're safe," Abi said. She imagined Petie or some of the other budding alcoholics coming into her mama's kitchen and putting their mouths to the fridge to bite off the ornaments. She had to admit it wasn't outside the realm of possibility.

The final new purchase was a box of tissues with hearts all around and, on the center of each of the four side panels, a picture of an owl holding a tissue that read, "Be Mine."

"I got this for your daddy," Mama said, tearing up a little. "To take with him to treatment."

The box of tissues was suddenly sad and important, as if it was—to Abi's mama—a truly precious cure for cancer. It caused a stirring of something Abi hadn't felt since she was a little girl. She'd mostly assumed Mama and Daddy didn't love each other. She thought they just stayed together as a habit, one that neither had the will to break.

"Let's go outside for a smoke," Abi said.

"Good idea," Mama said.

They leaned against Abi's Volvo. Abi examined her mother's boots. They weren't so bad.

"I want to come see you at work sometime, Mama. Maybe you can show me some boots I might get, and we could have lunch."

"You'd wear a bra, wouldn't you?" Mama asked, glancing at Abi's braless chest.

"There's really not much there, you know, that needs support."

"You've starved yourself trying to be skinny like a model. And this giving up meat, I'll never understand. I bet you don't have any red blood cells left after going these years without a steak or even a burger."

"That's not how it works, Mama."

Her mother took a long drag. "Abigail, what's going to happen to all of us?"

Abi kicked at the gravel. "He might respond well to the chemo," she said. "We gotta keep our spirits up."

"He is so handsome," Mama said. "He'll lose all those fine curls. You got to make sure he eats. Real food, not just salads."

Aunt Sister's voice rang out, "Don't you get in that canoe, you hear?"

Abi heard her nieces and nephews in the distance, no doubt getting into trouble. It was February, but the daffodils and crocuses were already budding, and the big tulip tree down by the water was blooming. It was always the first sign of spring—those big buds opening.

Abi and Mama finished their cigarettes without talking. Abi lit another cigarette and handed it to her mother, then lit one for herself. A small act of love, like her mother's agreeing to her plan. Love so strong it overpowered Mama's need for control.

"Please, can you two try to call me, Abi? It would mean so much to me."

"Okay, Mama."

Daddy appeared at the door, toting his suitcase, which must have been nearly as old as he was, and barely used.

"Abi will take good care of you, hon. You know she's good at that." Mama turned to Abi. "You *are* good at that. Now, wait right there, you two."

Mama hurried inside to fetch his going-away present, the box of tissues that read, "Be Mine."

When Daddy accepted it, he hugged Mama and said, "I've always been yours."

Abi was again reminded that they were a family in crisis. She was so glad that she had Landon downstairs, someone who could and would handle any kind of mental or emotional issues that might come up during this first round. She told Daddy this as they headed toward I-59. Abi's old Volvo station wagon was beginning to have problems. If she went over fifty-five miles an hour, it started shaking badly. She kept it at fifty and hoped her daddy wouldn't notice how slowly they were going.

When she got on I-65, the city rose to their left, and she saw him gazing at it. She realized he hadn't been to Birmingham in years, and so much had changed.

"Feels like I'm in New York," he said.

"Not quite, Daddy. But close enough."

"I don't remember this many buildings downtown."

"That's the medical center all sprawled out over Southside. You'll be in one of those buildings."

He rolled down his window and hung an arm out to the wind.

"I'm gonna take the Fourth Avenue exit, rather than the Green Springs exit I generally take, so you can see the university."

She showed him the building where she attended most of her classes. They drove by the hospital. He had been referred to an oncologist at the university, rather than the hospital in Bessemer, which was closer to the family compound. Abi turned onto Eleventh Street and paused at St. Andrew's Episcopal.

"That's where Landon goes," Abi said. "Well, she went once, on Christmas Eve. I helped her dress that night. She was stunning."

They passed the corner market. Abi pointed it out.

"That's where most people buy their food, just so you know. I don't really shop there. You won't find much fresh fruit or veggies, but the cigarettes are cheap, and they have good popsicles. I never outgrew them, you know."

He patted her leg.

"And there," she said, "is where I do my laundry. Right by the store."

"I wish I could get you a washer and dryer."

She waved the suggestion away. "I don't even have hookups. Landon does, but I don't."

She turned right on Cullom Street. "Here we are," she said.

As she pulled up to the curb, Abi spotted Landon on their porch.

"Will!" Landon called, waving.

"Come on up with us," Abi said as they approached the front steps.

Abi had moved all of her workout equipment to one side in her extra bedroom. She and Mr. Kasir had assembled a twin-sized bedframe he had found in the basement of one of his properties. Mr. Kasir's basements were not for the tenants' use. Rather, they were places where he stored things that people left behind. Abi and Landon still marveled that he had come up with the frame only hours after Abi asked him to be on the lookout. As for the mattress, it was new, still in its wrapping. Abi knew Mr. Kasir had bought this for her, even though he pretended to have salvaged it. He brought along Jason, who had grown quite a lot since Abi last saw him, to help get the mattress up the stairs. They also had a set of sheets and pillows, which Mr. Kasir told her were from Mrs. Kasir's linen closet. The Kasirs had been so good to Abi since they found out about her daddy's cancer. A few days after bringing the bed, Mr. Kasir arrived with a bedside table.

Abi watched her daddy take it all in. First, he surveyed the big room, which held Abi's TV, shelves, books, CDs, DVDs, and aquarium. Cinderella and Grits were asleep on the couch. There was a desk for Abi's computer. The screensaver echoed the nearby aquarium; yellow, turquoise, and red fish swam across it. The room was a bit dark, but Abi figured her daddy might want it that way when he came home every day following his chemo. Everything would be geared to his comfort.

"Daddy likes to sleep on the couch, or at least rest there," Abi told Landon.

A big, old, comfortable chair was next to the sofa.

"You can sit there when you're watching him," Abi instructed.

Daddy walked into Abi's kitchen, and she and Landon followed. Her cabinets were free of clutter, as were all the surfaces. No knickknacks for Abi. No sprucing up necessary. A table for two sat by the window. Abi kept the window open to let in fresh air. It was the only room in the place that got adequate sunlight.

Right before Abi left for work, after getting Daddy settled on the couch, she took Landon to the kitchen and opened the fridge, pointing out the food inside.

"I stole all this from work last night, once my boss was too coked to notice or care." She gestured to a big bowl covered with aluminum foil. "There's a big salad and two kinds of dressing, and pasta with different kinds of cheese. You can see the big Ziplocs there with the best yeast rolls you'll ever eat. Henry, our bread maker, is the greatest. Call the pasta *mac and cheese*. He'll like that. And if he doesn't, there's some

shrimp scampi, which I'm sure he's never had. Help yourself to whatever you want. I've made a pitcher of sweet tea. And there's ice in the
freezer. He likes cold tea over ice, even in winter. He doesn't drink
anything hot—tea or coffee or hot chocolate, nothing. He believes all
liquids should be cold. I know it's weird, but it's just a family thing."

"I'll do it right," Landon reassured her.

Abi gave her a big hug. "I know you will, Landon. And I can't tell
you how much I appreciate it. I won't be home till midnight, so don't
think you have to wait up for me. He'll probably fall asleep on the couch
around nine. Maybe if he does, you can throw a quilt over him. You
know where my quilt stand is?"

"I think I've got it," Landon told her.

"Tomorrow's his first day of treatment. He might be anxious. I know
I am."

Abi led Landon back into the living room, kissed Daddy on the cheek,
then headed to her bedroom to get dressed for work.

LANDON

"Thank you for being so good to my Abi," Will said.

Sitting across from him in Abi's living room, Landon tried not to study any particular part of his body. But she didn't want to stare too hard into his eyes either. In another life, she would have told him that the first thing she noticed about a man was his eyes. They were either flat as buttons or alive, had depth, sparkled. She would have told him that his were the latter.

She was having trouble making small talk, not usually a problem for her.

Landon knew from Abi that Will had worked in construction. She could have guessed that from his physique—the broad forearms, warm brown from years of working outdoors, the spread of his shoulders under his flannel shirt. He looked healthy—too healthy to be sick. She wanted to tell Will that he looked ready for the fight. She wanted to tell him how lonely she had been. She wanted to be off her medicine, but she knew it was there to keep her from indulging in short-term hedonism over long-term happiness. She wouldn't hesitate to say all these things if she were manic.

Instead, she asked him if he needed anything from the kitchen.

"I'm fine, but thank you," he replied.

"So," she said, choosing to skip over small talk altogether, "tell me the story of your life."

He laughed. "How long have you got?"

"As long as you want."

Will coughed a few times, dry and sharp, and it took Landon aback. It was the first time that he seemed sick. Landon went to the kitchen to get them each a glass of water. When she returned, she saw that Grits had crawled into Will's lap.

"Abi tell you the story of how she got this cat?" he asked her. "Ever since she was a child, she's loved God's creatures."

Oh, Landon remembered, *the God thing*.

"So tell me about yourself, Will."

And he did. He told her that he had grown up just a few miles from where he was living now. Both of his parents were killed in a car accident, so he was raised by an uncle.

Landon told him about her brother.

"I'm so sorry to hear that," he said.

"It was bad," Landon said, nodding. "But keep going with your story."

"After I came back from Vietnam," Will continued, "I went to work construction for my uncle. I met my wife when I was doing the carpentry on a place for her family. She was still in high school. We married, and then Abi came along a few years later. We tried to give her whatever she needed, but I never made enough money to give her what she deserved."

Landon waited to see if he'd continue without a prompt from her. When it was clear that he was looking for direction, she asked him, "How are you feeling about your diagnosis?"

He retrieved the tiny Testament from his pocket. "It's not just the New Testament, this little book. It's got the Psalms in it, too."

He carefully turned the pages; to Landon, they looked especially thin and vulnerable between his fingers.

"Like this one," he said, landing on the page he was looking for. "'Bless the Lord, O my soul, and forget not all his benefits: Who forgives all your iniquities; Who heals all your diseases; Who redeems your life from destruction; Who crowns you with loving kindness and tender mercies; Who satisfies your mouth with good things; so that your youth is renewed like the eagle's.'"

"I like that," Landon said.

"Abi is having a hard time with all this."

Landon nodded and looked at him to see where he wanted to go with this. She worried momentarily that Will would try to save her. But he must have sensed her discomfort.

"So, tell me about *your* life."

He smiled, and those eyes of his went straight through her. She didn't want to talk about her life. It was only other people's lives she wanted to hear about.

"I don't think I can tell you my story tonight; there will be plenty of time for that later."

"I'd like that," he said. "I'd like that very much."

This was, she knew, a good place to leave it. "Well, I'm going to head downstairs to my place," she told him. "I need to walk my dog." She fetched a piece of paper and a pen from Abi's desk. She wrote her phone number on it and put it inside Will's blue Testament on the table by the couch. "Call me if you need anything, okay? Abi left food for you in the fridge. There's some top-notch mac and cheese in there. And sweet tea, of course. And there's ice in the freezer. Feel free to come knock on my door if I can do anything for you. The porch swing is a comfort, too. I sit out there a lot and just listen to the night. I'll come check on you in a little while, just to make sure you're all right."

"Let me give you a hug," he said, standing. "Thank you for being so good to Abi. And to me, too."

Landon left feeling high. Their goodbye hug had lingered. But as she descended the stairs, she wondered if she was misinterpreting everything. She wasn't going to fall in love with Abi's father. She wasn't going to attempt to seduce him. She would keep an intimate distance, like she had with her patients when she was practicing.

Back in her apartment, she turned on the TV, flipped the channels until she found election coverage. She tried to get into the spirit of the campaign, but she found herself thinking of her daughters.

A few minutes before nine, Landon went upstairs to see if Will needed anything. He was stretched out on the couch, asleep. Per Abi's instructions, Landon spread the quilt over him. She checked on the cats. Though Abi had told her they usually slept curled in the folds of her comforter, Landon found them wide-eyed under the bed. She whispered their names, tapping her fingers gently on the floor, but they made no effort to move. She guessed they were freaked by all the changes in the apartment. But they would be fine once Abi got home.

SAM

I n deciding when he'd head to the Laundromat, Sam tried to choose a time when there wouldn't be a crowd. That way, he could use one of the three chairs and the one folding table—the place was tiny—to review for his engineering test tomorrow. He could use Landon's washer and dryer, he knew, but he liked the Laundromat. It helped him focus.

It was eight o'clock in the morning, and the place was empty. Sam divided his lights from his darks and put four quarters into two machines. Once they got going, Sam pulled a chair up to the folding table, opened his backpack, and retrieved his textbook, notebook, and highlighter. Engineering. Not Sam's first choice for a field of study, but he'd received a scholarship as part of a minority recruitment program. He took the scholarship money, hoping for the best. Poppy had been so excited. He told Sam that an engineering degree meant a good job with good pay. Sam hoped Poppy was right about this. Jet, with her history degree, was working in a bookstore for minimum wage. He hadn't seen her for several days. It worried him, knowing she had a habit of disappearing, then reemerging a week later in some kind of crisis.

Until recently, he hadn't cared much about where Jet was, but his feelings for her had gone from resistance to something like brotherly affection. And the campaign, of course, had brought all the neighbors closer.

He always started his studying by rereading the quote at the front of his book: "Scientists study the world as it is; engineers create the world that has never been." This was starting to resonate more and more with Sam. He had always been cautious and reserved. He was active in high-school sports but never believed his coaches during the pep talks before games; the assumption by the coach that they'd win—that they had to win—always made him uncomfortable. A loss didn't make him mad or sad; it made him embarrassed, which was worse.

That dread, that fear of embarrassment, was why he initially rejected Obama's campaign. He was so dead sure he would never get involved in the seeming impossibility of electing a black man president. He was afraid of his neighbors' embarrassment when Obama lost, of how it might reflect on him. But now that he had been drawn into the campaign—against his will, almost, as if something mysterious were leading him forward—he had to put these fears away.

After he moved his clothes into the dryers, he called Poppy. At first, there was no answer, so Sam waited a few minutes and then tried back.

"Poppy!"

"Sam. I couldn't make it to the phone in time. So glad you called again, son."

He pictured Poppy sitting at the old-fashioned telephone table with the rotary dial phone, fully dressed but also wearing his bathrobe and house shoes. He thought of his brown eyes, less defined because of the cataracts.

"Where are you?" Poppy asked.

"I'm in a Laundromat doing my wash. And I'm studying in here, too."

"I didn't know a place like that was conducive to studying." Poppy chuckled. "It's so good to hear your voice, boy. You get that girlfriend of yours to bring you down here like you said during your break in school. I wish I had the money to get you your own car. Maybe we'd see you more."

"I'm fine," Sam said. "Remember, I can walk to school and the Laundromat and the corner store. And Tanya likes coming to see y'all."

"That's right, that's right," Poppy said.

"I'm still worried about Obama," Sam said. He leaned forward. He also talked a little louder than usual because Poppy's hearing was going, just like his sight.

"Let me tell you what's gonna happen, so you can stop worrying."

"Yeah?" Sam said, leaning over so far in the chair that he was almost on his knees.

"Hold on, Sam. I need to get a drink of water from the faucet."

Sam held on, staring at his Nikes. He wasn't wearing any socks. All his socks were in the dryer. He saw a girl pass by on her way to the corner store. She was wearing a nice shirt and tight jeans but looked worried—cocaine, he guessed. Then again, he shouldn't judge. She might not be using anything at all, despite the likelihood around there.

"I'm back," Poppy said.

"Got your water?"

"Got my water. Now, what I want you to do after your laundry and studying is to look up and say, 'Barack Obama.' That's all you gotta do, since I know you probably don't have a habit of prayer. But if you just say somebody's name and let it rise into the blue sky, God will know what you mean. Or you might do something tangible like go to the headquarters—I'm sure they got a nice one in Birmingham—and tell them you're there to help. They'll probably have you make phone calls or whatnot. But if you don't have time for that, just remember to toss his name up in the air. God's got great antennae; he will hear and know. Now, remind me, when are you coming back down this way?"

"Spring break."

"That's right, that's right."

. . . .

Sam held the hamper in one arm, letting it rest on his hip. When he turned onto Cullom Street, he saw Abi in front of him on the sidewalk. She looked like she was at the end of her morning run. She stopped on her porch and did some stretching.

When she turned to the side, she spotted him. "Sam!"

"Hey, Abi. Come over," he said. "I've got something for you."

She made her way to his place, still sweating from her run.

"Need something to drink?" Sam asked.

"Water, please," she panted.

Sam got a bottle from the fridge. "For you," he said, handing her the bottle and a small baggie. "And this is for your daddy."

"I'm sorry, I can't afford—"

Sam stopped her. "Landon's already got this. She told me not to let you fight her on that."

"She is so dear," Abi said softly.

"So, tell me what it's been like," Sam said.

"Well, he did relatively well with his first round of chemo. His cycle is one week on, then three weeks off. So I took him home, and I'll go get him when it's time for cycle two. The chemo did make him sick. So thanks, the weed really helped."

She was sitting on the couch. Sam sat in the chair and leaned forward.

"This might sound stupid," he said, "but how do they give it to him? I don't know anything about cancer. Guess you've had to educate yourself."

Abi asked him for a piece of paper and a pen. She seemed glad to answer his question.

"I've learned so much," she said. "Okay, so the human body is made up of millions of cells that vary in shape, size, and function. In healthy tissues, new cells are created during cell division, a process called mitosis. When cells become old, they self-destruct—kind of like people do." She laughed and twirled the pen in her fingers. She drew little circles and lines and spirals as she talked. "The cells die, a process called apoptosis. I may not be pronouncing that correctly. Anyway, a delicate balance has to exist between the rate at which new cells are created and the rate at which old cells die. Cancer develops when the balance is disrupted and cells grow out of control. Chemotherapy is a type of treatment that uses strong medicine to stop the growth of cancer cells. Have you taken any biology courses?" she asked, pulling her hair back into a makeshift ponytail. "You don't have any rubber bands, do you?"

He laughed. "No. Let me turn on the AC."

"No, no, I'll be fine. So, once the drugs enter the body, they destroy cancer cells by preventing them from growing or developing or multiplying during mitosis. Depending on the stage you're in, chemo can be used to cure, stop from spreading, or relieve cancer symptoms. Unfortunately, chemo also harms healthy cells, especially those that divide quickly, like hair, blood, bone marrow. So that's where the hair loss comes in. Hair loss, nausea, fatigue, suppression of the immune system. That's why my dad has to avoid people who might be sick, even if it's just a little cold. Am I boring you?"

"No, no," Sam responded quickly. "I swear, these are things I've always wondered. My uncle had cancer, but I was too young to know what was going on."

Abi finished her water and set the bottle on the table next to the paper where she had drawn the geometric shapes.

"I'm gonna ask Poppy to say a prayer. What is your daddy's name?" he asked her.

"Will," she replied. "Recently saved, so he'll appreciate the prayers."

"All right, Will. You are getting prayed for by the best of the best."

Abi laughed. "I think he has a crush on Landon."

"Oh, yeah?"

"Well, the first night, I had to work, and she looked after him. I took him to all his treatment rounds every day during the week. Every night, even though he was weak and sick, he wanted me to go get Landon. We played Scrabble and poker and watched a lot of episodes of *Upstairs, Downstairs.*"

"You caught a vibe between those two?" Sam asked.

"Well, I don't know. Just that he wanted her around. He barely knows her."

"So, what do you think of all that?"

"Whatever makes him happy, eases his pain, causes him to . . . well, to hope. To look forward to something. It's supposed to improve his chances of successful treatment."

Sam nodded. "How did they do the treatments? Were you there with him?"

"Oh, yeah," Abi said. "They put him in this big blue leather lounge chair, get an IV going. The first time, they gave him a sedative. For a while, he seemed to be asleep, so I just watched TV. It was hard not to look around at everyone else. Afterward, he seemed fine, but he got sick a little later. We smoked up, and he was able to drink a smoothie I made for him. So thanks again."

"Don't thank me," Sam said. "Thank Landon. She's the one who insisted on paying."

"Oh, I will. I certainly will."

ABI

Abi noticed that her aquarium was leaking and knew it was just a matter of time before it seeped through her floor to Landon's ceiling. She scooped the fish out and put them in a bowl of water. She pulled the oxygen tube out of the tank and turned the lights off. She lugged the aquarium to the bathtub and, with the help of a sieve to hold the rocks, was able to pour out enough water to make it manageable to carry downstairs and onto the lawn. Once she was outside, she turned it upside down and dumped out most of the tiny, colorful rocks. She and Landon didn't have a spigot, so she got the hose and stretched it to the spigot next door. She washed the inside of the aquarium and wiped the corners with the paper towels she had brought down with her.

She was in a quandary about what to do next, since she didn't know where the leak was. She decided to take it to the pet store where she had bought it, Fred's Pets.

A pair of parrots wandered loose at the store. When Abi approached the counter, one of them began squawking at her, "Hello, missy! Hello, missy! Hello, missy!"

The owner, Fred, was smoking a cigarette and letting his ashes drop to the floor. "What can I help you with?" he asked, although Abi sensed he didn't really care to know. The shop was hot, despite the collection of fans Fred had set up around the room.

"I have an aquarium in my car that I got here awhile back. It's leaking, and I can't find where. I have two fish in a mixing bowl at my place."

While she talked, he flipped the pages of a magazine.

"So," he said, and finally looked her in the eye, "you are here because . . . ?"

"I don't know why I'm here," Abi said, realizing it herself just now. When she left the house, she had intended to get her aquarium patched up. But suddenly, it felt like too much. One more broken thing she didn't know how to fix. "I think my fish days are over. I should probably get rid of the aquarium, right?"

"Up to you," he replied.

She got her thoughts together. "Will you take the fish?" Abi said. "I've got them at home."

"You could always just flush them."

"What? No, I couldn't. They're tropical."

"You live nearby?"

"Yes."

"Put them in a big jar," he began, and reached under the counter. He retrieved a huge jar that was spotted with mold and mildew and God knew what else. "Put them in here and bring them back to me."

"Are you going to flush them?" she asked, then caught sight of an iguana creeping toward her across the dingy linoleum floor. Instinctively, she ran behind the counter, ducking a little. When she straightened up, she found herself standing shoulder to shoulder with Fred.

"You okay today?" he asked her. He smelled like fish and sweat.

"Well, I was until I saw the pool of water on my floor."

"Just go get the fish and bring them to me."

"And you will find them a home?"

Fred laughed. "A new home? This isn't the Humane Society."

Abi's eyes welled up. She realized she should have gone to the big-box pet store near the mall, but it was too late.

"My daddy has cancer," she sputtered.

"So do I," he told her without looking up from the magazine. Then he sighed and raised his eyes to her. "Just go get the fish. I won't flush them, I promise. I have a big aquarium of my own at home with lots of tropicals. I'll take them home with me. And you can just throw your aquarium in the dumpster."

"Thank you," Abi said, relieved. "Thank you. I'll be right back."

"Hello, missy!" the parrot said.

Abi cried all the way home. She threw Fred's moldy jar into the trash and found two clean ones in a cabinet, jars that previously had held stewed tomatoes from the family garden, tomatoes Mama had insisted she take home after a visit last fall. Abi turned on the kitchen faucet and filled the jars, cracked half a tab of water treatment into each, then used a strainer to scoop the fish out of the mixing bowl and into their temporary homes. She was still crying.

Without waiting for her emotions to subside, she secured the fish in their jars and went downstairs. She wanted to be invisible. She hated crying in public. She wanted everybody to think she was fine, just fine. She buckled the fish jars into the passenger seat and drove back to Fred's.

He didn't look up when Abi put the jars on the counter.

"I'm back," she said. "Hello."

"Hello, missy!" the parrot said.

Fred looked up at her.

"Here are my fish. Remember?" she asked.

He nodded and picked up one of the jars, peered into it at the fish.

"What kind of cancer do you have?"

"Prostate," he said. "I'm having a radical prostatectomy in a few weeks. The doc is cutting it out."

"I hope things go well for you," she told him, and started crying again.

He came from behind the counter and opened the store's door for her. At first, she thought he was kicking her out, but he walked her to the Volvo and opened that door for her, too.

"Hope your father makes it. Don't worry about the fish. I promise not to flush them."

Abi nodded and wiped her face with her hands. Fred closed her car door gently behind her and headed back inside, lighting a cigarette on the way. It couldn't be good for the animals, all that smoke. But it was his business. He could do whatever he wanted in Fred's Pets.

On the way back home, she thought about Fred and wondered how he was paying for his treatment. Daddy was lucky enough to have some insurance from the military, but Abi guessed Fred wasn't so lucky. And neither was she, should something happen to her. But it wasn't going to stay that way. She would have a master's degree and a job with benefits. She was going to be a professional, secure.

But things could change even then, Abi knew. She feared for Landon. She feared that her friend was traumatized by the divorce and hoped that Landon would start working again soon. She was on the way down the ladder, and Abi was on the way up. And for a brief moment, the two women were sitting side by side on their rung.

. . . .

Her daddy tolerated the first round pretty well. He didn't lose his hair during his three weeks at home. Sam's weed helped curb his nausea. Even Mama accepted the fact that marijuana was part of his treatment. She didn't try to hide it from Sister and them. Abi could see that Daddy's illness was changing her mother, who had even gone to the bookstore next to JCPenney and bought a book about the medical marijuana crusade. Abi liked to picture her all dressed up in a snakeskin jumpsuit, lecturing Sister on the importance of legalization.

Abi started to respect her mama's going to work. And it gave Abi a reason to take care of her daddy. In many ways, the illness was drawing them all closer. Her parents had kept it relatively together all these years. She might not have moved to Birmingham had there been tension between them. A couple of her cousins had stayed at home in order to keep their dysfunctional families from completely falling apart. They would never leave because they harbored the unfounded belief that they could fix things. Then the years had accumulated. Nobody got it together. There were drunken fights, infidelities, and pettiness. Compared to the rest of the extended family, hers was undoubtedly the most loving. Mama and Daddy never raised their voices to one another. Sure, she was closer to Daddy, but since his illness Abi had started to see her mother in a different light. Her parents had been married forever. And they never used her as a pawn in their disagreements, never tried to persuade her to take sides. Abi was an only child. She didn't have to share their love with a sibling. Growing up, she had occasionally wanted a brother or sister, especially when Mama was going on. But in the end, she was happy having them all to herself.

She thought of Mr. and Mrs. Kasir and their only child, Abe Jr.—how they must have felt watching his demise. The Kasirs had never tried to hide their problems from Abi. She had been renting from them for so long that they were like family. And they were so good to her, the way they had found the bed for Daddy before he began his treatments, the way Mr. Kasir brought Jason along to help. Jason, had grown up to be a source of pride and abiding affection for the Kasirs. In a way, Abi identified with him. Both of them had beaten the circumstances of their upbringings.

These thoughts occupied Abi's mind for the rest of the day. She didn't feel bad about giving the fish to Fred, who also had cancer. Everything worked together, in a way.

LANDON

L andon's phone rang.

"It's Will," he said.

"Do you need me?" she asked, trying to sound professional and less excited than she felt.

"I'm sure you're busy."

"No, no. Just finished cleaning a bit," she lied. "Be right up."

The door to Abi's apartment wasn't locked. She knocked anyway, then went in. If he was resting on the couch, she didn't want him to have to get up.

"I'm in here," he said.

She walked into the living room. He stood, and she was as always aware of his height. He drew her close and hugged her as if his life depended on it. Maybe it did, Landon thought. She didn't know what to say or do. She pulled away and looked around the room.

"Here," he said. "Would you mind just sitting and talking to me? I need a distraction."

He was wearing jeans and a white, slightly rumpled oxford shirt with the sleeves rolled up, revealing his forearms. His wedding band

142

appeared to be a bit loose on his finger. Maybe he was losing weight. Landon couldn't tell.

They took a seat. On the coffee table was his tiny blue Testament, along with his pipe and baggie.

"I need to smoke before I try to eat," he told her.

She gestured to his Testament. "Is that the only Bible you have?"

"I'm afraid so."

"I need to give you one of mine. I have several."

He packed the pipe, lit up, then offered her the bowl.

"Just one puff, maybe. Or two," she said.

"Or three?"

She smiled at him, took a hit—trying, a little more than she'd care to admit, to look cool—then coughed most of it back up. She felt a buzz immediately.

"This isn't like what we smoked back in the day, is it?" she asked him.

He laughed in agreement. She watched his hands as they lifted the bowl and worked the cheap plastic lighter.

Will put the pipe down and leaned back. "Do I look stoned?" he asked her.

"You do."

They were quiet for a moment, until Landon noticed the absence of the whirring aquarium pump.

"What happened to the fish?" she asked.

"Abi said the tank was leaking, and she had to get rid of it."

"And the fish?"

"She took them to the fellow who owns the pet store. Can't recall his name."

"Fred?" she asked. "Fred's Pets?"

"You'll have to ask her about it. I got the short version of the story."

"Fred can be an asshole. I hope he was nice to her," Landon said. "I can't bear the thought of anybody being unkind to Abi. I know she can take care of herself. It's just that she has a tender side."

Will picked up the Testament and moved the purple ribbon page marker to one side. "I wish I hadn't told her I've been saved."

"Why?" Landon asked.

"It scared her."

Landon got up and turned on a lamp. It was dusk now, and the room was dark. She felt Will's eyes on her.

"I like that skirt you're wearing," he told her, still holding the Testament.

"Thank you. I've had it for years. I sewed the patches on some torn places."

"Who tore it?"

She looked at him. He was trying to hide a smile, and she knew he was teasing her.

"Oh, all the men grabbing at me," she said.

"All at the same time?" he asked, his eyes traveling from the skirt to her eyes.

"And I fought all the others away because it was only you I wanted."

"Did we tear up the skirt dancing?"

She was relieved that Will didn't seem taken aback by her comment. She wondered how long they might keep on with this story they were making up together.

"Yes," she replied. "It was the nature of the dance."

"In my dreams," he said, and smiled at her. Then, as if he suddenly found himself in deep water he couldn't navigate, he let his eyes fall back to the Testament. "So, you've got a lot of Bibles? What's your favorite verse?"

"I've always felt that if you believe the first five words in the Bible, then you believe in something."

"'In the beginning God created,'" he said. "I'm right with you on that."

They grew quiet, neither knowing which way to go now.

"Do you miss your husband?"

"Yes. And no. Mostly yes."

"How could anybody leave you?" he asked.

"I was a mess, Will."

"You don't seem like a mess to me. You know, people hear I've got cancer and they feel sorry for me or scared for me, but I'm telling you, the past month has been wonderful. Getting to be with Abi, living part-time in Birmingham, meeting you. Aside from having poison pumped through my body, I'd say it's been good."

"We need some music," Landon said, rising and walking to the table where Abi's computer sat open. "You ever listen to Buffy Sainte-Marie? I downloaded this for Abi the other day. See if you remember it." She turned the sound up and waited.

When the music started, Will stood up. "I know this," he said.

"'Until It's Time for You to Go,'" Landon told him. "One of my favorites."

Will took Landon's hand, pulling her toward him. They danced and held on to one another. Landon leaned her head against his chest. She knew that, in vastly different ways, they both needed something from the other. The future was up for grabs. For both of them. They had more than survival to hope for, pray for. There were wars raging in them that had brought them together—her divorce, his cancer—yet, like Mr. Kasir and his girl in France, their time together would be fleeting. Landon knew this. It rested on his continued illness, without which his life would go back to normal. What possible reason was there for seeing him if all was well? Landon didn't want to destroy a marriage. And more than that, she didn't want to cause Abi any pain. She wanted only to dance. Even after the song was over, she wanted to keep dancing.

Will took Landon's face in his hands. She kept her eyes downcast. She knew if she looked at him, it would hurt, like staring into the sun. She might cry. She might go limp; her legs might give way.

"We won't be alone again until my next round begins."

Landon nodded but still didn't look up. She closed her eyes. She had no words. The music had ended. She had no map, no compass, no guide, no way to move, no clock, no metronome, no lifesaver, no eyeglasses, no song.

"I'm sorry," she whispered, eyes still closed.

"Don't be."

She kept her eyes closed and let him lean over so as to bring his face to hers. Their foreheads touched. He was moving in tiny increments. His lips brushed her cheek. She felt thirteen, on the verge of falling, thrilled and terrified. His lips searched her cheek, then found her mouth. He kissed her like she always wanted to be kissed but seldom had been—just lips touching lips. She knew what Mr. Kasir meant by his girl's kiss being a question. Will let his lips linger on hers.

When it was over, he led her back to the chair where she had been sitting before the dance. He sat back down on the couch.

"Are you all right?" he asked her.

"Yes," Landon said honestly. "Very much so."

"I want you to be all right."

"And I wish that for you," she whispered.

"I need to lie down," he said.

"Of course. Let me get you a pillow." She hurried to Abi's bedroom and retrieved one for him, fluffing it as she returned to the living room. "Are you hungry?"

"No, not yet."

"Do you need to be alone?"

"No, please don't go quite yet."

"I've got all the time in the world," she assured him.

He raised an eyebrow and smiled. He was still playing, but it was light fun again.

They played their game for a long time—making up stories about the past, pretending they had known one another and wanted one another back.

"Remember the time we were playing football and I tackled you and straddled you, pinned you to the ground with your hands over your head, my hands pressing yours?"

"Remember that party when we left our dates on the dance floor and ran to the parking lot to make out?"

"Remember the night you told me you used to be scared of losing gravity, so I got on top of you so you wouldn't fall off the earth?"

When this was over and Will felt like he could eat, Landon ordered a pizza and got him a beer from the refrigerator. It was time for her to go, but she sat on the floor. He was stretched out on the couch. She got on her knees so her face was next to his. This time, she looked him straight in the eye as she touched his lips with her finger. He did the same to her, each of them tracing something on the other's lips.

"What did you write?" she asked.

"My initials."

Whatever was happening was nothing to fear. She was back in familiar territory again: taking care of somebody. But the kiss was tucked away inside her. There, they were on the dance floor, basking in what could never be, would always be, theirs for the remembering.

JET

The lawyer Stephanie hired for Jet was reassuring from the beginning. He explained that the cops were outside their jurisdiction, so the arrest couldn't stand. He'd have it resolved quickly.

Jet had called Abi to let her know what was going on, and to tell her she was staying on for a week but would be back to Birmingham. She chose Abi because she had known her longer than the other neighbors.

Stephanie offered to drive her home, but Jet insisted that she'd done enough. She took the bus.

When the bus pulled in, Jet spotted Abi leaning against a concrete wall, smoking a cigarette. She reminded Jet of Paul Newman.

When Jet got off, Abi smiled and embraced her. They walked through the station and out to the curb, where Abi's Volvo was parked unapologetically in a no-parking zone.

"I've always thought of rules as suggestions," Abi said.

Jet threw her tote bag into the backseat. Because Jet's clothes had been in her car at the time of the arrest, Stephanie and Caroline had taken her shopping—a new pair of jeans and six tees of varying colors.

Once inside Abi's car, Jet sighed.

"How bad was it?" Abi asked, and lit another cigarette.

Jet shook her head. "I panicked when they arrested me. But that's not what I've been thinking about. I've been chewing on how it all worked out for me. Getting to know Stephanie for who she is—my mother. That was like heaven. And Caroline, too. Knowing I have a sister. They tried to make it like a vacation for me—lying by the pool, wading in the Gulf, telling bad jokes."

"Oh, sweetie, that is wonderful."

"How something so good could come out of . . ."

"I understand," Abi replied. "In a way, that's how my daddy's illness has been."

"How's he doing?" Jet asked.

"We'll know Monday. He has an appointment with the oncologist. He'll let us know whether or not the chemo has worked. And depending on that outcome, we'll discuss the next step."

Jet stared at the people on the sidewalk by the Greyhound station. Many of them held up signs that read, "Homeless" or "Hire me" or "Feed me." Then she spotted a woman who held a sign that read, "Heal me." The words caused a quickening in Jet. The woman reminded her of Violet. The Birmingham police had brought Violet to the shelter on Jet's first night there. It turned out that everyone there knew Violet well. That night, she wore sunglasses, even though it was dark out. She said a man beat her with a gun. The volunteers checked her out and didn't find any injuries. But they didn't turn her away because, for whatever reason, she needed to be sheltered. And she never left. She was Jet's guide in the underworld.

"Look at that woman's sign," Abi said. "Are you going to get Father Patrick to come save her?"

"She doesn't need saving," Jet replied, rolling her window down.

"Don't say anything to her," Abi said.

"I won't, don't worry."

Jet wasn't in a hurry to get to Lenny's apartment to pick up her car. She needed time to adjust to being back, time to think. Abi turned on the radio, searching the stations for a song she might like. A breeze picked up. Jet leaned toward the door, hung her head out the window, and let the sunlight take her face. She closed her eyes as if she were still at the beach, tanning.

Then, without opening them, she said, "How's Sam?"

Abi took her hand, and Jet opened her eyes.

"I don't mean to be harsh," Abi said, "but do you think maybe you're attracted to him because you can't have him?"

"Boyfriends always let you down in the end, don't they?" Jet asked.

"Girlfriends can let you down, too," Abi replied.

"It must be nice to have a choice like you do."

"A choice?"

"You know, liking men *and* women. Maybe that multiplies your chances at getting somebody who knows how to love you right."

"Little sister," Abi said, "that's not really how it works."

"I wish you were my big sister."

"I am," Abi replied. "Also, don't get so hopeless about guys. The only men in your life are either taken or in their nineties or gay or priests. You haven't met a lot of eligible fellows lately."

"I guess that's weird," Jet said, cracking a smile.

"It's safe," Abi said, and started the car. "Relationships aren't so great. That's why I'm happy it's just me and the cats."

"Do I need a pet?"

Abi shrugged. "Couldn't hurt."

LANDON

Landon was in her front yard planting some tomatoes in a space she had cleared with a hoe. Spring had not brought her the melancholy it had in years past, though she wasn't sure why.

She transplanted the Big Girls from a flat into the ground. A bandana held back her hair, but she had still worked up a sweat. She stopped and wiped her forehead on her sleeve. That's when she saw Mr. Kasir's truck coming up the street.

"Mr. Kasir!" she hollered, waving a gloved hand.

He pulled over. Landon wasn't sure if he was there to see her or not. Generally, he called first when he planned to visit.

He rolled the window down, and she walked over to his truck. She leaned forward and apologized for the way she looked.

"You planting tomatoes?"

"I am. Is everything all right?" she asked him.

"I'm fine. I'm on my way home from my attorney's office and just thought I'd drive by Cullom to see if all is well, and I see that it is for you. How is Abi's father?"

"We'll know on Monday if the chemo's working. Why don't you

come inside?"

"I don't want to interrupt what you're doing."

"Don't be silly. I need to cool down."

Landon noticed that he had a harder time than usual getting onto the running board of his truck. He held the steering wheel with his right hand and his cane in his left. Once on the curb, he hesitated, needing to get his bearings. Landon had noted before that his arthritis was getting worse. She had never seen him have to catch his breath, though. It worried her.

Once inside, she turned on the window air-conditioning unit and got the lemonade she had made from scratch the day before. And as always when she was with Mr. Kasir, she used her good china and crystal. She dropped a few ice cubes into the glasses and took the pitcher to the table, where she poured both of them a glass.

"Homemade, isn't it?" he asked after taking a long sip.

"When life gives you lemons . . . ," she replied.

"Ah," he said. "The real trick is putting in enough sugar."

"You wouldn't believe how much sugar is in here; it's enough to make us feel high as a kite. I can't drink alcohol, so it's important for me to have my own good things to indulge in."

"You're a sweet girl," he replied.

"I'm glad you think that."

Landon waited for a clue as to what was on his mind.

"The reason I've been at my attorney's office is because I'm changing my will," Mr. Kasir said finally.

Landon nodded and moved closer, as he clearly wanted to choose his words carefully.

"I don't want to burden you with this, but my son, Abe Jr., is in jail for possession of narcotics with intent to distribute. Oh, did you hear about our little Jet? She called to tell me. She knows I won't judge. Anyhow, back to my son. They were strong painkillers, and I can't recall the name of them."

"Oxycontin," Landon said.

"That's it. How did you know?"

"Industry hazard. Oxy's as strong as heroin, and just as addictive. It is easy to overdose."

Mr. Kasir nodded. "You are a smart girl."

"It's just that I had plenty of patients who were dealing with addiction." She put her hand over his. "What addictionologists tell us is that a person stops growing emotionally at the age when they began using. Like, let's say that Abe Jr. started using at eighteen. That means that, in many ways, he's still eighteen."

Mr. Kasir pulled a handkerchief from his pocket, took off his glasses, and wiped his eyes. Landon knew his generation had been taught that men didn't cry. She wondered where all those unwept tears were stored—maybe in the heart. And one day, the heart couldn't take any more and just stopped.

"Tell me," she said softly.

"It hurts me to think he never grew up and never will. All these years, I've tried to help him, but he would not change. A few weeks ago, when my grandson, Jason, came over to tell us that Abe Jr. was back in jail, something inside me finally broke. Or rather, was finally resolved. We even looked that word up in the dictionary. I was at peace and decided on the spot that I was through with him, that I wasn't going to get him out."

"Often, that's the best thing you can do."

"But what you said about him still being eighteen, it makes me want to reconsider."

Landon leaned closer. "You're doing the right thing. What does Mrs. Kasir think, and Jason?"

"Oh, they were thrilled. My wife started going to all the Al-Anon meetings and got herself to a good place. She stopped worrying over him long ago and devoted herself to Jason. She got healthy, and I was sick. As sick as Abe Jr., the way I enabled him."

"I cannot tell you how brave you were to have made this decision," Landon said. "I'm sorry I even said that about his still being eighteen. That can go only so far, for so long."

"You're a good listener," he said.

"I'm your tenant, and I'm grateful to be. I'm also your friend, right?"

He nodded and stuffed his handkerchief back in his pocket. "So that's what I was doing this morning," he said. "I was making some real changes before I lost my resolve. I saw my attorney and told him the properties—all of them, not just the ones here on Cullom—should go to Jason after his grandmom dies. I know it's the right thing. There is a tiny part of me that I fight, the lingering notion I can save my son."

Landon nodded. "But this is where your faith comes in, right?"

"Right."

"And I am also here for you. Always. Just as you are for me, right?"

"That's right," Mr. Kasir said, patting her hand. "But why did it take me all these years to leave it be?"

"You were trying to be a good father."

"You think so?"

"Yes. And that's something, believe you me."

"I've been trying for a long time. I'm almost ninety years old."

They sat quietly for a moment, both lost in their thoughts. Finally, Mr. Kasir took the piece of shrapnel from his pocket. Landon knew he wanted to move the conversation back to the war, the girl.

"Tell me."

"Every day, she came for me," he said, picking up exactly where he left off. "The last time I saw her was like the other times. She came to get me, wearing the white cotton dress she had worn the first time. I knew my platoon was starting to pack up. I knew she'd come back the next day, and we'd be gone. I was glad we didn't have language at that point. I didn't want to give her the bad news—that we were moving on."

He continued, "We were lying on the grass in the meadow. I remember a new moon in the sky, a tiny crescent so bright it looked like gold. She turned to face me. There is a difference between wanting something and needing something. I knew it then. We were so young. Maybe she knew I'd be leaving soon, because we stayed there too long. We weren't thinking about the war. To us, just then, it didn't matter. When we think we're in love, we throw danger to the wind, don't we?"

"Yes," Landon said. She allowed herself briefly to think of Will.

"Forgive me for pouring this all out. Sometimes, it seems that the more I tell you, the more I have left to tell."

Landon was, as always, mesmerized by Mr. Kasir's love story.

"And before we got up to walk home . . . ," he began. He picked up the piece of shrapnel.

"Did you kiss her?"

"Yes," he said. "Yes. And this is the part of her I carry. The war would take over. I was going to see more men die. That first day on Omaha Beach had been so horrific, but war doesn't let up. It feels endless, when you're in it. I wanted to pack her up and carry her with me, keep her safe with me—as if that was safe. I tried to remember Mrs. Kasir and the future ahead. We'd have children. I'd work every day and come home to her arms and a warm dinner, and we'd sit on the patio of a house we'd build and study the constellations. But I couldn't see the future. I forgot how to love Mrs. Kasir. I had nothing but the war and Carissa. War doesn't give a damn about love. I never saw her again."

Landon reached for his hand and held it. The sun came out from behind a cloud. They didn't say anything, even though Landon knew what she had to tell him. She had been thinking about it since the last time he visited. It was time to tell him. But sometimes, people think they want an answer to something, even though the answer only brings pain.

She stared at the pitcher of lemonade. It was green etched glass and had been her mother's. She heard the sound of Abi's broom upstairs, moving across the hardwood floor. She looked at her hands. Even though she had washed them when Mr. Kasir came in, they were still dusted in earth. She stared at the place on her finger, at that pale circle where the wedding ring had been. The sun couldn't get to it. Even though she had taken the ring off a year ago, the band of skin was still white. She wondered how long the discoloration might last.

Landon kept her hand on Mr. Kasir's and told him what she knew must be true. "I think I know what she was trying to ask you."

He took off his glasses and looked almost scared.

"I think her question was, *Will you come back for me?*"

Mr. Kasir nodded and inhaled sharply.

"It was a blessing that you spoke different languages. How could you have answered that question, knowing it would break her heart, and yours, too?"

"You're right," Mr. Kasir said.

"But she lives on in a place in your heart. And it's not a dark place."

"Oh, but to me, it is," he replied. "Once we moved on, I started feeling that I had betrayed Mrs. Kasir. But I also betrayed Carissa. Even without a shared language, I should have told her I was leaving."

"I know so little about war," Landon said, thinking of her father, her daughter. "But I do know what it's like to have to move on. That is what I've been doing for as long as I've been your tenant. I have been moving on. And it hasn't been easy. I wish I could see my daughters. I fear for my oldest, who will be in Iraq soon. I long to hear my ex-husband's voice. I mean, I have talked to him on the phone, but I long to hear a hint of our old love, just a word to betray that he might come back for me."

"I forget," Mr. Kasir said, squeezing Landon's hand. "I hate it that you are alone. Most of my tenants are children. They seem to be happy living alone, just to be out of their mama and papa's control. You don't know what you've lost until long after you lose it. How long were you married?"

"Thirty years."

"My, my," Mr. Kasir said, shaking his head. "But you are building a new life."

"That's right. I'm building it through you, through Abi and Jet and Sam, this neighborhood, this apartment. I was building it when you pulled up, planting tomatoes in my yard, putting down my roots. My new life is starting. And in a way, you are my new father. Growing up, I never felt safe like I do here. I never felt cared for the way you care about me. I never knew when my father would lash out, and I never knew why my mother allowed him to. But she must have been scared, as scared as I was. And we make mistakes. We can't save everyone we love."

Landon put her hands to her cheeks. They felt hot. She shouldn't have told all this to Mr. Kasir.

"So you do know about war," Mr. Kasir said. "That was your war, Landon Cooper."

"I suppose so," she said, and self-consciously looked at her watch. "But now I've kept you too long."

"You know better than that." He lifted the piece of shrapnel from the table. He examined it closely, moving it around so as to get every angle. "I don't think I've told you this. Every platoon gets a medic, lovingly referred to as 'Doc.' You train with them, eat with them, and share every hardship. We love them; they love us. When someone gets hurt, the first call is '*Medic!*' So I'm your medic, and you are mine—moving on together, despite our wounds."

Landon walked with Mr. Kasir back outside, and the two surveyed her tomato plants.

"I'll bring you some stakes," Mr. Kasir said, sounding like his regular self again. "And don't forget to clip the suckers at the bottom. You want all your growth in the fruit, not the leaves."

ABI

Abi waited until Jet pulled out of the parking lot of Lenny's apartment, just to make sure that her car started. Lenny was out and had left Jet's keys under a planter by his door.

It was Saturday. Two more night shifts, and then she'd pick up her daddy for his Monday-morning appointment. She had a quiz on Thursday and felt she needed to go ahead and study for it. Monday was going to be the day of reckoning.

When Abi pulled up against the curb in front of her house, she noticed the new tomato plants that Landon must have planted. Once inside her apartment, she headed straight for the couch and her stack of textbooks. She lit a cigarette, trying to focus on sociology rather than Monday's appointment. They had all agreed that, no matter what the outcome, Daddy was to spend Monday night with her. She looked to where the aquarium had been and saw the water stain on the hardwood floor. She hoped that Fred had taken her fish home like he promised.

The chapter she was studying was titled "Life at Home." The first section covered the topics "What Is Family?" and "Diversity in Families" and "Sociological Perspectives of the Family." The second section, called "Changing the World," included "Who Can Marry," "Forming Relationships," "Talking about Kin," and "Selecting Mates."

She paused.

She knew her mama worried over her being single. According to her textbook, she wasn't really driven by the romantic concept of chemistry. She actually was driven by what society selected for her—homogamy, meaning mates who were similar in class, race, age, religion, and education; or propinquity, the tendency to choose people who lived nearby. But neither of these concepts interested Abi. Maybe it was because her life was cut in half. There was trailer-park Abi, and there was Birmingham Abi. Trailer-park Abi never dated, held on to the memory of Marcia and the pond in Tennessee. Birmingham Abi had dabbled with Scott, a lawyer, and Celeste, a masseuse, had a one-night stand here and there. She had nothing in common with any of them, including their neighborhoods.

And the thing was, Abi wasn't seeking a mate in the way that the textbook and Mama assumed she was. She liked being single. She had worked so hard to get where she was. She was only now beginning to understand herself. Why bring another person into the equation to muddy all that up? She loved the restaurant staff like they were her family. She loved the neighbors on Cullom in the same way. She wasn't opposed to having a little fun when the mood struck. But that had nothing to do with love. It was as if she were married to herself. Her old self in the trailer had married her new self in Southside. In this respect, she was beginning to feel complete.

Abi read and reread a passage about the development of intimate, romantic relationships—they were not something natural; they were socially constructed to appear natural.

She felt the same way about religion. She knew it as a construct, and not one she was particularly interested in participating in. The situation with Daddy had, of course, stirred up her unwillingness to make this intellectual surrender. People such as Daddy and Landon caused Abi to question her agnosticism. They were both so smart, yet they believed. Mr. Kasir had his Lebanese church, and even Jet had found something special, thanks to Father Patrick. Sam was always talking about his granddaddy's preaching. And all of them had told Abi that they were praying for Daddy. She pictured him in the blue leather chair, among all the other patients. Surely, they all had people praying for them, but some were sure to get bad news. Did God not hear those prayers? The whole thing seemed random and senseless to Abi, like a cruel game of chance. But she wasn't ever going to let Daddy know that her doubts went this deep.

. . . .

Monday morning came none too soon.

On the way to the compound, Abi called Landon.

"I know how big today is," Landon said. "I'm thinking about you."

"I'm afraid I might come apart at the seams," Abi said. "The appointment's at one-thirty. Will you be home after that?"

"Of course. You know I never go anywhere but down the block and back with Alejandro."

"Will you come up when we're back?" Abi asked.

"I'll be glad to," Landon said.

"I mean, you've been in on all this treatment, and I know Daddy will want to see you, whether the news is good or bad."

When they said goodbye, Abi tossed her phone back into the passenger seat. Once she took the exit that led home, she wanted to go slowly. And quietly. She wasn't ready to face Daddy. Surely he was anxious, and surely they'd only amplify one another's fears.

It was still early, so Abi stopped at the small, familiar café just a few miles from her parents' place. The waitress approached her as she slid into a booth. She was young and had a word tattooed on her arm. Abi tried to make it out, but she didn't want to stare.

"What can I get for you?" The waitress was definitely a local. Her accent confirmed that.

"I'd like coffee and a cinnamon roll," Abi told her.

"That it for you?"

"Yes, thanks, that's all."

When the waitress returned with the order, Abi told her she liked her tattoo. She couldn't help asking what it said.

"Mike."

"Mike must be a special guy," Abi said.

The waitress smiled and shrugged.

"Do you have any others—tattoos, that is?"

The waitress glanced back at the man near the cash register, who was more than likely her boss, leaned forward, and whispered, "I have one right above my ass."

Abi smiled her approval. She thanked the girl for her breakfast and watched her walk away in her gingham shirt and blue jeans, the order pad stuck in her back pocket, the pencil behind her ear. Abi missed dressing like that at work.

She ate only half of the cinnamon roll and wrapped the other half in a napkin from the silver holder beside the salt and pepper shakers. She used to come here a lot when she had just turned sixteen and gotten her driver's license. She hadn't eaten here in years. In the past, the waitresses wore what looked like nurse's uniforms, puffy white numbers with a big pocket in front for the pad and pencil. Abi couldn't imagine her waitress in that getup.

She picked up her check. The coffee and roll came to $2.50. She paid up front, then approached the waitress and handed her a five. She knew from experience that the tips people filled in when they signed their credit-card receipts didn't always make it to the waitress.

Back in her car, she phoned Daddy to tell him she was almost there. When she arrived, he was sitting on the concrete stoop, his old suitcase beside him. Abi saw that her mother's car was gone. She must have been working the morning shift.

Abi got out of the car and gave him a long hug. "As handsome as ever," she told him.

And he did look good. He had lost only a little bit of weight. Abi could see it in his face. But all in all, he didn't look like a cancer patient. He still hadn't lost his hair. His blue eyes matched the sky. He looked excited, maybe even happy. How could he be so jubilant on a day like this? She didn't ask him why, of course, because she was sure his answer would have something to do with God.

She reached down to pick up his suitcase. "You staying all week?" she asked, noting the unexpected weight of the bag.

He laughed. "Just a change of clothes for tomorrow. The city's making you weak."

Abi didn't want to leave right away. But she knew that, one way or the other, she would bring him back to the trailer the next morning. If things were good, there was no reason for him to stay. If things were bad, there wouldn't be any further treatments right now, and Mama would want him home with her.

"There's half a cinnamon roll in the glove compartment, if you want it," she said.

"I have something to tell you that you will love but not believe," Daddy said. "Your mother is talking about voting for Obama."

Abi was stunned. "Are you kidding me?"

"Honest to God." Apparently, it was all part of Mama's sophisticated new self. "She almost gave Aunt Sister a stroke when she announced her intentions."

Abi just shook her head, feeling like she owed a bit of thanks to JCPenney.

. . . .

Abi wanted to get to the medical center early. She circled her car up the parking deck. The crossover was on the fourth floor. She spotted an empty place right by the elevator. She tucked the parking ticket into her jeans pocket and her wallet in the other. Her keys were on a carabiner hooked to her belt loop. A purse would have made more sense, but she had always hated carrying one.

When they opened the doors on the far side of the crossover, the Oncology Department stared them right in the face. They checked Daddy in, but rather than being led to the chemo room, they were asked to have a seat there in the waiting room. Big windows filled the space with light, which must have been an attempt to make the wait feel less grueling. A table of magazines was beside the chairs where they sat.

"I just can't read celebrity gossip right now," Abi whispered.

"Those people holding magazines aren't really reading theirs either," Daddy whispered back.

Abi nodded. This wasn't like a waiting room for internal medicine or family practice or pediatrics. This was oncology. Everybody involved—from the patients to the receptionist and the other clerical workers behind the window—knew that oncology was a special and dreadful place to find yourself.

Abi played with her keys. She snapped and unsnapped the carabiner nervously. Daddy wasn't talking. She wasn't going to hide behind a magazine. It was all about stoicism now. A brave face. She wondered if her daddy was praying. Whatever was in his file was already there. It was too late to change anything now.

Daddy whispered to her, "Where do you think Dr. Ravi is from?"

She laughed.

"Is that not an appropriate question?" he said softly.

"Not really, but I don't know how much political correctness matters on the oncology floor," she whispered. She felt like they were kids misbehaving. It helped. "I think he's probably from India. Do you want me to ask him?"

"No, no. You know, your mother is calling black people African-Americans now."

"That's a lot better than what she used to call them."

Daddy was laughing now, too. A lady who was dressed to the max glanced at them, looking up from her magazine. She was reading *House Beautiful*. Abi thought about nabbing it on the way out to give to Mama.

A nurse holding a chart walked into the waiting room. "William," she called. She didn't say Daddy's last name, but he was the only man who looked up.

Abi held Daddy's hand while they followed the nurse.

"Here," the nurse said, and opened the cracked door to a spacious office. "Have a seat."

Abi was surprised. She assumed the nurse would weigh him, take his temp, check his vital signs. But none of that mattered. The verdict was in.

The walls were covered in framed diplomas and Picasso prints. The carpet was plush and blood-red. Dr. Ravi's desk was huge. It held nothing but her daddy's file, a pen, and a stack of what appeared to be blank paper. Another big window let in a beam of sunshine.

Abi looked for dust particles in the light but didn't see any. She guessed the staff took great care to avoid too much dust in the air. Still, the office didn't feel sterile. Three lavender irises bloomed from a pot on a side table. Abi wondered what her blood pressure was right now. She looked at Daddy, but he was sitting with his eyes closed. The clock on Dr. Ravi's wall read 1:35. She took a few deep breaths.

Dr. Ravi entered the room and closed the door behind him. He shook Daddy's hand, then Abi's, before he sat behind his desk. With everyone in place, the desk seemed bigger, like an interminable boundary separating doctor from patient, known from unknown.

Dr. Ravi wasted no time. He didn't even open Daddy's chart. He simply looked at both of them and said the words.

"I have good news, William."

Abi grabbed her daddy's hand.

It was only after delivering this one statement that Dr. Ravi opened the file.

"The chemotherapy is working for you. For right now, the tumors have shrunk. And there is no indication that any of them has metastasized. So," he said, closing the file, "right now—and I want to emphasize this—right now, you are in good shape. Right now, the prognosis for you is good. Tumors can reappear later, and if they do, we will work together again. But all in all, your body is healthy. For a man your age, you are in remarkably good health overall. Had you not been, the chemotherapy would have been a lot harder on you."

"Oh, thank you, Dr. Ravi," Abi said, realizing her voice sounded like a kid's.

"I'm happy when I have good news," the doctor said. "This can be good, or it can be just a lull. I will want to see you again in three months. If you're still healthy, then it will be six months, and eventually it will be once a year. Any questions?"

"No, sir," Daddy said, standing to shake Dr. Ravi's hand again. "Thank you for taking such good care of me."

"Some days, it's good to be an oncologist," he replied.

They stopped at the receptionist's window to make a three-month follow-up appointment.

When they cleared the Oncology Department and were walking on the crossover, they let loose. All their pent-up anxiety made them both delirious. Abi skipped along, as if playing hopscotch. Daddy held out his arms and whirled around, as if dancing with an invisible partner. Despite her fear of high places, Abi stopped and looked over the side at the cars moving along the street. How could she ever have been afraid of anything? The doctor's words of warning that the tumors might return weren't lost on her. But the good news was all about remission. Daddy danced up to her and wrapped her in a hug. They stood there, embracing on the crossover. Abi wasn't crying. She was fearless.

LANDON

Landon went to the corner store at noon and bought an avocado and cottage cheese. When she returned home, she scooped the fruit out of its skin, then shook a bit of salt and pepper over it. But she wasn't hungry. She was too worried about Will.

"I think we need a walk," she said to Alejandro, leaving her meal on the counter.

She grabbed his leash, and the dog—on command—jumped out of the wicker chair, wagging his tail and hopping up and down.

Outside, the sky was perfectly blue. Not a single cloud.

Landon and Alejandro started the climb. When they reached the top of the hill, Landon turned around and stared at the city below. All the trees were now bearing green leaves. Spring had obscured the buildings. She turned left, toward the alley that would take her back home. She let Alejandro stop and sniff.

In the past, this was the time of year when her daughters played softball. Earlier in the week, her older girl, Danner, had deployed to Iraq. Landon hardly knew what to make of it. How could the daughter of two former hippies be in the Marine Corps? Never in a million years would she have guessed that the military would be Danner's choice. But like much in life, Danner had been changed by 9/11. After the first plane hit, her principal had made a solemn announcement over the PA and sent the students to their homerooms. Danner was glued to the television from the moment she got home, long into the night. After that, she didn't smile much. She lost interest in boys, even though they were knocking the doors down. And before she graduated, she visited a recruiting office and signed on for a two-year stint. She told her parents that she was interested in avionics and hoped to be stationed in Pensacola. Landon pictured that it would be almost like college—not too far from home, her daughter studying hard, working long hours in a hangar, far from any danger. But when Danner called her from specialized training at Twentynine Palms, it became clear that wasn't going to happen. Now that her daughter was overseas, Landon worried about silly things, like how hot it must be. Was Danner staying hydrated? All that sand and wind. Would it tear up her eyes? Worrying about the little details kept Landon from having to worry about what was most frightening.

Landon pulled gently on Alejandro's leash to get him walking. He had found a bit of interesting information and was sniffing a clump of weeds from all angles.

"Come on, buddy."

When they reached the dumpster, Landon stopped. Beside it were a sofa, chairs, and a table. Clothes poured from torn plastic bags piled next to the furniture. It wasn't an unfamiliar sight around the properties that Mr. Kasir didn't own. When somebody moved, they often piled their unwanted stuff back there, not bothering if it didn't make it into the dumpster. There was usually a reason it was unwanted, but Landon liked to check it all out anyhow. She couldn't help it. One man's trash was so often her treasure.

A voice called to her from above. "Hey, Landon!"

She looked up. It was Sam, leaning over the railing of his back balcony.

"Looks like somebody got evicted," he said, gesturing to the alley furniture.

"Sure does. You know who?"

"No," he said. "Want to come up? Talk primaries?"

"I would, but Abi's daddy gets his report today. I'm supposed to meet up with them."

"Let me know," he said.

"I will."

Landon and Alejandro followed the alley toward her backyard. Blackberry vines were growing wild along a barbed-wire fence. They would be ready for picking soon. Once they were so ripe they bled purple onto her fingers, she would make a cobbler, just as she had used the pecans from a neighbor's yard in the fall to make a pecan pie. She had even located a pear tree two blocks over and had taken to scavenging fruit that dropped to the pavement. What started as a quirky preoccupation was fast becoming Landon's way of life. She wondered how long she could survive on pecans, pears, and blackberries. *Foraging*, Abi called it. It made Landon feel like a wild animal, which she didn't really mind. She glanced back at the dumpster to the bags of clothes. It was so tempting.

Sometimes on a walk, Landon would spot a plant she wanted from somebody's yard. After dark, she'd return to snip a blossom or two. Abi had taught her how to do this. "They'll never know it's missing," she told Landon. "And anyway, if they truly love nature, they would want to share it."

Sometimes, these occasional finds were more pragmatic. Like the hammer Abi had rescued from beside the dumpster—the one she waved at the frat boy who'd passed out in Landon's lounge chair.

Landon and Alejandro returned from their walk just as Abi's car was turning onto their street from down the block. Landon quickly unleashed the dog and let him inside, then took a seat on the porch swing. She didn't want to appear too eager to know how it had gone at the doctor's office, in case it was bad news. But Abi rolled down her window before she even finished parking and gave her a thumbs-up.

Landon made the sign of the cross. She wasn't Catholic, but it seemed appropriate.

Abi and Will got out of the car and walked to the porch. Landon embraced Abi and kissed Will lightly on the cheek. Both of their faces were flushed, and their eyes were glimmering. Will had dodged a bullet for now. They all had.

"Come on inside," Landon said, and opened her door. "Tell me everything."

Abi told her what they'd learned from Dr. Ravi—that the tumors had shrunk, that the prognosis was good.

"He did add that it could return, but today is a day to celebrate. I'm going upstairs to get some beer."

"Just because you're well doesn't mean you can't come to visit, right?" Landon asked Will.

"Abi and I have already talked about that. I'm going to make it a point to come up from time to time. And can I call you sometime? To catch up?"

Landon got a pen and a notepad from the secretary drawer. She wrote her number down and put it in his shirt pocket. Suddenly, they were holding hands, studying one another's eyes as if they both were looking for the same thing and the answer was to be found.

They were not young. His life with his wife would move on. Landon's life with herself would move on. It was enough just to have danced.

SAM

In June, Obama became the presumptive Democratic nominee. Sam kept hearing from his friends that if Obama survived the primaries, he would win the general. It was starting to become real, yet Sam still couldn't believe it.

The summer wore on. When he wasn't in class, Sam was glued to the TV.

The campaign announced its decision to opt out of accepting public financing for the general election. Obama was the first candidate to do so since the system was implemented. It was clear to Sam that the news anchors were all about Obama. Everyone was excited. The lengthy nomination process meant that Obama had operations in nearly every state, firing on all cylinders. Yet the Gallup tracking poll showed Obama and Senator John McCain in a dead heat. Obama picked Joe Biden as his running mate.

The convention opened on a hot August night in Denver. Both Bill and Hillary Clinton were given a night to speak. But Obama's speech would be delivered to one hundred thousand people at Invesco Field, home of the Broncos, on a night that happened to be the forty-fifth anniversary of Martin Luther King's most famous speech.

That night, Tanya got off work early in order to drive Sam to Greene County so he could watch the speech with Poppy. Sam and Tanya rarely discussed the race. Sam figured maybe she was like he had been at first—too afraid to believe it might happen. She picked him up at four o'clock. Right before they entered Greene County, they stopped at a grocery store so Tanya could pick up what she needed to make chicken spaghetti.

"You wait in the car," she told him, smiling. "You'd just be in my way."

He smiled back and watched her walk away. She was still in her work clothes. She wore a tight blue dress and stilettos. He was amazed anew at how beautiful she was. Her dark skin was lit from the inside. She had the longest eyelashes he had ever seen. And she was always dressed to the nines. He looked forward to the day—after he graduated from the university and had a job lined up—when he would ask her to marry him. Half of Greene County would come to Birmingham. Tanya's church was big and bright and a good place for a ceremony. Her extended family, all from Birmingham, wasn't as big as his. She always seemed amazed at how many of Sam's people showed up for the simplest Sunday supper. Tonight, though, there was to be no gathering. It would be just Tanya, Poppy, and Sam.

When they arrived at the old homeplace, Poppy was sitting in a folding chair on the porch. He stood when he saw the car pull up. He was in his usual attire—trousers and a shirt, with his bathrobe and house shoes on. Only when he went to work at his store did he take off the robe and shoes. Or when he preached and wore his good suit. But at home, he dressed for a cold winter night no matter what season it was.

Tanya hugged him and kissed his cheek before heading to the kitchen.

Sam pulled Poppy close. He was a good bit taller than his grandfather, and it seemed that every time he saw him, Poppy was shorter.

They headed inside to the living room. Sam sat in the rocker where his grandmother used to soothe whatever baby was at hand. Poppy sat in his old green chair. Stuffing leaked out of a few spots where the dogs had chewed away at the material.

"Tell me how you've been," Poppy said.

"I actually have some big news," Sam replied. "Next summer, I'll be eligible to go to a developing country with a group called Engineers Without Borders. I'm interested in getting clean water to people."

"So you're going on a mission," Poppy said, nodding. "I'd say that makes you a missionary."

"I'm not a good enough person to think of myself as that."

Poppy propped his legs on the ottoman, settling in. "Who says you're not good enough? You weren't even born yet when President Kennedy said in his inaugural speech, 'Let us go forth to lead the land we love, asking his blessing and his help, but knowing that here on earth God's work must truly be our own.'"

Sam let that sink in.

"You understand what I'm getting at, don't you?" Poppy asked.

"Yes, sir. I do."

"One of the greatest things about growing old is watching your children and grandchildren begin to understand their destiny. You think Tanya in there will be all right about you being gone all summer?"

Sam looked at Poppy. "She never tries to interfere in my life."

"Lucky boy," Poppy replied with a smile.

The aroma of onions and peppers cooking in the big cast-iron skillet filled the room. Though his grandmother had died many years ago, the smell of good home cooking always reminded Sam of her.

It was August, the dog days of summer for Alabama. Poppy's house wasn't air conditioned, but he had an attic fan and oscillating fans in almost every room. A cool breeze from yesterday's rain helped circulate the air.

Sam could see Poppy's dahlias through the window. Poppy prided himself on the prize-winning flowers. They were red, pink, and yellow. They grew tall, the blooms the size of basketballs. One year, Poppy grew one that looked to be the size of a steering wheel. He didn't know what to make of it. But he did enter it in the county festival, its stem so long and thick that it of course won the blue ribbon. Sam didn't remember this from his boyhood, but he had heard tales of it. Even though the county had since abandoned the flower competition, Poppy still grew the big dahlias. He said he had a special recipe for good earth. Nobody knew what he put in the soil, but Sam carried the memory of getting up early one morning when he was young and watching Poppy take a bag of coffee grounds to mix in the dirt beside the plants.

"I see your dahlias," Sam said, gesturing to the window beside Poppy's chair.

"They're pretty this year, aren't they?" Poppy asked.

It was of course a rhetorical question. They were always spectacular, and Sam treasured the bit of farmer's botany that Poppy had passed on to him. Not that Sam was ever likely to grow flowers. But it was a knowledge he treasured because it came from Poppy. Everything he knew about nature was tied to Poppy. Whenever Sam was around him, life made perfect sense. He wondered how he would make sense of anything after Poppy died. But he couldn't dwell on that. It was too heartbreaking.

Sam leaned toward him. "There are some video games that you play with people from anywhere in the country. I was playing after class, and one guy was from Denver. He stopped playing and said, 'The stadium's filling up. I need to go.'"

"That so? Should we turn on the TV?"

Poppy flipped it on, but it was only the commentators prattling on from their studios.

"Turn the sound down, Poppy. If I listen to them, I'll get nervous. Are you still praying for his safety?"

"Oh, yes, son. Every day."

"Looks like he's gonna need it. That stadium's gotta seat a hundred thousand people at least."

"That's right, that's right. I got up early this morning and went outside to pick a few tomatoes. And by the way, show them to Tanya, would you? They're in a basket on the back porch. Ask her if she'll be kind enough to peel and slice them to eat with whatever she's cooking in there."

In the kitchen, Tanya still had her stilettos on, though she had put on an apron over her blue dress.

"Don't you want to take those shoes off?" Sam asked her.

She was cooking the chicken in the iron skillet and had water boiling for the spaghetti. She looked at him playfully. "I'll take them off when they start hurting my feet. Go away, you're making me nervous."

This was the story of his life—the women cooking in the kitchen didn't have time for the men. They were all about the food. Tanya's back was to him. He hugged her from behind, and she turned around with a big wooden spoon in her hand, wagging it at him like a finger.

"I'm going, I'm going. But Poppy said to tell you there are some ripe tomatoes in a basket on the back porch. Do you want me to get them?"

She whirled back around. "I'll do it. Go watch TV with Poppy."

She was working hard. Sam guessed that since she knew Poppy liked to have dinner at five o'clock, she didn't want to mess that up on her first solo outing in the kitchen. Sam saw that she had already set the table for three.

"You need to hold on to that girl," Poppy said when Sam returned to the living room. "She is so smart."

In Sam's family, this meant something more than just Tanya's obvious intelligence. It meant that she knew how to whip up a good meal in a flash, to use fruits and vegetables that made for a bright mouthful, to make enough food to feed an army. She'd make sure everybody's appetite was so satisfied that they'd push their plates forward, silverware and napkins on the dinnerware, and say something like, "I'm gonna bust if I eat another bite."

Sam agreed with Poppy. "She is smart, that's for sure. What do you think he's going to say in his speech, Poppy?"

Poppy hesitated, then replied, "It doesn't matter what he says. It's how he says it. This boy can preach. You know what I mean?"

"Yes, sir."

"I knew back in 2004, when he gave that speech at the Democratic convention. You weren't following politics yet, but we all knew that night that we had a preacher on our hands. And because he was black, he knew how to speak—with that crescendo to lead the crowd forward."

Sam smiled. He loved watching Poppy talk when he really got going.

"But son, let me remind you that I never, never thought this would happen in my lifetime. I couldn't even vote until 1965. How far we have come! Yes, Lord. Forty-five years ago, Dr. King dared to dream of a world where people would not be judged by the color of their skin. Tell me what it's like now, for you. You who live among white folks."

"Yes, but I could marry only a black girl."

"Well, now, that is something your aunts and uncles would certainly expect."

Sam laughed. "Yeah, buddy. I'd hate to see the looks on their faces if I showed up one Christmas with a white girl. But Poppy, in Birmingham, it's not unusual to see a black man with a white woman holding hands, walking down the street—and oftentimes pushing a baby stroller."

"I can't even picture that," Poppy said.

"It is a different world now, Poppy. But then again, Obama's mixed. So why do we call him a black man?"

"Well, I guess if you're a half-black man, then you live like a black man," Poppy said.

"Supper's ready!" Tanya called from the kitchen.

The two men stood and headed for the table.

"Oh, sugar, you've outdone yourself," Poppy said, peeking under the pot lid at the chicken spaghetti.

Once seated, they joined hands. As always, Poppy didn't bless only the food. He used the occasion to say whatever was on his mind.

"Father, God, thank you for this food and the hands that prepared it, and use her hands also to do your good work on this earth. Bless my boy, Sam. Give unto him a sound mind, a clear vision, a strong and good heart. And give unto your son Barack the protection you have promised us. 'For we wrestle not against flesh and blood, but against principalities, against powers, against the rulers of the darkness of this world, against spiritual wickedness in high places.' Help him be strong in you and in the power of your might. 'And to stand therefore, having his loins girt about with truth, and having on the breastplate of righteousness; and his feet shod with the preparation of the gospel of peace; taking the shield of faith, and taking the helmet of salvation, and the sword of the Spirit, which is the word of God.' Amen."

Sam opened his eyes and tilted his head. "Isn't that from the Bible?"

Poppy looked at Tanya. "See how good this boy is? He knows his scripture."

Tanya smiled and nodded.

"Yes, Sam, I borrowed a bit from the book of Ephesians. Hard to improve on the classics. Oh, I hope they have enough security tonight."

Tanya took his hand. "They will, Poppy."

After dinner, Tanya took up the plates. There was no dishwasher, so she'd have to wash them by hand. Sam and Poppy went back to the living room. Poppy turned on the TV. The stands at Invesco Field were full of people, and so was the field. The crowd shook American flags to the beat of Bruce Springsteen's "Born in the USA." Digital signboards flashed "America" and "Obama." Roving spotlights sprayed the audience. People were shouting, "Yes, we can!" Signs read, "Change We Can Believe In."

"The time is growing near," Poppy said, looking at his watch.

Sam looked at Poppy sitting in his chair, watching the TV set that had not always brought good news. He had told Sam about how he watched Bull Connor's dogs and fire hoses used to break up protests. He had also told Sam about watching TV when the message was delivered that JFK had been shot and killed, when RFK had been shot and killed, when Medgar Evers had been shot and killed, when Dr. King had been shot and killed.

"Are you nervous?" Poppy asked.

"I'm excited," Sam replied.

The crowd was already wild. It seemed that everyone had a flag to wave, making for a sea of red, white, and blue. The thing that was most striking to Sam was all the white folks standing with the black people, visible whenever the camera closed in on clusters of the audience. Sam wanted to know precisely what Poppy was feeling, but he didn't want to disturb the moment.

Poppy was leaning forward in his chair. He had moved the ottoman aside so he could plant his feet firmly on the hardwood floor. Jennifer Hudson sang the national anthem. Poppy put his hand over his heart as she delivered the song.

Sam called out to Tanya.

"I'm right here," she said softly from the doorway.

Obama finally took the stage, and the crowd roared for what felt like an eternity. Sam felt goosebumps rise over his arms and up his neck. When he could be heard, Obama started thanking people, and then he did his thing. He delivered his speech, pausing from time to time to let the crowd roar.

Sam recalled how much crap Michelle Obama had gotten when she said that, for the first time in her life, she was proud of her country. He felt that way, too. He remembered how cynical he had been when Jet and Abi first appealed to him to get involved in the campaign. How scared. But now his conflicted heart was resolved.

"This campaign has never been about me," Obama said. "It's about you."

Sam felt the knot in his throat growing.

"'We cannot walk alone,' the preacher cried. And as we walk, we must make the pledge that we shall always march ahead. We cannot turn back. America, we cannot turn back."

"Tanya," Poppy called as the speech ended, to a swell of cheers.

"I'm here," she said again.

"Come in here, sugar. I want to tell both of you something."

She walked in and sat beside Sam on the couch. Poppy leaned forward. Sam watched his eyes. He had something spiritual to say. His eyes always changed when this was the case, as if he were looking not necessarily *through* you, but more like behind you or above you. He got his handkerchief from his pocket and wiped his brow.

"Did you hear what he said in that piece of scripture at the end?"

Sam and Tanya nodded, waiting.

"'Hold firmly, without wavering, to the hope that we confess.' Not 'the hope that we profess.' No, it's the hope that we *confess.* Anybody can profess to having hope or faith. But not everybody can confess that they have it. To confess this is to make yourself exposed, malleable, and human. Some people say they don't need God. We confess that we do. We profess when we're standing up. We confess when we drop to our knees. And so, when people ask us if we believe, we are brave to be willing to confess that we follow after something we cannot yet see. But we will in time. Remember, Sam, that verse from the second chapter of First Corinthians: 'Now we see through a glass darkly, but then face to face.' And to quote another bit of scripture, Jesus said to Thomas, 'Because you have seen me, you have believed: blessed are they that have not seen, and yet have believed.' So, when Mr. Obama told us, 'Hold firmly, without wavering, to the hope that we confess,' we realize that we do walk by faith, not by sight."

. . . .

On the way back to Birmingham, Tanya and Sam were quiet for the first few miles. It was a hot, muggy August night. But instead of using the air conditioning, Tanya rolled the windows down as they drove along the two-lane road that, in a few minutes, would connect them with the interstate. She let her hair blow in the wind. She was driving barefoot. Sam held his arm out the window like he used to as a kid, trying to keep it straight against the force of the wind.

That night, he had felt something he'd never felt before. He understood the historic gravity of what had happened and was still happening within them and between them. Sam felt like Poppy had married the two of them right there in the living room. They were in love, but it encompassed so much more. Rather than looking at each other, they were looking together in the same direction. Sam wasn't sure where all this powerful energy would take them, though he was going to begin with Engineers Without Borders.

Tanya finally broke the silence. "I think I'm going to quit my job. Go back to school."

"For what?" Sam asked, understanding exactly where Tanya was coming from.

"International relations."

It stunned him. He put his hand on her leg and squeezed. The night was dark. All they could see was the headlights before them. But that was all they needed to see because what was illuminated could carry them all the way home.

LANDON

October chilled quickly that year. The last day of the month brought with it first frost. The dogwood trees were lit up by red berries. So were the hollies, nandinas, and winterberries. The leaves from the maple, oak, hickory, elm, and poplar trees that grew along Red Mountain showed off fiery reds, deep golds, burnt oranges, and sunny yellows. It still puzzled Landon that most people would choose spring as their favorite time of year. In autumn, the leaves danced in the wind right before they landed, then carpeted the earth with warm color. One of her favorite memories of Nick was walking home with him from school, the two of them skipping through piles of leaves. Sometimes on weekends, they raked the leaves into a tiny hill into which they then dove.

She and Nick were born in October. Their mother had always insisted on separate, simultaneous parties, so no one had to buy two gifts. Nick had boy parties; Landon had girl parties. The girls had the front yard, where they could play hopscotch or jump rope; the boys were in the backyard, where the configuration of the trees allowed first, second, third, and home for their games of whiffle ball. Then their mother would call them all inside to open gifts and eat cake and ice cream together.

Mother had to make sure they were all cleared out by five o'clock because that's when Daddy came home from work. The sight of too many children in one place made him jittery. By five, their birthday gifts had to be tucked away in their bedrooms, their party clothes removed and replaced with clean pajamas, their sticky hands and faces rinsed. But despite this, year after year, their mother made the celebrations work. When they got older, there was no way to keep the boys separate from the girls. Nick and Landon and all their guests spent those later parties chasing each other from the backyard to the front in a hormonal, disorganized game of tag.

Landon remembered the rare joy of those birthday parties as she and Alejandro returned from their afternoon walk. When she got close to her house, she noticed Mr. Kasir's truck. But it wasn't Mr. Kasir at the wheel. Landon squinted. Instead, the driver appeared to be a boy around the age of her daughters. Landon realized this was Jason and felt a chill in her gut. Something wasn't right.

And then it hit her, even before Jason stepped out of the truck, even before she stopped in her tracks, even before she saw his face up close, his red eyes moist, his hands trembling. She knew why he was there.

They stood on the sidewalk. He was having a hard time getting the words out.

"He's gone," Jason said. "Went to sleep last night and just didn't wake up. My grandmom wanted me to come see you. She asked that you tell the others, said you were special to him."

"I need to sit down," Landon said.

They sat on the sidewalk in their agony. Landon unleashed Alejandro to allow him to play in the grass, but the dog stayed right by her side, as if he knew she needed him.

"I really loved him," Jason said.

"Oh, I know you must have. We loved him, too, and we weren't even kin."

She was torn in different directions. On the one hand, she wanted to be calm for Jason. She guessed it might be his first death. It had happened to her around his age, when she lost Nick. On the other hand, she felt weak, wanted to cry. There had been many deaths in Landon's life since Nick, both family and friends. But this was different. It was different because she was different. This was her first loss in her new life.

"Thank you for telling me," Landon said. "It's a comfort. Just like Mr. Kasir, always taking care of tenants in distress."

Jason allowed himself a small smile. He picked at a clump of weeds. "Granddad told me these things are so strong they can break through concrete."

The two stared at the weeds as Jason twirled them between his fingers, as if they were a kaleidoscope, as if one turn could change everything.

Landon didn't ask about Mrs. Kasir because she knew that Jason was already taking on more responsibility than he needed. Instead, she took his hand in hers.

"You will get through this."

Jason nodded.

"Do you have friends or a girlfriend you need to call? I'll tell the rest of the tenants on the street."

"I have a girlfriend. I called her before anybody, Mrs. Cooper."

"Please, call me Landon."

He looked around the neighborhood. "I want to remember people's names. It's Abi who lives upstairs?" he asked.

Landon nodded.

"And Jet across the street? And Sam two houses up? Roy across the street, who grows vegetables in the front yard. Tina, who has the problem with window jumping. And Sid, who subs and is into vitamins. And who else? Oh, and Nicole, who works at the bank."

"That's right," she replied. "You covered it all."

"He had other property in Southside, but my grandmom said those renters would learn about it later. She just wanted me to tell y'all face to face. He loved this street more than the others."

Landon smiled.

"I like that," Jason said, gesturing to the Obama '08 sign in the yard.

"I'm glad."

"Granddad would have voted for him."

"You think so?"

"I know so. Do you know where our church is?" he asked her.

"I do."

"It will be there, but I don't know yet what day or what time."

Landon guessed Mrs. Kasir's neighbors or church friends were helping her make the arrangements for burial and for an obit in the *Birmingham News*. She was glad that Jason wasn't handling everything alone.

She squeezed his hand. "Don't worry. I'll find out."

"Will you come to his funeral?" he asked, looking into her eyes.

Landon found the question disarming. As if she needed to be asked. Maybe he didn't know yet just how many people truly loved his granddad.

"I wouldn't miss it."

Landon and Jason continued to sit on the sidewalk. Her mind was racing now with the story of the girl Mr. Kasir had entrusted to her. The story the clergy would deliver as a eulogy might include the Silver Star he received for his valor on Omaha Beach. But Carissa would be missing from it. It was something she would keep inside, never telling a soul.

Jason stood and held his hand out to help her up from the sidewalk.

"I guess I should be going," he said. He paused, then added, "I'll be overseeing the properties for my grandmom. I want to be like my granddad. I want you to tell the others on Cullom not to worry if their rent isn't on time, and to call me if other problems come up. I brought this card with me." He pulled it out of his shirt pocket. "This is my phone number and address. This is where you mail your check to me at the first of the month."

Landon saw that he was standing tall, perhaps allowing his new-found sense of responsibility to override his grief.

"I'll make sure the others have it," she told him.

After Jason left, Landon went inside and threw herself on her bed like a fitful child. Mr. Kasir was almost ninety years old. People would say something simple like, "He lived a good, long life." *Not long enough!* Landon thought. And she knew Jason and Mrs. Kasir must feel the same way.

Alejandro jumped onto the bed with her. She petted him and told him what had happened.

She wasn't ready to tell anybody else yet. Instead, she went to the kitchen and saw that she had all the ingredients for a Veg-All casserole—a day-of-the-funeral food most Southern women knew how to make. She opened two cans of Veg-All and poured the contents—carrots, potatoes, celery, sweet peas, green beans, corn, and limas—into a pan. She grated two cups of cheddar cheese and mixed that in, then a chopped onion and a cup of mayonnaise. She topped it with Ritz cracker crumbs, then poured melted butter over the top. She set the oven at 350 and the kitchen timer at thirty minutes.

Landon wondered what men did with their grief, if they couldn't hide their tears in the preparation of food. She searched the internet for florists in the city and chose the first one that came up. She used to order flowers from a shop in Homewood, but it didn't feel right to do so now. Landon requested the card to read, "From all of us on Cullom Street." Landon wondered who would have the hardest time and knew it would be Abi.

She went back outside to see who was home. Abi's car was there. So was Jet's. Sam didn't have a car, so she had no way of knowing, but she was pretty sure he had morning classes. She'd get Jet or Sam to help her tell the others.

She went upstairs and knocked on Abi's door.

"Who is it?"

"Landon."

"It's unlocked. Come on in."

All the windows were open. The afternoon sun warmed Abi's apartment. She was on the couch studying. She had a big textbook in her lap and a yellow highlighter in her right hand.

"What's up?" she asked Landon.

Landon sat on the couch. "Well . . . ," she said, searching for the right words.

Abi must have understood that something bad was contained in that pause because she put her book aside, got a cigarette, and walked to her kitchen for the ashtray. She didn't sit down.

"I have bad news," Landon told her.

"What is it? Who is it? Who died?"

Landon nodded. "It's Mr. Kasir."

Abi dropped her cigarette into the ashtray and collapsed onto the sofa next to Landon. They wrapped their arms around each other and held on the way lovers did, face to face. Landon put her fingers in Abi's hair and brushed away the tendrils from her face. For a long time, Abi said nothing. She just held on. She didn't ask what had happened or how Landon found out. None of that mattered. The thing that mattered was that he was gone. Landon held her tight.

Then Abi released from the hug and stood. "So Daddy gets to live, but Mr. Kasir has to die. Is that the way God works? Who told you?" she asked, wiping her face on her sleeve.

"Jason, his grandson. You've met him, right?"

"Yes," Abi replied, retrieving her cigarette.

"He told me his granddad went to bed and never woke back up. And don't worry, I'm not gonna say, 'At least he didn't suffer.'"

"I'm glad you know better than that."

"Believe me, I know all the stupid things people say when somebody dies. I've been at this business since I was twenty-five and lost my brother. The funereal platitudes, all the clichés."

"I'll get it together here in a minute," Abi said, wiping her face again. "I suppose the service will be religious. Where do you believers think we go after we die?"

"I don't know. People have different ideas of heaven."

"But I'm asking you."

They had been over this before, but apparently Abi wanted to do it again. Landon could see that Abi wasn't sad over Mr. Kasir. She was mad.

Landon didn't say what she was thinking—that to be angry with God was to acknowledge his existence. Abi went over to the mantel and returned with the metal cross from her daddy. She threw it toward the kitchen.

"Fuck that!" she shouted. She whirled back to look at Landon. "If there were a God, I'd have a word or two to say to him. Like, 'What the hell is this all about?' Life, I mean. If there is a better place where we go when we leave here, why wouldn't he just tell us?"

"Probably because everybody would end it if we knew there was something better than this incomprehensible place."

Abi ignored this. "My daddy was happy when he got saved. He wasn't even afraid of dying. Why can't I feel that way?"

"Are you afraid of dying?"

Abi ignored this, too. "Couple weeks ago, I asked Daddy if he believed in the virgin birth. You know what he said back? He said, 'If my God can fling a handful of stars over the night sky, he can surely get a virgin pregnant.' He wasn't trying to be funny. He meant it. And then there are those reincarnationists. They are real strange. Like, when Mr. Kasir breathed his last breath in the middle of the night, did he suddenly reemerge as a baby, born to some woman on the other side of the world? Or is he a butterfly in the backyard? Soul migration is a cop-out for people who know better but have to hang on to some kind of belief. Like, when we put Mr. Kasir six feet under, his soul—whatever that is—will have escaped his body, and God will have to make a quick decision about where it will go, depending on what lessons Mr. Kasir failed to learn. I mean, really. Mr. Kasir? How could a man so kind be forced to do this life thing all over again? Surely, he finished all his lessons, all his homework. If God isn't in charge but there is reincarnation, we might find Mr. Kasir at the Humane Society, at the mercy of people who will pass by him and either reject him or adopt him.

"And that gets me into territory I know you don't want to hear. Like the pro-lifers who believe life begins at conception. They stand by the entrance door to the clinic, picketing. But they also stand outside the exit door, where they tell each woman not to worry, that her baby is in God's hands, and they'll be reunited after the woman herself dies. I know you don't run with these nuts, but don't you believe in the same God? Or maybe there are two Gods, a liberal one and a conservative one. Who the hell are we? Why are we here? Is this a dream? If God is real, why didn't he give us some clues, like a pathway of breadcrumbs to show us the way to his place? If you and my daddy can make this intellectual surrender by believing, why can't I? Have I not suffered enough to be relieved of this horrific loneliness of a nonbeliever?

"Don't for a moment think I don't want to be like you and Daddy. But I can't. I used to think that religion was for ignorant people. Then I met you. Then Daddy got saved. That forced me to question both myself and you. I'd give anything to be able to believe. But it isn't possible. Not if I'm honest. Not if I use my brain. I don't like fairy tales. I never have. My mama says I'd whine when an animal talked in a storybook. So, what? I'm a realist? Is that what I call myself? I don't want to label myself as an atheist or an agnostic, even. I'm just Abi.

"And another thing that bothers me is when people say they're able to give you the date, the time, the moment when they 'saw the light.' Like it's an actual light going on. With a time stamp and all. Well, like I said, it's an intellectual surrender I can't and won't make."

Abi had stood holding an unlit cigarette during the entire rant. Now, spent, she lit it.

"So, what kind of food are we going to take to the Kasirs' house?"

"I've made a casserole," Landon said.

Abi drew hard on her cigarette. "I'll go over to where I work and steal some yeast rolls."

"That'll be great. I know how good they are. Will your boss mind?"

"He won't even know. I'm cozy with the bread maker."

"I've already talked to a florist. The card will be from all of us."

"You've been quick, haven't you?"

"It's the way I cope. Food and flowers. Did you know that Mr. Kasir changed his will just a few months ago, gave his properties to Jason after his grandmom dies? He didn't want Abe Jr. to inherit them, ever."

"Jesus," Abi replied. "So Jason's life is about to change, isn't it?"

"Yes. It broke me up when he told me he was going to be the kind of landlord his granddad was, that he understood sometimes people don't have the money in hand to pay the rent, that he'll work with them, with us, just like Mr. Kasir did."

"I'm going on over to the restaurant. You have that casserole ready. Then we'll take it all over to Mrs. Kasir. I don't know if you've ever been around them, but she took care of Mr. Kasir. She adored him. And they were married forever."

"You know," Landon said, just realizing, "I never went to Mr. Kasir's house. He always came by ours."

"What did you and he talk about when he would come over?"

"He talked about the war," Landon said. She burned to tell Abi about Carissa. But she owed Mr. Kasir her silence, even though he was gone.

Abi got her keys, wallet, and cigarettes.

"I'm going. I just . . . This is all I can do. Rolls. That's all I have to offer."

Landon thought of the story in the Bible in which a widow gave only a couple of coins for church. And Jesus sat down and began observing how people were putting money into the treasury, how many rich people were putting in large sums. But the poor widow came and put in two small copper coins, which amounted to a cent. He called his disciples and said that the poor widow put in more than all the other contributors. She gave all that she had.

But Landon wouldn't in a million years tell Abi the story.

For a moment, Landon thought of Will's tiny blue Testament. He was still doing well in remission. She missed him.

"Why am I doing this?" Abi asked before heading out the door. "Fetching some food."

"It's just what we do," Landon replied.

ABI

Abi sat on a stool in the kitchen and watched Henry the bread maker at work.

"So, who passed?" he asked.

"My landlord."

He nodded and dropped small balls of dough onto a baking sheet. After Henry filled the sheet, he put it in the huge oven, washed his hands, and pulled over another stool to sit beside her.

"Okay, sweetness," Henry said, moving his stool close to hers. "Now, tell me. I wouldn't expect a tenant to be so moved. Tell me what you loved about him," he said.

Abi looked down at their hands. She was afraid to look him in the eye because she might get choked up. The rant she delivered to Landon had left her depleted, exhausted, and more than a little embarrassed.

"His name was Abraham Kasir. He wasn't like most slumlords."

Henry interrupted. "You don't live in a slum, do you?"

"Of course not," she replied. "I'm just being cynical. It's how I deal with shit."

"Okay. You do what you need to do, sweetness."

"It's just that nobody in the neighborhood has much money, and he understood that. He didn't have a greedy bone in his body. It's like he wanted us to be a family."

"And is that the way it is in your neighborhood? A family?"

"Yes. We all need each other that way."

"Most folks single?" Henry got up and opened the oven door to make sure the yeast rolls were rising.

"I'm going to miss him so much," Abi said.

"'I go and prepare a place for you,'" he replied.

"I guess that's from the Bible."

"Sure is."

She had no arguments left in her. She took Henry's hand, put it to her lips, and kissed it. He pulled her a bit closer, put his arm around her, and cradled her head.

When the bread had risen and baked, Henry took out the sheet and brushed each roll with melted butter. After they cooled a bit, he got two baskets from one of the cabinets and lined them with cloth napkins. Then he carefully covered each basket with other napkins.

"Won't they miss the baskets and napkins?" she asked—they being the owners.

"Nah. They don't know, they don't care."

Henry walked Abi to her Volvo and opened the door for her. He kissed her on the forehead.

"This is a small, good thing you're doing," he told her. "And life's about doing one small thing for one small person. That's all that matters."

She nodded, told him thanks, then goodbye. She put the baskets in the passenger seat, turned on the radio, and drove in the direction of home, crossing the mountain that separated the haves from the have-nots.

JET

Jet sat on Sam's couch. She was wearing her black stockings and a denim skirt. Her long, dark hair was pulled back with a clasp that looked like a giant spider. She had taken off her cape and laid it beside her. Sam had been playing an Xbox game when she arrived, and she could tell by the way he kept glancing at the screen that he might want to keep playing. But of course, he was hospitable and loaded a bowl. She crossed her legs slowly and watched his eyes slide over her. For a moment, she believed she might be able to find some desire in him, but he averted his gaze to the TV again. He had muted the sound.

When he got up to get her a beer, she followed him to the kitchen and looked out the back, where the dumpster was overflowing in the alley. He was handing her the bottle when they heard a knock at the door.

"Is it Tanya?" she asked, a bit alarmed, even though nothing was going on.

"No, she's still at work."

When he opened the door, Jet saw Landon. She wasn't wearing a smile.

"I'm glad you're both here," she said. "I don't like being the bearer of bad news."

"What is it?" Jet asked her.

"Mr. Kasir died."

Sam remained standing, as if in respect for the dead, and didn't sit until Landon told them what she knew—that Mr. Kasir went to bed last night and didn't wake up this morning, that Jason had come over just an hour or so ago with the news. Since Jet didn't know what to say, she waited. Landon told them in a hushed voice that he had died in his sleep.

Jet looked down at the carpet, as if she had not heard the news. Finally, she whispered, "When's the funeral?"

"I don't know yet, honey," Landon said.

"It hasn't been so long ago that I had to bury my daddy." Jet rose as if in a stupor. "I'm going to bake a pound cake."

"That's perfect," Landon told her. "I've got a casserole, and Abi's gone over to where she works to nab some fresh-baked yeast rolls. A cake is great. I can take the food over soon as the cake is done."

Jet nodded. She was neither happy nor sad. She kept looking at her hands—palms up, then palms down, then clasped and unclasped, as if she had lost a ring, not Mr. Kasir.

"What kind of casserole?" Jet asked Landon.

"What?"

"What kind of casserole did you make?"

"Veg-All."

"Did you use Ritz crackers crumbled on top?"

"Yes," Landon replied.

Jet managed a smile. "Then we can bury the dead."

. . . .

Back at her apartment, Jet lit a black candle for Mr. Kasir. She went to her vanity, sat down, and brushed her hair, one hundred times in all. She had read that this was the way to have healthy, vibrant hair but had found that it also relieved stress. She watched the black wax until the first drop spilled over the tip and ran down the height of the candle to pool in the lip of the candleholder. She needed a bit of time before she started baking.

The first time she met Mr. Kasir, she was still living in the Episcopal halfway house. Father Patrick was with her that day on Cullom Street.

They sat on the porch and signed the lease right then and there. Jet wasn't sure why Mr. Kasir took a bet on her. She was still trying to shake her time as a prostitute, her anger and her fear. But Mr. Kasir was kind. He treated her like a granddaughter from day one. That was why she had called him to tell him about getting arrested. She knew he would be nice—and he was, of course. He didn't chastise her or dismiss her. He simply wanted to know who had paid her bond. He told her that if she was in financial trouble, she could be late on the rent. He knew the story of her life, and he didn't want her going backward.

The first time Stephanie and Caroline came to Birmingham, shortly after the arrest, Jet called Mr. Kasir to come meet them. He had been his gentlemanly self. Jet introduced him to Caroline, who seemed suddenly shy. Stephanie had asked him questions about his family, his properties, even where he went to church. Jet could tell that Mr. Kasir was impressed by her. A smile never left his face as he answered her mannered questions. Jet had been aware of how stunning Stephanie was in that moment, how she held herself, how she talked a bit louder than usual after she noticed his hearing aids.

Now, Jet reached for her phone and called Stephanie. She didn't answer, so Jet left a message that Mr. Kasir had died. It still didn't seem real to her. But it was time to bake.

Cooking was like one hundred brush strokes to Jet; it was soothing. She got two sticks of butter, two cups of flour, one cup of sugar, four eggs, and vanilla extract. It was amazing that she had every ingredient she needed. She preheated the oven, greased and floured the pan, then beat the butter and sugar with her electric mixer on high speed. She added the eggs one at a time, splashed in some vanilla, and gradually added the flour. That was it. She put it in the oven and set the timer.

She found one of the blank note cards her mother had bought for her when she almost got married. They were intended for thank-you messages but of course had sat unused since Jet called off the wedding. Today, she was glad she had saved them. She wanted to write to Mrs. Kasir.

Dear Mrs. Kasir,

I'm so sorry about Mr. Kasir. He was the kindest man I've ever met. I can't imagine life without him, and I'm sure you must feel that way. We're all so happy to know that Jason will be our landlord. I hope you will be comforted by his presence. He's just like his granddaddy. When I found out a few minutes ago about Mr. Kasir, my thoughts went immediately to you. And they will remain so in the coming days.

Love,
Jet

She didn't say she'd be praying for her because that would be a lie. She wasn't praying. She was baking.

She put the note card in an envelope and got a stamp from the box—her mother had also provided postage for the never-to-be-written thank-you notes. A picture of the flag was on the stamp. That was fitting, she thought. Mr. Kasir was a patriot.

She went to the porch to leave the note for the mailman, securing it to her box with a clothespin. She knew that Landon was going to take the food to Mrs. Kasir later that day, but she wanted her note to arrive in a couple of days, after the initial shock had subsided.

She sat on her steps and looked up and down the street at all the houses that held Mr. Kasir's tenants. It was as if his spirit was still around. Every time the wind swept through the leaves of the hickory tree in Landon's yard, she felt him. A butterfly landed on the ledge of the porch. It was an orange monarch. It, too, seemed to herald Mr. Kasir nearby.

"I love you," Jet said aloud, as if Mr. Kasir were there to hear her. She listed for him all the times he had helped her. She wasn't talking to God. She was talking to Mr. Kasir.

When she heard the timer go off in the kitchen, she went inside and used her hand mitts to pull the cake from the oven. It was perfect. It wasn't going to fall.

Cakes can fall and have to be made all over again. Leaves can fall and carpet an entire yard. People can fall and get back up again.

LANDON

Since Abi and Jet both had work, Landon ended up taking the food to the Kasirs' alone. She arranged the casserole, cake, and yeast rolls in an oversized picnic basket that once belonged to her mother. She loaded the car and took the high road over the mountain.

The Kasirs' yard was big. A gazebo on one side had climbers that somebody had trained to grow up to the top. She guessed that maybe Jason kept the lawn mowed and that Mrs. Kasir planted the flowers, some of which were still blooming, despite the first frost. She pulled the big basket from the passenger seat and carried it to the front door. She was surprised by the lack of cars on the street. She had assumed the house might be packed with church friends or family. But when she rang the bell, only Jason greeted her and invited her into an empty living room. She handed him the basket.

"Grandmom!" he called.

He led Landon to the kitchen.

Mrs. Kasir stood up from the table and hugged Landon. "How sweet of you to drop by," she said.

Landon had met her once before, but it was late one frigid night during her first winter at the apartment, when Mrs. Kasir had driven her husband around to make sure all the tenants had left their faucets dripping. That night, Landon had walked around to the driver's side to say hello, but it was dark and she didn't have a good look at Mrs. Kasir. Now, in the light of day, Landon took her in. Her hair was dyed a golden strawberry blond. Her eyes were hazel. She did not look old, even though Landon knew she was almost ninety. It was as if she were surrounded by an aura of grace, the way she took Landon's hands and smiled.

Landon caught sight of the spread of food on the table and reasoned that friends or family had been there earlier to bring their offerings.

"Please stay for tea," Mrs. Kasir said.

She accepted, hoping Mrs. Kasir wasn't just being hospitable. Sometimes, Landon recalled, it was the unexpected person, rather than those who had to come calling, who brought the most comfort.

"Jason, could you fill the teapot for me, hon?"

He did what his grandmother asked, then took the food from Landon's open basket and set it on the table with the rest.

Landon sat at the table and thanked Mrs. Kasir for asking Jason to deliver the news in person. Mrs. Kasir's hands were folded on the table. She was wearing a bright blue dress and a string of pearls. Landon was certain that she wanted to present herself as a woman in charge of her feelings.

Mrs. Kasir peeked under the foil at Landon's casserole. "Oh, a Veg-All. Nobody else thought of that."

Landon told her the cake was from Jet and the bread from Abi.

"I love the smell of yeast rolls, don't you?" she asked Landon.

"I do," Landon replied.

Mrs. Kasir turned to Jason and said, "Hon, use the Earl Grey teabags."

"Yes, ma'am."

"Isn't he the best boy in the world?" she said.

"Oh, indeed, he is," Landon agreed.

They drank their tea while Jason munched on the rolls.

"I have to show you something," Mrs. Kasir said, smiling. "Go get the ledgers, Jason."

Jason disappeared into another room and returned with Mr. Kasir's stack of spiral notebooks.

Mrs. Kasir laughed as she told Landon how every renter had his or her own private ledger. "But they are more like journals," she went on.

"He made these entries that seemed superfluous. Oh, Abe—he was quite a character, wasn't he?" she said, and shook her head.

Landon smiled and took her hand. "Yes, he was. A legend."

"The nicest man in the world," Jason inserted.

"You are right about that," Landon said.

"He was compelled to help people," Mrs. Kasir went on.

She stood, walked to the drawer that held silverware, and sat back down with a fork in hand. Carefully, she pulled the foil back and scooped out a bite of the Veg-All.

"Mmm," she said. "Do you make it the standard way? I taste something special."

"Well, I did pour some melted butter—more than is called for in the recipe—over the Ritz crackers crumbs."

"Ah," Mrs. Kasir replied. "That's it."

Jason got up from the table and went to the living room. Landon guessed he wanted to give the women privacy.

Mrs. Kasir took off her earrings and put them on the table. "I guess I don't need these, now that the church friends have gone," she said. "I know you don't mind how I look, do you, Landon?"

"I think you look beautiful."

For some reason, this caused Mrs. Kasir's eyes to fill. "I apologize," she said.

Landon reached over and squeezed her hand. "I understand."

Mrs. Kasir dabbed her eyes with a napkin and asked, "Are you acquainted with grief?"

Landon told her about Nick's young death, and that she had lost both her parents many years ago. She didn't know how much Mr. Kasir had told his wife about Landon's past and present struggles.

Mrs. Kasir reached for one of the spiral notebooks. She came to a red one that had "Landon Cooper, 1627 Cullom Street" printed on the cover. "I need to jot some things down," she said. "And what better place to do it than in your notebook?"

For a moment, Landon feared that Mr. Kasir might have mentioned the girl in his notes. Or that he might have put the photograph of herself at twenty-one in a side pocket. But Mrs. Kasir went straight to the back and tore out a sheet.

"I need you to help me remember some things," she said.

Landon sipped her tea and nodded.

"First of all, don't you think we should have the funeral day after tomorrow?"

"Have you talked with the funeral home about it?" Landon asked.

"Jason!" she called.

He appeared immediately and pulled out a chair for himself.

"Didn't the funeral director tell you that it would be day after tomorrow?"

"Yes," he said. "Then, or we'll have to wait until next week." He turned to Landon. "I can't remember if I told you I'm studying music at the university. My granddad's funeral will have the best music in the world. The service will begin with Aaron Copland's 'Fanfare for the Common Man.' A soloist will later sing the old Shaker hymn 'Simple Gifts,' which was the inspiration for Copland's *Appalachian Spring*."

Mrs. Kasir turned to Landon. "If Jason thinks it's what we ought to do with the music, then that is what we will do. He is also putting together a eulogy for our priest, Father Mark. We're Catholic, you know."

Landon nodded. "I know. I know where your church is. It's beautiful from the outside, and I am looking forward to seeing the inside. I told Mr. Kasir that I used to think it was Greek Orthodox. But he set me straight on that."

"Here," Mrs. Kasir said, and put the piece of notebook paper and a pencil in front of Jason. "Write all this down, hon. I mean, the order of things—the processional, the solo, the eulogy, the surprise recessional. I know we have to follow all the rituals of the church, including the Eucharist. But you will talk to Father Mark for me about the music, won't you?"

"I will. And the soloist is one of my friends from the Department of Music. She'll knock your socks off when she starts to sing, ' 'Tis the gift to be simple.' Do you know that tune?" he asked Landon.

"Yes, I do, and how perfect for your granddad."

"Listen to me, Grandmom," he said, and broke into song.

> 'Tis the gift to be simple, 'tis the gift to be free
> 'Tis the gift to come down where we ought to be,
> And when we find ourselves in the place just right,
> 'Twill be in the valley of love and delight.

For a moment, neither Landon nor Mrs. Kasir said a word, they were so moved by his baritone voice and the lyrics that so personified Mr. Kasir.

"Can't you feel his spirit?" Landon said.

She often found herself talking to the deceased at night or when she felt most alone. And she never stopped talking to some of them, particularly Nick. She prayed more to those she'd lost than she did to God, in fact. She was certain they would hear her and pass along the information to him.

Now, she basked in the invisible presence of Mr. Kasir, along with his wife and beloved grandson. Landon reached for Mrs. Kasir's hand, then Jason's, as if they were a family about to give thanks for their supper. But they didn't speak. Instead, they sat quietly holding hands.

Finally, Jason smiled at Landon and asked, "You sure you're not a priest?"

"Afraid not," Landon replied.

After Jason and Mrs. Kasir had a rough draft of the order of worship, Landon stood.

"I need to be going," she said softly.

Mrs. Kasir stood alongside her, then hugged her, lingering in the embrace for a moment, then backing up to study Landon's face.

"You are special," she said. "Just like Abe told me. Keep us in your prayers."

"I will. And I will see you at the funeral."

When Landon got in her car, she looked back and saw Mrs. Kasir standing on the porch, waving. As she drove away, she kept sneaking glances in the rearview mirror, only to see Mrs. Kasir standing by the screen door, still waving until Landon turned left and she fell out of sight.

THE NEIGHBORS

The funeral was held two days later at Mr. Kasir's church. Landon, Sam, and Jet all piled into Abi's Volvo and drove to the church together.

They chose a pew at the very back.

The extended Kasir family gathered in the vestibule. They were to lead the processional down the aisle. Jason was holding his grandmom's hand. At the front of the church were the brass and percussionists—friends of his from the Department of Music at the university. He waited for "Fanfare for the Common Man" to begin. He spotted the Cullom Street neighbors in the last pew and was somehow humbled by their presence. The drummer heralded the beginning stanza of Copland's piece.

When the trumpeters sounded the clarion call, he took a deep breath and whispered to his grandmom, "Here we go."

They walked hand in hand, leading the rest of the family. Only his father, Abe Jr., was missing, still doing time. Jason quickly dismissed that thought. He felt something—pride, perhaps—that he had assembled this group of friends to perform. The music felt special.

Jason held his head high as they moved down the aisle. This wasn't something he had anticipated—the power he felt, knowing he had done a good job with the funeral planning, his final act of helpfulness for his granddad.

The pew for family members at the front of the church was marked by purple velvet ropes. He unfastened the one on the first pew and helped Grandmom along until she was seated.

The priests led the rest of the processional, followed by the pallbearers, who carried Mr. Kasir's body in a flag-draped coffin. Jason hadn't known he would be so moved by the fact that it was to be a military funeral.

At the back of the church, Landon leaned forward to check on Abi, who was in the aisle seat. Abi was staring straight ahead. She felt uneasy being in a church. Her heart was racing. She hoped her body wasn't going to revolt and send her running from the service. But when the incense was released, she relaxed and leaned against Sam.

"Wow," he whispered reverently. He associated incense with weed. But here, in this place, its power caused a quickening in him—like the feeling he often had when Poppy's preaching started its crescendo.

Abi took his hand. "This isn't what I thought it would be like," she whispered.

"You all right?" he asked her.

Sam was surprised and touched that she let him hold her during this moment. Abi was fighting back tears. She prided herself in her ability to dodge hysteria, to be stoic in the face of catastrophe, to hide when hurt. But Mr. Kasir had been part of her life for so long.

Landon again checked on Abi and was relieved to see that she was finally letting herself grieve.

Jet looked down at her hands, folded in her lap. This was so different from when her daddy died. She didn't have to love Mr. Kasir; he wasn't kin to her. But she had loved him, and he had caused her to realize that she was worthy of love.

The priest spoke of Mr. Kasir, his family, his service to the country, and his work as a landlord. "Mr. Kasir helped those who had chains they could not break, a song they couldn't sing, a path they couldn't find. I have never, during a funeral, asked what I'm about to ask, but I feel I must do this. If Mr. Kasir personally helped you find your way, will you please stand?"

Jason rose from the first pew at the front of the church. His grandmom reached for his hand so as to stand, too.

Landon saw this and was moved. How had Mr. Kasir helped her, his wife, find her way? And then she understood—they had lived and loved together for over sixty years. Landon cried for them but also for herself, thinking of her own marriage, of the years spent with Robbie. They had witnessed one another caught in chains they could not break, a song they could no longer sing, a path they could no longer go down together.

Landon stood, thinking of how Mr. Kasir had helped her find her way forward.

Jet rose. Then Abi. Then Sam.

Jason turned to see who was standing. It was nearly half the people in attendance.

"Look how young these people are," Landon whispered.

"Other tenants," Jet whispered back.

"Will you all join me," the priest concluded, "in celebrating the life of a man such as this?"

Those who were still seated rose, and the priest asked for a moment of silence. Then the rites, and finally the Irish blessing: "May the road rise to meet you. May the wind be always at your back. May the sun shine warm upon your face, the rains fall soft upon your fields. And until we meet again, may God hold you in the hollow of his hand."

The recessional began. An acolyte extinguished the candles. The sound of recorded music began.

"What is that?" Abi said.

"It's Pat Metheny," Landon told the group. "'Last Train Home.'"

"Pat who?" Jet asked.

"I guess some churches allow secular music," Landon said as they filed out.

They packed back into Abi's Volvo and joined the other cars to form the procession to the cemetery.

"Turn on your lights," Jet told Abi.

"Oh, that's right."

"Look at those cars pulling over," Sam said as they drove toward Elmwood Cemetery. "I can't believe people still do that."

"It's one of those old Southern traditions that never die," Landon replied.

At the grave, Mr. Kasir's friends and family gathered under the canopy surrounding the coffin. The priest read a passage: "'For I was hungry, and you gave me something to eat; I was thirsty, and you gave me something to drink; I was a stranger, and you invited me in; naked, and you clothed me; I was sick, and you visited me; I was in prison, and you came to me. The disciples asked when they had done those things for him, and he replied, Inasmuch as you do unto the least of these, you do it for me.'"

A prayer was recited. The flag was folded and presented to Mrs. Kasir. A lone bugler played Taps. He was clearly just a kid, a volunteer student, but he hit every note perfectly and, in this way, played Mr. Kasir home.

Jet realized her father was buried here. She hadn't come to the cemetery in years. As she looked out over the acreage, she decided that maybe it was time to start coming again.

She joined Sam and Abi, and the three of them walked back to the Volvo.

Landon waited until the family members rose from their folded chairs under the canopy. Then she walked in the direction of Jason and Mrs. Kasir.

"It was a beautiful ceremony," she told Mrs. Kasir.

"Didn't Jason do good with the music?" Mrs. Kasir asked, patting her grandson on the arm.

"Oh, yes," Landon replied.

They embraced. Mrs. Kasir was so much older, yet Landon felt a new bond with her. They were both living alone, without their men, but Landon knew Mrs. Kasir was going to be fine. And in that moment, for the first time, she knew she also would be fine.

. . . .

The next time the neighbors were all together was election night. A month had passed since they'd buried Mr. Kasir.

They met at Landon's. Abi, Sam, and Tanya. Jet and Lenny and his boyfriend, Brett. Jason and his girlfriend, Carly. Jet had invited Jason. Nobody thought he'd come. But he did. He thought his granddad would have wanted him to.

Landon, Tanya, and Carly sat on the couch. Abi took the lounge chair. Jet sat on the floor. Sam stood. He needed to stand. He was still worried, even though it was going to take a miracle for McCain to pull out a victory. Sam was almost too nervous to watch CNN.

Every time a new state was called for Obama, the tenants toasted.

"Sam, it's gonna happen," Abi said. "You've got to sit down."

"Can't," he said, shifting his weight from one foot to the other.

"Call Poppy," Jet suggested. She was clutching her own phone in her hand, occasionally texting Caroline and Stephanie.

"Not now," he replied.

And then, finally, it happened. The network projected Obama to be the next president of the United States. Abi went to her knees and put her face in her hands. Sam and Tanya raised their hands like they were in church. Jet jumped around the room, hugging Lenny and Brett, Jason and Carly. Landon sat dumbstruck, trying to hear the TV.

"Let's just listen in to what's happening at Grant Park in Chicago," the TV commentator said before falling silent.

It was a sea of flags. Some people were cheering; others looked stunned; some were crying. The network switched to New York for a view of Times Square, then to Atlanta, Los Angeles, Paris, London, and ultimately Kenya, where Obama's African family members were dancing in the streets.

"I didn't for a moment think this would happen in my lifetime," Landon said to nobody in particular.

Abi was still on her knees. She was thinking about her mother—how she had, in the end, not only accepted a black man but actually voted for him. Abi felt like the problems they had in the past were erased. She was going to call Mama and tell her how she would always remember her vote—what she did for Abi, for her friends, for her country.

Abi stood and hugged Jet. "Little sister," she whispered.

Jet hugged Abi tight and perhaps for the first time in her life felt proud of herself. She never for a moment had doubted that Obama would win, that he deserved to win. And at this moment, she felt she did, too. Jet looked at each of her friends, lingering on the two couples. She saw the way that Sam was looking at Tanya, the way Lenny had nestled into the crook of Brett's arm on the sofa. She knew that their lives would be better because of what had happened that night, and she knew she was a part of that. Alabama had gone for McCain. Work was still to be done in their state. But it didn't matter right now. This was the time to be happy for what had come to pass.

Finally, the crowd at Grant Park quieted for an announcement.

"America, here is your next first family."

The house was rocking. Cell phones were ringing. On the TV, Bruce Springsteen was singing "The Rising." These friends, from all different worlds, had their moment in time, and it was good. It was good.

After Obama's speech, everyone stayed on, getting drunker.

Jet pulled up a playlist from Obama's campaign on Landon's computer and turned the volume way up—"Your Love Has Lifted Me Higher," "Signed, Sealed, Delivered, I'm Yours."

Sam finally called Poppy. He knew it was late, but he couldn't resist.

Poppy answered the phone quickly, as if he'd been awaiting the call.

"Poppy!" Sam shouted.

"Sam! My boy!" Poppy answered.

Poppy's voice was wavering. Sam figured he might have been crying. He thought of how Poppy had helped him understand that a black man could make history, could be president.

Poppy, as always, had a piece of scripture just right for the moment. "'All things work together for good to those who love God,'" he said, "'to those who are called according to his purpose.'" Then, "I hear that party going on, wherever you are. Go be with your friends."

After he hung up, Sam held Tanya tight. He looked into her eyes and saw their whole future—marriage, travel abroad, their own family, children who could be anything they wanted.

Jet had brought a bottle of champagne. She uncorked it and passed it around the room. Stephanie had already texted, "Congratulations!" as if Jet had personally made it happen—this historic night.

Jason sang along with the music. He felt so exhausted from everything that had happened since Granddad died, and yet he was excited for what was to come. He had started pulling for Obama once he saw the neighbors' signs in their yards. They couldn't all be wrong. Now, he understood that the new president wanted the whole country to be like the neighbors on Cullom Street, taking care of each other. He stood and pulled Carly to her feet. They danced, clumsy and happy.

Landon picked up Alejandro, who was hiding in a corner, dazed and unhappy with their rowdy houseguests. She carried him to the front porch. It wasn't that she wanted to get away from her party. She just wanted to listen from a distance as she held Alejandro on the porch swing.

Once, she had dreamed she could fly. And she had shot straight up into the sky. She looked back and saw the backyard she'd grown up in. She knew she'd return to earth. But for a brief moment in time, she wanted to keep flying, glancing down at her life on earth, gazing at the trees, the seasons, the friends, the neighbors. Now, as she walked back toward her door, to the neighbors dancing inside, she thought once more of Mr. Kasir, where he was now, and where they would all be in the by and by.

ACKNOWLEDGMENTS

My deepest gratitude goes to John Neel, Nancy Nicholas, Bob Weathers, Ashley and Trey Kuehl, Neil Gambrell, Dennis Covington, Mark Burnette, Carolyn Sakowski, Anna Sutton, Steve Kirk, Lizzy Nanney, and all the people at John F. Blair, Publisher, who believed in the book.